A TALE OF
TWO FREDDIES

AN ARNIE & ZELLIE COZY MYSTERY

Eric Small

ERIC SMALL BOOKS

St. Augustine, Florida

Disclaimer: This is purely a work of fiction. Any resemblance of any character or any situation in this book to any person or situation is unintended and purely coincidental. The characters and places, other than nationally known entities which are also used fictionally, are figments of my imagination. Middletown, New Jersey is a real place, as are Monmouth County and the neighboring towns such as Red Bank and Eatontown. Many of the depicted streets actually exist, but the town descriptions are intended to provide general geographical information only, not as completely accurate portrayals.

Eric Small Books
P.O. Box 840003
St. Augustine, FL 32080
www.ericsmallbooks.com
Book Layout ©2017 BookDesignTemplates.com

A Tale of Two Freddies - Eric Small -- 1st ed.

For My Mom - A wonderful, caring, and supportive parent.

Acknowledgments:

This book would not be possible without my wife Denele's unwavering love, support and encouragement, and her many helpful comments and suggestions during the writing and editing process.

I greatly value and benefit from the love, support and encouragement I regularly receive from my family – my mother Sally, my brother Steve, and my sister Nancy, as well as from my late father Richard, whose love of books and reading had much to do with my own love of words.

A big thank you to Rik Feeney (RickFeeney.com) for permitting me to use his cover design for Brazen Gambit as a model for A Tale of Two Freddies.

Thank you to Middletown, New Jersey for its excellent sense of humor in tolerating multiple fictional murders in that great town. It was an excellent place to grow up, and remains a nice place to live.

To my nephew Tommy, who wanted to be in my next book – you're now in it.

CHAPTER ONE

With the grace of a dancer and the practiced skill of a seasoned food service vendor, Eddie executed a deft pirouette over the sleeping figure on the floor. Ever oblivious, my dog Lazlow had plopped down to snooze in the center of the busy store.

Eddie manages the Moo Mart, a convenience store/coffee shop in Middletown, New Jersey, where we all live. It has comfortable couches and tables for the coffee drinkers, and several aisles of small packaged grocery items and refrigerators filled with milk, juices, and soda.

We had adopted it as our office with Eddie's tacit agreement, although we all doubted that the owner of the franchise would approve. Eddie reasoned that if we bought coffee every day, that made us customers. Also, I think he just likes us.

"We should take part of the money to go to the Caribbean," Zellie said. "I'm thinking Turks & Caicos. Sipping some sort of fruity drink with an umbrella while reclining on a chaise and pretending I want to go windsurfing."

"I think I'd rather pretend I'm going jet skiing. But the Turks & Caicos part of it sounds nice."

Zellie Morgan and I have been best friends almost since we were born down the street from each other. For a long time, we kept away from a romantic relationship, reasoning that we didn't want to risk messing up our strong friendship.

Zellie had a short-lived marriage to a real louse, and my first real love turned out to be a criminal. We got together after solving our first case, and we're both enjoying it immensely. We should have hooked up much earlier, but were too scared. I'm still jealous if a guy so much as looks at Zellie, and she hates it if she thinks a woman is flirting with me and I don't shut it down right away. And we still worry about screwing up our friendship. So nothing has changed, thank goodness.

We're still best friends, close as ever, and partners in the A to Z Agency, solvers of exactly one case. One that put some substantial funds in our agency bank account, due to the reward money from information leading to the capture and conviction of some bad people, my lost love Jennifer included. Or at least I think so. There was a plea deal with her and very little information after that. I made a mental note to call the Assistant U.S. Attorney and ask about it.

Anyway, about the money. We were at that moment deciding what to do with it. We were sitting in our office, and Eddie was bringing over our coffee.

"You should think about investing the money in your business," Eddie said, setting down our coffees. "Like renting an actual office. Anyway, don't you want to wait until it's cold around here to get away to a warm place?"

"You're no fun, Eddie, you know that? We're just dreaming."

"Speak for yourself, buster," Zellie said, smiling. "But you have something on your mind, I can tell," she added, looking up at Eddie. "Sit down and tell us what's bothering you."

Eddie sat down, looking miserable. "The thing is..." he stopped to take a breath. "The thing is... I kind of have to evict you."

"Evict us?" I asked. "Are you in trouble with the boss? We would never want to get you in trouble. I know we've used this as a rent-free office and all, but we buy coffee, and I thought Mr. Hooten might even like the publicity we brought to the place with our first case."

Tom Hooten owned the Moo Mart franchise, and people held him in high regard for his marketing acumen, having transformed many places such as this into lucrative businesses. But he also had a nasty disposition and often mistreated his employees.

"That's just it, Arnie. It was okay when you two were under the radar. Mr. Hooten didn't even know about it. But you're celebrities and all now. The Moo Mart is famous for being your office. Mr. Hooten took my head off when he heard I'd let you use the place for the A to Z Agency. He said it would bring 'undesirables' to the place, and numerous other people to 'abuse' his hospitality, as he put it."

"Eddie, we're so sorry. The last thing we want is to get you in trouble," Zellie said. "We'll leave right away," she added, reaching for her purse.

"Absolutely. We wouldn't hurt you for anything." I agreed, getting to my feet.

"I feel bad about this, guys. And what Mr. Hooten doesn't understand, is that your notoriety has almost doubled our business. You'd think Mr. Hooten would appreciate it. He's supposed to be such a marketing whiz and all."

"Just tell him you evicted us. Don't get yourself in trouble." I extended my hand, and we shook.

"Thanks guys. I was nervous about telling you. And I'll miss you, and all the excitement."

"We'll miss you, too," Zellie said. "But we're still allowed to buy coffee, right? We're not barred from the place, are we?"

"He never said that. Of course. You can buy coffee. That's our business." Eddie brightened at the prospect of our continuing visits, and we bid him goodbye.

"So where should we set up shop?" I asked as we walked out of the Moo Mart, holding Lazlow's leash as he trailed behind me. Lazlow never pulled on the leash, and heeling was not his forte. He liked to walk behind, sniffing everything.

"We could try AB," Zellie suggested, referring to Audacious Bagel, one of the more unusual bagel restaurants in Middletown, or anywhere else.

Audacious Bagel, or AB as the locals called it, served specialty bagels that at first, made a bagel traditionalist like me cringe in abject horror. But our favorite waitress at AB lured me into trying one of the delectable concoctions, and I'm hooked. Everyone in Middletown ate at AB, but it was unsuitable as a replacement for the Moo Mart.

"Nah, they'd kick us out as soon as they saw what we were up to," I said. "Also, they'd never let Lazlow in the door. And I'd hate to put Delilah in the same position we put Eddie." Delilah, our favorite waitress at AB, played an important role in our first case.

"We might have to get an actual office. Maybe it's time," Zellie said. "We won't impress potential clients by meeting them at a coffee shop."

"Our only client so far met us at the Moo Mart without making a single complaint."

"That was different, and you know it. Are you opposed to us getting an office?"

"Nah, I was just being a contrarian. Sorry. I think we'd like it."

"Okay, good. And no time like the present. Let's drop Lazlow off at home and go find a real estate broker to show us some offices."

"Okay with me. Is it okay with you Lazlow?" I asked, looking down to the end of the leash where Lazlow was lying down licking his privates with reckless abandon. "I mean when you're done with whatever it is you're doing, that is."

Lazlow rose, and promptly pooped on the parking lot blacktop. Then, he turned around as if to say "who did that?" He then leaned down to sniff at it. At that point, I pulled him away with the usual disgust I have under such frequent occasions. Without saying anything, I handed the leash to Zellie, who was doubled over with laughter, and knelt to pick up the poop with one of the bags I keep in my pocket for these things. Did I mention that dogs are disgusting? Well they are. It's a good thing we love them so much.

I deposited the bag in a nearby dumpster and got into my car. Zellie sat in the passenger seat of my brand-new Chevy Suburban, with Lazlow situated in the back. My old car, a classic 1966 Chevrolet Impala named Matilda, no longer functioned, and sat in my garage. Stalling out at a crucial time in our first case relegated her to the ranks of the unreliable.

My new car possessed a smooth ride for an SUV, heat and air conditioning that worked well, leather seats, power windows and doors, and every gadget imaginable, from Bluetooth to a GPS to front and rear cameras and stabilization systems I didn't even understand. Its spacious back seat provided ample space for Lazlow to sleep in comfort, and in all respects served as the perfect vehicle for my needs and those of the A to Z Agency.

Still, I hated it. And I refused to name it. I wouldn't countenance such disloyalty to Matilda, sitting by herself all day in my garage. We'd shared many experiences, and I felt comfortable riding in her. I lost count of the number of times I'd tried to fix her to no avail and came within a whisker of throwing in the towel. But I hadn't given up. I just told no one.

Zellie helped me pick out the new car, convincing me to look with the very sensible argument that I needed reliable transportation. She's right. I couldn't deny that fact when Matilda had let me down at a moment of particular importance, one that involved Zellie in a very personal way.

So we hopped in the Suburban and headed home.

CHAPTER TWO

We dropped Lazlow off and gave him some fresh water and a doggy treat. He ate the biscuit, lay down on his bed, and fell asleep in an instant.

"That dog could teach at a sleep clinic," I said as we left. "An aircraft taking off over his head wouldn't disturb him in the least."

"He's just tired from taking care of all that important doggy business," Zellie responded in a lame defense of my lazy, but loveable dog.

"What important business is that?"

"Well, you know, sniffing stuff, begging, eating, pooping. Stuff like that."

"Sounds exhausting," I said with a smile.

"Well it is for him."

"Obviously."

"So where should we go?" Zellie asked, as we got into the car. "Do you know any real estate brokers?"

"No. I've never bought or rented any property. Ever. I live in my parents' old house. And so do you."

"True. I suppose we could Google real estate brokers," Zellie said, reaching for her phone.

"Why don't we do what everyone used to do before there was an Internet?"

"The phonebook? I don't even know if they're delivered anymore."

"I thought we could drive around in the general area we're interested in and walk into the first real estate broker's office we see."

Zellie giggled. "After first studying all the listings plastered on the wall outside, getting distracted by all the unrelated listings, speculating on whether we want to buy a house that's listed there, and more or less forgetting why we were looking."

"Of course."

"Okay. That sounds fun."

Driving around looking for a broker meant driving down Route 35, a busy thoroughfare containing most of the town's business. Smaller side roads with businesses existed in the town. Some might even have had real estate offices, but Route 35 remained our best bet.

And we found one right away. Its facade appeared a little questionable, but we had vowed to go to the first broker we saw, and Fate chose this one, next to a pizza parlor in a strip mall, with a huge sign bearing the words "Real Estate" embossed in large gold letters. With some trepidation, we parked the car and walked to the front of the office.

Calling it an office might be too strong a word. Peering through the front window, we only saw a lone desk with a single chair, although an adjacent door suggested the possible existence of an office beyond. Large letters emblazoned on the wall behind the desk read "Real Estate," along with some smaller words below we couldn't make out. No one sat at the desk. Even worse, the broker had pasted only three real estate listings to the front window, and each looked cut out of the newspaper.

"We might as well go in. There's nothing to look at outside," I said, setting my jaw.

"Um, Arnie, this is bad. Shouldn't we find one that's.... well... more reputable looking?"

"We said we'd go into the first real estate office we saw. This is it. Where's your sense of adventure?"

"Maybe they're closed," Zellie said, with hope in her voice.

I tried the door. "Nope. Let's go in. We can always go to someone else if this doesn't work out."

Zellie muttered something indistinguishable that sounded very much like "That's guaranteed." But I ignored it and charged ahead. Once inside, we could read the words "Massage Parlor" underneath the real estate sign. We looked at each other with the shared intention of getting the heck out of there, but before we could do so the door opened and a thin, brown haired woman with white framed glasses burst out.

"Hello, hello. Welcome," she said, with ebullience. "I'm Melissa Caron. Right this way," she added, pointing at the door from which she had emerged. She paused for a moment. "I'm by myself today, so I will have to do you one at a time. I hope that's okay. How about you go first, big fella? I'll get to the little missus right after we're done. You can sit in and watch, ma'am. No hanky-panky here, no way. A therapeutic massage, that's it."

"But..." I sputtered.

"I mean it."

"We know you do," Zellie said, in a soothing voice. "We were here to see a real estate broker. It's clear we made a mistake. We'll go now. Sorry to take up your time."

"Real estate? That's me. The massage stuff is just a sideline. The real estate business has dried up, and I used to spend so much time massaging people's egos to get a listing, it was a natural. You know what I mean?"

"I do," Zellie said. "I used to be in the public relations business."

"Whoa. That's the big time. You must have gotten good at slinging it."

"She was the best," I said, putting my arm around her. "No one slung it better than Zellie."

"Thank you... I think."

"Yup, best in the business." I suspected that Zellie wouldn't tolerate this much longer, and I was right.

"Okay, that's enough," she said. To Melissa, she pointed out the obvious. "You don't have many listings. We saw only three on your window."

"Oh, I have many more listings. Sit down and tell me what you're looking for."

We must have looked skeptical because she went into massage mode. Literally. She offered to give us free massages if we'd just listen to her. We agreed. Not because of the massages, but because she seemed so earnest, we thought there was no harm in listening.

"I have a list of office space for rent in Monmouth County. Do you want to stay in Middletown, or look elsewhere?"

"We want to stay in Middletown," Zellie said. "It's where our client base is located."

I laughed to myself. Our client base consisted of no one. We had only had one client ever, and that had turned out...well, in a strange way. But I liked Zellie's enthusiasm.

"Yes, Middletown," I agreed.

"Okay, let's see. Ooh, I have the perfect thing for you. Check this out." She motioned for us to come around the desk and we looked at her computer monitor. "It's right off of Route 35. "It's a house."

"But we're looking for office space." I thought she was a complete loony, but Zellie showed interest.

"I kind of like it. And it has lots of parking for our clients." Zellie turned and whispered in my ear. "When we get them."

Distracted as I was by Zellie's soft lips brushing my ear, I managed to croak my agreement. "It's a better fit than a stuffy office building. Can we go look at it?"

Melissa looked pleased. "Of course. I'll set up an appointment. Is tomorrow at 10:00 a.m. good for you?"

"Works for us." I said, after glancing at Zellie and getting her nodded agreement.

"Great. Now I promised the two of you massages. Would you like them now, or should I give you a voucher for future use?"

"Better just give us a voucher," I said. "Thanks."

Melissa rifled through the top drawer in her desk and pulled out a glossy brochure with the name "Melissa's Massages" on the front, slid in two vouchers and handed it to Zellie. "The vouchers last for one year. And I'm great at it, if I do say so myself. Very relaxing."

* * *

Zellie looked at the brochure while I drove us home. "She has formal massage training, Arnie. Maybe we should take her up on those massages." She rubbed her neck. "I bet she could fix this crick in my neck, and that hip thing you always gripe about."

"Where'd she get her training?"

"It says here that she went to the Central New Jersey School of Massage Therapy."

"So... she went to 'Rub U?'"

"Looks like it. She's a trained massage therapist, go figure."

"I hope she's a competent real estate broker."

"Well, she found us at least one place to look at. And I like the idea of a small house, instead of an office building."

I smiled. "So that all of those clients we have can park with ease."

Zellie leaned over and kissed my ear, giving me the shivers again. "Right," she said. "We've worked hard today. How about we head to your place for a little rest and recreation?"

I stepped on the gas. "Sounds like a fine idea."

CHAPTER THREE

We drove over to AB to meet Ted and Marla for our morning breakfast date. The hostess ushered us to our regular table in Delilah's section, where our friends already sat talking with their heads close together like a couple of lovebirds.

"Looks like those two are getting along well," Zellie remarked as we headed to the table. "I think it's good for both of them."

"Me too," I agreed. "Ted needs to settle down."

"Like us?" Zellie said with a smile. "Best friends for decades, lovers for a couple of months."

I grinned. "Maybe not like us. I think they're doing that backwards."

We greeted the two of them and sat down. Delilah appeared in an instant, like a hovering apparition. She wore a baseball cap bearing the AB restaurant logo, with her long dark hair tied up in a ponytail. She sported snug designer jeans and a red T-shirt with the words "I'd Climb Mountains for an Audacious Bagel" emblazoned across her chest.

"A little suggestive, isn't it, Delilah?" I asked.

"Why, whatever do you mean?" She winked at Zellie when she said it, and Zellie cracked up.

"You got him again, Delilah."

"He's way too easy to make blush." Everyone laughed at my expense, even me. Delilah and I had sparred like this ever since the place opened for business several years ago. We gave her our orders and chatted with our friends.

"Eddie evicted us," Zellie started.

"You know it wasn't much of an office, right?" Ted asked, more than a little bit facetiously.

"Well, it wasn't much, but it was ours," I said, defending the Moo-Mart's honor.

"It wasn't even yours. It's a coffee shop."

"Nonetheless, it was our place of business."

Marla fumbled in her purse for something and she pulled it out and passed it across the table to us with a chuckle. "My card," she said. "I know I'm a criminal attorney, but I couldn't resist taking on this case."

"And what case is that?" Zellie demanded.

"Why, representing you in the eviction action. A clear violation of the terms of your lease. The case is open and shut."

"We don't have a lease. It's a coffee shop."

"A month-to-month tenancy, then."

"Nope."

"An oral agreement to let you conduct business in their establishment?"

"Not even close. They just tolerated our presence if we bought coffee."

"Aha! Adverse possession. It will be my greatest case."

"It would be your greatest defeat, Marla."

"It would be my greatest defeat," she agreed. "So, what's next?"

"We're looking for office space," I said. "We're meeting the real estate broker this morning."

"What broker are you using? Most of the attorneys I know use Trans World Real Estate Partners. It's a big full-service broker."

A mischievous smile crept into Zellie's face. "I bet they don't offer the services our broker does."

"Oh, I think you'll find that Trans World can address all of your needs."

"Do they give massages?" I asked.

"What?" Ted and Marla both exclaimed, jaws agape.

Zellie and I smiled in quiet contentment, letting this information sink in.

"Our broker is Melissa Caron," I said.

"Melissa's Massage Parlor? That Melissa?" Ted asked.

"That's the one."

Marla looked at him. "Ted, how do you know about Melissa's Massage Parlor?"

"Well, I've been there," he said, hanging his head. "It's legit. Really. She's a licensed massage therapist. Recommended by my orthopedist for my back issues. I forgot she was a real estate broker."

"Well she is." Zellie said. "She's helping us find office space. And we have coupons for free massages, too."

Marla looked doubtful. "I can put you in touch with someone at Trans World."

"Nah, I think we'll take our chances with her. Don't you think so, Zellie?"

"I'm sure she'll be fine at helping us find an office. Although I admit I would think twice about listing my home for sale with her."

"Are you thinking about selling your house? Perhaps considering moving down the street?" Marla teased.

"That's not the present intention," Zellie answered, as we all turned our heads toward her with rapt attention. She looked at me for a long moment, then added playfully, "Although it is possible that someone may sell a house in the neighborhood at some point. One never can be sure of these things."

Ted and Marla pressed both of us on our plans, but we remained unyielding in our silence on the matter. We enjoyed their speculations. But no specific plans existed other than us talking about living together, which we did anyway, alternating between the two houses depending upon our mood. We agreed not to rush, given the delicate steps we'd taken to convert a lifelong friendship into a full-blown romance. We wanted to enjoy falling in love, and any decision about formal cohabitation had no urgency.

After finishing our coffee and bagels, we bid Ted and Marla goodbye, and headed to the real estate office. Melissa greeted us like old friends and suggested we go in my car. She told us our first stop as we piled into my SUV.

"You said you wanted to stay in Middletown, but a listing just popped up for a building in Red Bank. It might be a good fit for you."

Glancing at Zellie, I saw her shrug, signifying it was okay with her.

"I guess so," I said. "Where in Red Bank?"

"It's off Broad Street." Broad Street is the main street in downtown Red Bank. "Um, very off of Broad Street. But nearby. Sort of. It's called the Buckles Building. I haven't seen it, but I understand it's nice. And the rent is cheap for Red Bank."

Zellie and I both yelled at the same time. "No!"

Melissa asked what was wrong, and, turning around to face her, Zellie explained that a shady private investigator named

Jack Buckles owned the building, and that our experiences with him were most unpleasant.

Melissa nodded. "A competitor, I get it."

We didn't bother to explain further. I guess Buckles is a competitor of a sort. A licensed one, I thought with disgust. He is a sleazy, dishonest, greedy son of a bitch. We didn't want to go near him, much less rent space from him. And his building was a dump. I knew it first-hand. But we let Melissa think it was just respectful competition.

"What else do you have, Melissa?" Zellie inquired.

"Good office space is hard to find, but I have that listing I mentioned yesterday for a small house in Middletown, right off of Route 35, that you will have no trouble adapting into an office." She said it in an odd combination of real estate broker enthusiasm and doubtfulness she was showing us something that might work out.

I glanced at Zellie, who gave an almost imperceptible nod. She caught Melissa's inflection. But we remained undeterred.

"Sounds great," I said. "Tell me which way to turn."

Her enthusiasm restored, Melissa gave me directions, and we soon pulled up in front of a small, blue cottage right off of Route 35 as promised.

"It's cute," Zellie exclaimed, moving her head in multiple directions at once. "This is way better than a stuffy office building."

More uncertain, but willing to give it a chance, if only because Zellie liked it, I gave a swift reply. "Sure. Let's look inside."

Melissa led the way to the door, which bore one of those "Broker Only" key containers. She fumbled with the combination, and, after a few errant attempts, pulled out a key and held it up. She seemed proud of her effort, so I felt obliged to say something.

"Great," I said.

Zellie nodded with eager anticipation, and Melissa unlocked the door. We walked into a small entryway lit by a single bulb overhead. No fixture, just a single bulb. And a forty watt one, too. Very, very poor illumination in the foyer.

Still, the place had its charm. A dark entryway, but it featured high ceilings, crown moldings, and old-fashioned large floor to ceiling windows that would let in significant light if someone had bothered to clean them once this century. And it looked already set up as an office of sorts, with two large bedrooms, each with its own bathroom, and outlines of desks on the floor. It looked cozy and cute, and might serve its purpose as an office. It was apparent that the people who owned or rented this place before used it that way.

Zellie had already moved in, dashing with excitement around the house, claiming the office on the left as her own. She ran a finger on one window, and expressed her disgust, saying at the same time it would "clean right up." Looking up at the tall sheer curtains still hanging from curtain bars mounted high above us, she muttered something about "getting rid of them, pronto." Pointing at the single bulb in the foyer, she mapped out the places we would (she would?) go to pick out a "classy chandelier."

"Isn't this place perfect?"

I nodded. "I like it a lot. But we don't even know what the rent is, and we should get more information about it. It's the first place we've looked at. Shouldn't we look around more?"

"We should get the details, but I don't think we need to look anymore unless the financial arrangements don't work out."

She looked at me with those beautiful big brown eyes, and I melted, as I always do. I'd look at those eyes all day long, every day, if I could. I nodded at her in acquiescence. "Okay. Maybe I'm just being overcautious." I turned to Melissa. "Let's sit down and go over some details."

"Great," she replied. "It's still morning. We can head back to my office and go over everything."

I gave an inquiring look at Zellie.

"Works for us," she said. She kissed me on the cheek and took my hand. "Let's go."

As we walked toward the front door, Zellie let go of my hand and pointed toward the ceiling. "An attic," she exclaimed. "Storage space for our case files."

"Yes, all of our one case file, "I said, laughing. "But we can hope that number increases."

Zellie grabbed the rope to pull down the fold out stairs to the attic. But she couldn't pull it down. "It's stuck." I took the rope from her hand and gave it my best shot. It gave a little, but didn't open.

"I think it's catching on something up there, or a heavy object is on top of the fold out stairs." I gave the rope a firm grip, and an enormous tug. The door opened and a large object came tumbling out.

"Look out! It's a person!" Zellie screamed from her vantage point to the side.

Melissa let out a wordless frightened cry, and closed her eyes, like a child assuming danger doesn't exist if not seen.

I hunched my shoulders and ducked, my brain not comprehending the source of the peril.

CHAPTER FOUR

The corpse barely missed my head. For that's what it was, a dead body. It had fallen to the ground and lay prone in front of us. I shivered, and turned to the others, who both stood shaking, probably in shock. We did a group hug and remained silent in a show of respect for the prone body in front of us.

No one said a word. We stared at the body. For my part, I felt a little sick. I have a sordid history with dead bodies. I get queasy. And that's a gentle way of putting it.

"I think he's dead," Melissa ventured.

"Well, he's not sleeping. He's definitely dead," Zellie said.

I forced myself to look at the body. "No question about it," I agreed.

Everyone fell silent again as we studied the body. It was a man of fifty or so, about five foot eight inches tall (or long, as we were viewing him from above), a little on the heavy side, with dyed dark hair. He wore a white dress shirt with dark blue trousers, and had a pair of glasses in his top front pocket, that looked crushed by his fall out of the attic. I offered a question.

"How did he die?"

Everyone looked again at the body.

"No blood," Melissa said.

"Wasn't bludgeoned," Zellie offered.

"He doesn't look strangled," I added.

"Maybe he got locked up there and starved..." Melissa start-ed, then added, "but that's just stupid. I mean, look at him. It would take that guy a year to starve, and he looks, I don't know, more freshly dead."

Zellie and I nodded agreement. "No sign of starvation," I said.

"I wonder who he is," Zellie said. She turned to Melissa. "Do you know who owns this place, and who occupied it before the landlord put it up for rental?"

"I have no idea who rented it before, but the landlord is a business, Monmouth County Properties, LLC."

"We'll have no trouble finding the owner of that compa-ny," Zellie said. "Can you check to find the name of the prior tenant?"

"I think so," Melissa replied.

"I hate to interrupt this discourse," I interjected, "or to in-terfere with your thought process, Zellie, but we need to call the police."

"Well, of course we do," Zellie replied. "But no harm in start-ing our investigation right away."

"What investigation? It's a dead body in a place we thought about renting."

"A place we still want to rent, don't we? A little matter of a dead body shouldn't deter us. It's Karma, or serendipity, or something. A client falls into our laps, so to speak."

"A client? He doesn't look like he can hire anyone."

"A mere technicality. We have no **technical** right to investi-gate, either," she said.

"He's not a real client, Zellie."

"Neither was our first client, and that worked out pretty well."

I sighed. "You've got me there. But why can't we get clients in the normal way? And ones that want us to investigate something?"

Melissa just listened to our discussion, but finally spoke up. "You guys are real private eyes?"

"Sort of," I acknowledged.

"Yes we are," Zellie said.

"And this will be your office?"

I sighed. "Yup. Right after we call the police, we can go sign the papers. If ever there was a sign that this is the place for us, it's a dead body."

CHAPTER FIVE

W e called the Middletown police. I hoped against hope that the officers who showed up were not the same ones who we dealt with in our previous case, but no such luck. None other than Tweedle Dee and Tweedle Dum (or is that Dumb?) responded to our call. I tried to stay polite.

"Hello Officer Madison, Officer Dunston," I offered weakly.

"Fischer. Not you again." Dunston scowled when he said it. He looked over at Zellie and gave her a wink. "At least you have your pretty bimbo with you."

Oh no, I thought, here it comes.

"Look here, Officer Dimwit," Zellie said, her eyes flashing daggers at Dunston. "The next time you refer to me in that disrespectful way, you'll be making your snide comments in a soprano. Show some professionalism, you ignorant snot."

Dunston just smiled at that, risking infuriating Zellie further. He looked over at Madison. "She's a fiery one, I like that."

Zellie was about to say more, but I took her hand, and she stayed silent, satisfying herself with giving Dunston a dirty look.

"Watch your manners, Chester." Melissa spoke up.

Dunston looked up, startled, and confused. Melissa was standing to the side, and he didn't see her at first. "Melissa, what are you doing here?"

"And stand up straight, Chester. Throw those shoulders back. Haven't I taught you anything?"

Without thinking, Dunston straightened his posture at her command. "How is this?" he asked. Realizing where he stood, he resumed an imperious tone.

"I mean it, Melissa. Why are you hanging out with them? I'm not convinced that they didn't kill this guy. Or you either, for that matter. And somebody, tell me what we have here," he barked.

"Chester, what we have here is a dead body. And don't be silly, of course we had nothing to do with it. I was just showing this place to Mr. Fischer and Ms. Morgan. We opened the attic and this body tumbled down here. None of us ever visited here before. It's a multiple listing," she added.

"Melissa, you're my massage therapist. How did these two corrupt you? And stop calling me Chester. It's Officer Dunston."

"You are well aware I'm a real estate broker and a massage therapist, Chester," she said ignoring his attempt at formality. "It's written right on my door."

"All of this is very interesting," Madison interjected, in a feeble attempt to restore decorum to the situation. "But we have a potential homicide to investigate, and the three of you are the sole witnesses. We'll need you to come down to the station."

"For what purpose, Officer?" I asked. "You've already heard the sum total of all we know. We were looking at this place as a possible rental. We've never been here before, and we've never seen this poor man before. What more could we tell you in a trip to the police station?"

"We have to get formal statements from you," he said.

"You just got them. Type them up and we'll stop by to sign the papers after we've concluded our business. We're happy to cooperate. And it's not like you don't know where to find us."

"Did you touch anything?" Dunston asked.

"Not the body. He fell down out of the attic when we opened the door and landed right there. I used my cell phone to call you guys right away. But we all walked around this place for a while before we opened the attic. We were deciding whether to rent it."

He looked at Melissa. "Is there a current tenant?"

"Not as far as I know. My understanding is that it's remained vacant for a while."

"Okay. The coroner just arrived. We'll be in touch if we need anything else," he said officiously, closing his notebook. "And stop by the station to sign your statements by tomorrow at the latest. Thanks Melissa." He nodded at Zellie and me. "And thank you for your cooperation."

"Of course, Officer. Anything we can do to help."

When the officers left, we moved outside, and I turned to Zellie. "Wow, that was some change in attitude. I wonder what happened."

Zellie looked over at Melissa. "I think he didn't want to aggravate Melissa. If you weren't here, I think he'd have locked us up by now," she said.

Melissa laughed. "He's been a customer for a long time. And he credits me with fixing his bad back."

"Well, that's our good fortune, Melissa. Thank you. We'd be down at the station being pressured to make a full confession," I said.

"Yes. And they would have had us, too. We'd confess that we knew nothing about this, and couldn't know anything, because, hello, we've never been here before today." Zellie was fuming, but showed the glimmer of a smile, too.

"C'mon. Let's go. We'll drop you off at your office, Melissa, and you can get started on whatever papers you need us to sign. And thanks again."

After promising to provide us with the name of the owner and prior occupant of our new office, she bid us goodbye.

CHAPTER SIX

Arnie, we're looking for office space for our private investigation firm. Has it occurred to you we might have forgotten about something?"

"Phone service? Utility bills? Internet access? We'll need that. Better write that down." I stopped when Zellie held up her hand in the universal sign meaning stop.

"I've been reading about the requirements for getting a private investigator's license in New Jersey. Remember? We didn't have one, and the cops yelled at you during our first case?"

"An unforgettable experience, to be sure. But I forgot about it anyway. Maybe even actively put it out of my mind, to be honest. There was nothing pleasant about that set of events."

"Well, we need licenses."

"So we take a test and pay a fee. This is New Jersey. It can't be that hard."

"It's hard."

"What do you mean?"

"Well I'm sort of wrong about the 'hard' part."

"See, I told you. This is New Jersey."

"No, I mean it's not just hard. It's impossible!"

"How could it be impossible? Even Jack Buckles has a license. How could it be so hard if a dope like him has one?"

"Look at this list of requirements."

"Good moral character? We have that. Don't we? Don't tell me we have lower moral character than Jack Buckles?"

"Well, you were a securities trader, and I was a public relations specialist, but no, that's not it. Look above that line where it says 'five years prior investigative experience.'"

"It does, doesn't it? Frickin' New Jersey. Requiring prior investigative experience to get to be an investigator to get the prior investigative experience you need to be an investigator. That makes no sense. And it was hard to say. It's like needing money in the bank to get a loan. Oh, wait. You do. But how did Buckles get past that requirement?"

"I think he served as a police officer back in the late nineties."

"Whoa. That's almost too scary to think about."

"Yes, but more to the point, we can't meet that requirement."

"We'll figure something out."

"I'm all ears."

"Well, we could call the business something else, like public relations, or customer service, and just tangentially do investigating. For money. But not as investigators, no sir. Find a loophole. There must be one. Prior investigating experience. In what? Doesn't specify. I investigated good securities deals. That's investigating, isn't it?"

"I don't think that will qualify."

"Or the lettering on the door can make full disclosure: We are not licensed investigators, and cannot do investigations for money, and will not do so. If anyone wants investigating, they should go to a licensed investigator. If people want to volunteer information, we won't say no, though."

"Listen to yourself."

"Oh, I know. I'm just trying to find a way. It's amazing how low honest people will sink to pursue their dream."

"We won't give up. We'll figure something out... Arnie? What's going on in that scheming, plotting brain of yours?"

I hesitated. And thought a million thoughts at once, none particularly lucid. I didn't want to suggest it, and I sure as hell didn't want Zellie to go for it. But if it's the only way.... So I blurted out the idea anyway.

"We could ask Mike Mullen if he'd be interested in leaving the State Police, getting a private investigator's license, and joining our firm, and we would get our investigating experience with him as the one with the license." Did I say that? I don't want that at all. But it was too late. Now, I had to wait to see what Zellie would say. Maybe she'd just laugh it off as another hair-brained idea. But she just looked at me.

"Is that what you want, Arnie?" she intoned. "I guess it could work." Her inflection was doubtful.

"No. We shouldn't even ask." I began talking fast, my nervousness taking over my brain. "The words that came out of my mouth don't reflect how I feel. We don't want to work for anyone, and I want it to be just us anyway." I squeezed her hand.

"Well, that's a relief. I don't want that either."

CHAPTER SEVEN

I picked Zellie up later on and we went out for takeout coffee from a drive-thru fast food place. As soon as we started moving again, Zellie touched me on the arm. "We need to talk."

"I know. It's about my incredibly stupid idea for garnering the experience necessary to get our license."

"Yes. Incredibly stupid is a good characterization. In fact, add confusing, offensive, insensitive, hurtful and just plain stupid."

"You already said 'stupid.'" I offered helpfully.

"It deserves to be said twice," she snapped.

"Look, Zellie. I'm not minimizing it. It was dumb, I admit it. I'm very sorry. It is not what I mean or feel. Heck, I don't want Mike Mullen anywhere near you, much less acting as our quasi-boss. The only reason we started this agency is so we could spend more time together. We sure as heck didn't want to answer to any bosses."

"That's what I thought," she agreed. "But I need to be sure you don't want to change things. We're approaching our relationship in a vastly different way than when we started the business, as best friends starting a detective agency."

"We're still best friends. That hasn't changed."

"It hasn't changed for me either. But I need to ask you, Arnie, has our becoming lovers changed our friendship? It's what we worried about, remember?" Zellie's lower lip trembled a little when she said that.

"Who could forget? And emphatically no, Zellie. It hasn't changed our friendship one bit. In my mind at least, it has enhanced our relationship far beyond my wildest dreams. I get to love you as my best friend and as my sweetheart. What could be better than that?"

"Nothing," Zellie said. "It's the best thing we ever did."

"We both might have avoided a world of hurt," I agreed.

"So true," she said. "So why did you make the... what term did we agree on?"

"Incredibly stupid, I believe."

"Yes, incredibly stupid. So why say something like that?"

"I don't know."

"I talked to Marla, and she said it's just because guys always say dumb stuff. It's like a gene thing."

"Well, I phoned Ted, and he called me an idiot."

"I find myself agreeing with Ted, at least in this case." Zellie smiled. "But you're not an idiot, and you don't often say dumb things."

I knew why I said it, and was having a difficult time telling Zellie, which was funny because I always told her everything. But this was personal and directly related to our fledgling romance. It underlined my clear insecurity. But Zellie was more or less admitting that she was nervous about it, too, so I owed it to her to share my feelings on the matter. Feelings. Guys are definitely not good at that.

"I think I was testing you." There, I said it.

"You were testing me? You are such a moron."

"I'm pretty sure we've already established that."

Zellie took my hand. "Arnie, you don't need to test me. I love you. I've always loved you. Read my lips – I have no interest in Mike Mullen, or any other guy. You're the one. To be fair, I should say our new relationship makes me nervous sometimes, too. I don't want to lose our friendship, but I want to keep our romance."

"Me too. I love you, and I want it all. And if we're both a little nervous, it's okay. It's new and exciting. Just think of what we were missing while we ruminated and procrastinated, delaying this inevitable joy out of fear. I won't make that mistake again."

"**We** won't make that mistake again," Zellie said, squeezing my hand.

"Well, I'm glad we settled that. Our first relationship crisis. Completely resolved. Good to get that over with," I said.

"Yes, it is, and I'm certain we won't have any more," Zellie added with a giggle.

"Exactly. That was it. Over and done with. All relationship issues are a thing of the past." I was laughing, too. "Seriously, Zellie, this relationship stuff can be complicated. We never had these kinds of issues before."

"No, but we had best friend stuff. Let's face it, all interpersonal relationships present challenges. Ours is no different."

"I guess so. But sometimes I think we are a little different. Like for instance, why do we always have these kinds of discussions in a car we pulled over and parked because we couldn't wait even a moment longer to work things out?"

Zellie looked around. We sat in the breakdown lane of Route 35, with cars whizzing past. When Zellie said we needed to talk, I pulled over and parked on the spot. "Good point, she said. "We are different. Let's get out of here."

CHAPTER EIGHT

I put the car in gear and we were off. "Where to?" I asked.

"Let's go back to your place and fire up the computer. I want to find out who owns our new office and who rented it before us, and my phone is too small to do real research."

"Weren't we going to wait for Melissa to give us that information?"

"Yes, but there's no need for that. We can find out just as easily as she can, and I want to get this investigation going."

"We still haven't worked out the licensing thing. The cops will be none too happy to have us meddling."

"Are you saying we shouldn't investigate?"

I looked over at her. "Sit on the sidelines and let the two stooges investigate a murder which took place in our own office? Not a chance. But we should figure out a solution to our licensing problem. And not Mike Mullen," I added.

"No, not Mike Mullen. But I wonder...." She trailed off.

"Wonder what?"

"Just a half-baked idea. I'll let you know when it's fully baked."

"You do that," I said, chuckling.

We pulled into my driveway and got out of the car. As we walked to the door, I put my arm around her waist, and pulled her warm body close. She looked up at me with a beautiful smile, and we stopped right there, just enjoying the moment. Then I leaned down and we kissed, not waiting to enter the house. I think we might have disrobed right there, but we somehow made into the house and closed the door.

***

It was late afternoon when we turned on my aging desktop computer, retrieved from my old workplace. Yes, that computer, for those of you who remember our first case. I couldn't bear to abandon it, and no one objected to me taking it home. Zellie started her online search for information about the history of our new office. I sat down beside her and *kibitzed* while she worked. I distracted her by fiddling with her brownish blonde hair, which at this moment fell loosely on her shoulders. As I brushed a stray lock off her cheek and behind her ear, she gave an involuntary shudder, and turned to look at me.

"I'll get nothing done if you keep doing that." She paused and leaned over to brush my lips with a gentle kiss. "But keep doing it anyway."

She continued searching, and several minutes later cried out "Eureka!"

"Eureka? Are you serious? Does anyone use that word anymore?"

"I do," Zellie answered, her eyes beaming with excitement. "I checked the address, and found the identity of the prior tenant of our office."

"You did?" I looked at the screen, and read out loud "Ferdinand Darrow, Esquire."

"Yup. A lawyer."

"A lawyer named Darrow. How unusual," I said facetiously. "I wonder if he's a relative of Clarence Darrow. You know, the Scopes trial guy?"

"I know who Clarence Darrow was," Zellie said. "*Inherit the Wind*. Spencer Tracy, Frederic March. A classic."

"And I thought I was the movie buff. Do you think he's the dead guy?"

"You mean our client?" Zellie corrected me.

"I mean our dead guy client, yes."

"I don't know. Maybe there's a picture of him here. I'll keep looking."

"We're bound to find out soon, anyway. It will be in the newspapers, maybe even as soon as tomorrow."

"Arnie, that's so early twenty-first century. And I can't believe I said that. But nowadays, it will show up on the newspapers' web sites with near- instantaneous speed. And blogs, Instagram, Facebook, and Twitter before that."

"I guess I'm just an early twenty-first century kind of guy," I said with a smile. "Do we have a positive ID yet?"

Zellie stared at the screen for a few moments and then shrugged and expressed grudging acknowledgement that the news had not yet broken. "Anyway," she said, "we haven't eaten since this morning, and I'm starving. Let's get something to eat. We can check back later."

"Spaghetti here, or a steak and baked potato at Know Your Beef?"

Know Your Beef was a quirky steak place in Red Bank regarded as the current trendy place. The odd name came from its morbid presentation of menus containing names and pictures of individual cows from which your steaks originated. The owners were from a small farming town in Eastern Europe, and it's possible that some language and cultural differences existed. I think their somewhat misguided intention was to demonstrate the freshness of the beef they served. The original name of the place was "Fresh Beef" and almost no one went there. As soon as they changed the name, it became an overnight sensation. Just try to figure out human nature. I dare you. To be clear, the depicted cattle were not the source of your meal. The owners photographed the cows at a farm in New Jersey, and word is that those cattle will die of old age, presumably sipping cool drinks in rocking chairs on the porch. But the steaks are outstanding.

"How about the steaks?" Zellie giggled and added, "I'm in the mood for some Elsie butt and Mr. Potato Head."

"The potatoes don't have names."

"They do now."

"Why not? The whole idea is bizarre, anyway. I'll call and reserve a table for seven o'clock."

See, that's one thing I love about Zellie. She's beautiful and smart. But she's not a prude, and she can watch a ballgame or a raunchy movie without getting all girly about it. And she can laugh. It's like listening to beautiful music hearing her laugh. Okay, I know. Over the top. But I'm in love with her.

CHAPTER NINE

We took Lazlow for a quick walk, fed him, and gave him a treat. He settled right back onto his bed and fell asleep, and we headed out to dinner. After a delicious meal, we drove home the long way around by Route 35, as we both wanted to take a detour and just look at the cottage again. Pulling into the parking area, we gawked from outside at the bright yellow crime scene tape around the front entrance, and speculated about what the investigators found when they scrutinized the place.

"I'm sure they lifted our fingerprints and Melissa's. They're no doubt preparing the arrest warrant as we speak."

"I don't know," Zellie mused out loud. "This is a bizarre case. We don't even know how Darrow died. And we certainly don't know how the killer got the body up those attic stairs. That would take effort. And a single person couldn't haul him up there. Could the two of us even do it?"

"I doubt it. Maybe we could handle the weight, but a body would just be too awkward. I suppose the police could somehow think the three of us conspired to kill the guy, dragged his body up to the attic, and call them to report the crime."

"You don't believe they'd think that, do you?"

"No, I don't. Even those two are not that dumb."

"This will be a tough case to solve."

"Well, it fits the requirements for what we're allowed to do. We aren't investigating for money, so no one can accuse us of running an unlicensed private detective business. The law ties the licensing requirement to investigating for compensation. That's not the case here."

"Ooh, a loophole. I love those."

"Me too. But it brings up a teensy-weensie little problem."

"How we'll pay the rent."

"Bingo," I said. "We have enough for first and last month's rent as required by the lease, but the reward money from our first case will only go so far. I would just fund the expenses until we got off the ground, but with the liquidation proceedings of my former firm, I'm hesitant to use the buyout money until it's all sorted out. They can't touch my pension, but that only goes so far."

"We decided not to use personal funds, anyway. And I would never ask you to do it even if those funds were free and clear. You know that."

"I know. It kind of makes me think we should have listened to Ted about incorporating the business."

"We still can. I guess we took an informal approach."

"That's for sure."

Our formation of the business comprised picking a name, declaring that we were open for business, and hugging each other. Ted suggested we incorporate the business, much the way he incorporated everything, including his name, but we rejected the idea. We're just two best friends going into business, we told him. Why would we need a corporation? He had just shrugged and let it go, mumbling a few inaudible words.

Still, we had no business plan, neglected to provide for any operational funding, and now couldn't even use the Moo-Mart as an office. Not to mention that we had no experience and hadn't even known we needed a license to work as private detectives. Against all odds, however, we had solved a big case first time out of the box, and helped put away some nasty people.

"We'll figure something out. And we'll have the first month's rent paid, giving us at least a month to find an income stream."

"Piece of cake," I said. "We'll just focus on the case and let the chips fall where they may."

"I wonder if we could look at the coroner's report?"

"Fat chance of that happening. But someone will leak it to the news media. And see how I said news media, instead of newspapers?"

We both laughed.

"I guess we should head home," Zellie said. "There's nothing more we can do here."

"No, but we'll hear from Melissa tomorrow, and together with the information you already found, we can really start our investigation."

"Where to?" Zellie asked.

"I guess my place, if it's okay with you. We need to let Lazlow out."

"It's okay with me, but you know he has a bed at my place, too, and is always welcome."

"I know, and he likes it there. If you prefer, we can let him out, then bring him over to your place and stay there tonight."

"Either place is okay with me, but we should figure out this two-home thing at some point. We spend almost all of our time together, but ostensibly live in two separate places."

"We don't live in two separate places," I said, smiling. "Just two homes in which to cohabit. But your point is well-taken. We'll talk about it, I promise."

Zellie looked at her watch. "I guess 11:30 after a long day isn't the time for it. Let's let Lazlow out and then get to sleep."

CHAPER TEN

"Where are we going today?" Zellie asked, between sips of coffee.

"Let's go see Melissa," I suggested. "For two reasons. First, we can sign a lease for our new office."

"Better known as 'the crime scene.'" Zellie added.

"Right. And she can provide more information on the building owner."

"Also known as our future landlord."

"Yes. I suppose it might be a good idea to solve this case before we sign a lease, huh?"

"Well, it would be a little uncomfortable if our new landlord was involved somehow."

"Just a little. Nothing like having a murderer for a landlord. Okay, but we can at least check in with her."

"Sure. It's not like we have any other leads."

"I still wish we had the autopsy report," I mused, half aloud. "That would help."

"Our chances of getting that from Officers Tweedle Dee and Tweedle Dum are slim and none."

"But maybe..."

"What?"

"Just an idea. Melissa seemed to have an almost ironclad hold on Officer Dunston. Almost like she'd cast a spell on him. Maybe she'd be willing to help."

***

"Oh, that won't be a problem," Melissa said when we asked. We sat in her little office adjacent to two rooms containing massage tables, drinking some kind of tropical health drink she proffered. "Chester Dunston is a pussycat, a real gentleman. I'm sure he'd be delighted to give me a copy of the autopsy report. It's not like it's secret or anything. It's an official report. I'll have it for you later today. I'll just ask him to bring it along to his noon appointment."

"Thank you, Melissa. Officer Dunston doesn't care for us."

"I can't imagine why. You seem like such nice people."

She abruptly stood up. "I almost forgot. Some real estate broker I am. I have the rental documents for your new office, and that other information for you, about your prospective landlord. I'm guessing you don't want to sign a lease just yet, but it won't hurt for you to take the papers to go over with your attorney, so you can be ready to go when this nasty business is resolved."

"You're right about us wanting to wait a little while, but we hope it's not long. We like the place. Except for the dead body, of course."

"I know," she said. "It is such a bright and cheery place. Such a shame that a dead body almost fell on our heads. Very unpleasant." She curled her nose like someone encountering a bad smell. But her countenance changed to a sunny smile, as she removed a sheaf of papers from a file cabinet and handed them to us.

The rapid mood change jarred me at first, but I'd begun to see Melissa as someone who never let adversity ruin her day.

It was impressive. And that carefree, new age type exterior masked a sharp, intelligent woman. She was no fool.

CHAPTER ELEVEN

We waited until we returned to the car to look at the papers Melissa gave us. Zellie put the lease aside and eagerly scanned the other paper.

"Jayne Merriweather," she read aloud. "Executive Vice President, Many Counties Properties, LLC. With a nice logo reading 'MCP.' Offices right on Broad Street in Red Bank. I'll call to see if she is available now, or if we can see her later today." Zellie pulled out her cell phone and entered the number on the page in front of her. She said a few things into the phone, waited a few moments, and turned to me. "We're in luck. She'll see us now, if we get there in the next fifteen minutes. She has a meeting in a little more than a half-hour."

"Let's go."

It's a short distance from Melissa's office on Route 35 to downtown Red Bank, but there are a lot of traffic lights, so the four or five miles used up our fifteen minutes. But we arrived in time, and Ms. Merriweather's assistant showed us right in, with a perfunctory comment that she expected us.

She stood upon our entry and towered a full six feet, with long, straight dark hair, and an angular, almost hollow face, with a button nose that suggested surgical alteration. Not my type, although most people would consider her beautiful. But she had a hard line to her countenance, one that said she'd traveled around the block a few times. This was a tough cookie, no doubt.

She pointed to two chairs in front of her desk and invited us to sit down. "Now what can I do for you? My assistant could not state the purpose of your visit, just that you indicated its importance."

Zellie jumped in. "It is very important, Ms. Merriweather. We're investigating a homicide in one of your properties."

"I've already spoken to the police about that. Not that I could tell them much. He rented one our hundreds of properties. And anyway, what business is it of yours? You don't have badges, so you're not police officers. Are you private investigators? Who hired you?"

"First," I replied, "it's our business because we are the prospective tenants at the property, and almost injured by your dead renter. Second, we remain interested in signing a lease there, but have questions. As for the private investigator question, we do not precisely fit that definition, there being licensing requirements and other similar inconveniences necessary for us to assume that moniker.

"As for our client, I'd say I'd claim confidentiality, but you wouldn't accept that, as we have no true legal status. In fact, we have no right to ask questions at all. Anything you say is voluntary. You wouldn't have to tell us anything even if we had licenses, which we don't. But you will. You surely will cooperate with us."

"And why is that?" She sounded defiant, and she glanced at her watch. It did not look good.

"We have ways of convincing people to talk," I said. I couldn't believe I said that. It was something out of an old war movie. A bad one.

"Oh, and what are they?" Her eyes narrowed, but I plunged ahead.

"Well, we are always respectful. We are always polite, and are not pushy or arrogant in the least. Also, we always compliment the people we interview on their appearance. By the way, that's a lovely outfit you're wearing. The color perfectly suits your flawless complexion."

"Well, thank you..." she started, and then laughed. "Okay, you got me," she chuckled. "I really have little information for you, but I'll try to help."

"Thank you, Ms. Merriweather, that's very nice of you." I said.

"I don't think the two of you would get any information if not for people like me agreeing to help against my better judgment. Is that pathetic innocence thing you do just an act, or is there at least a tiny smidgen of truth to it?"

"It's all true," I admitted.

"It's our investigative method," Zellie said, sporting a big smile.

Ms. Merriweather looked at Zellie as if about to inquire whether Zellie was pulling her leg, then shrugged in apparent acquiescence. "You might as well call me Jayne. Everyone else does."

"Okay, Jayne. Thank you. What do you know about Ferdinand Darrow?"

"Not much. As I told the police, I only knew him as a name on the lease, and on rent checks. In my job, I review all of the leases, and look into prospective tenants' backgrounds and financials, but I don't interview them."

"What did you find out in your background check and financial review?"

"Well, that's usually confidential, but as he is no longer with us, there is no harm telling you that at least at the time he first rented the place, his finances were solid, and he had no criminal record. He was an attorney in good standing, with no sign of any disciplinary actions against him. In short, he was an acceptable tenant, and we leased him the property."

"When did he first rent the place?"

"Three years ago."

"Why are you renting it now?"

"What do you mean? He's deceased."

"You listed it for rent before the discovery of the body."

"Oh yes. I see your point. He gave notice he intended to vacate."

"How did he do that? In writing, on the phone, by e-mail?"

"In writing, by a letter, received in the mail about two weeks ago. It conformed with the terms of the lease. Notice is required in writing at least two weeks before a tenant vacates."

"Did his lease have a renewal option?" I asked.

"Yes. All of our leases have that feature. On their face they are for one year, but assuming a lease is in good standing, a tenant can renew it at a set incremental increase in the monthly rent."

"Was his lease in good standing?"

"Yes. He paid like clockwork. Never even a day late. We were sorry to see his notice of non-renewal. He was a good tenant."

"No problems with him at all? Not even with his clientele?"

"No. He was a trusts and estates attorney. It's not like he represented hardened criminals."

"So you never met him in person?"

"Not related to his renting the place. I believe I met him once at a charity event."

"What event?"

"I don't recall. It was only a brief encounter."

"Would anyone else here have met him? A building manager, perhaps?"

"Yes. Our building manager for that property is Patsy Bruder. She's in the field now, but I will have my assistant give you her contact information."

I looked at Zellie, who shrugged. We weren't getting anything more here, but I had one more thing to ask.

"Do you happen to have a copy of the notice of non-renewal Mr. Darrow sent?"

She smiled and held out her hands, palms facing each other. No, I'm afraid not. I gave it to the police." She gave an exaggerated look at her watch, and we took the cue, thanked her for her time and departed after first getting Patsy Bruder's contact information.

CHAPTER TWELVE

What did you think of her?" I asked Zellie as we got into the car.

"She's a sharp one, that's for sure."

"No question," I agreed. "But I don't know what to make of her. She cooperated, but didn't tell us anything."

"She told us some things," Zellie replied. "About his status as a trusts and estates' attorney, his finances, and about the notice of non-renewal."

"Yes, she did." I pondered for a moment.

"What's bothering you?"

"That stuff we could get on our own, so it cost her nothing to give it to us. The thing I'm most interested in is the so-called brief encounter with our dead guy at an unspecified charity event."

"You think it means anything?"

"I don't know. But I think we should find out. She was kind of sketchy about it."

"It could be just what she said. She doesn't remember it because it was so brief."

"Maybe. But it wouldn't hurt to cross-check her charity work with Darrow's and see if they had more than a chance encounter."

"Real investigative work. I love it."

"More like random flailing, but your description sounds better."

"Oh, get rid of that grumpy expression. We're good at this."

"You're right. We are good at it, in our own unique way."

Zellie rubbed her stomach. "It's lunch time, isn't it? Tell me it's lunch time."

"It's lunch time."

"Good. I'm starving."

"Okay. We're in Red Bank. Let's go to Jake's and get a sandwich. I'm dying for a Reuben."

"I'm getting a turkey club. Let's walk."

Jake's Sandwich Shop was a Red Bank staple, right on Monmouth Street. Around the corner from the real estate office on Broad Street we just visited. He served legendary sandwiches, piled high like those at the Carnegie Deli, where he worked as a kid. He wasn't a kid anymore. Jacob Rothberg was eighty years young, still presiding behind the counter, barking orders at the youngsters who worked there. They jumped when he told them what to do, but you could see their affection for him. Kind of like their surly on the outside but sweet on the inside grandpa. Heck, he treated all of us that way. Zellie and I have known him since we were kids. Although neither of us ever worked for him, he treated us like we were his former employees, and we indulged his whimsy.

"See those two people?" he barked at one of the two boys working behind the counter. "No not there, numbskull, over there." He pointed right at us. "Two of my best employees. If you could do one tenth of what they did behind this very counter, you'd own the place in a year. You'd kick me right out. Right out that door. I could just retire to Florida."

"You wouldn't know what to do with yourself in Florida, Jake," Zellie laughed. "Who would you harangue? You'd be a fish out of water there."

"I could just play golf and canasta all day, Zellie my dear."

"Oh sure, that would entertain you."

"It might. Maybe I'd like to try it out and see. What do you think, Arnie?"

"You're a deli guy. And let me tell you, my folks live in Florida, and they can't get good deli there. They come back from time to time, as you know, and the first thing they want to do is come here and get the real thing from you. What are you going to do, disappoint Mom and Pop Fischer?"

"Same with my folks," Zellie said. "First thing they want is to go to Jake's and get corned beef sandwiches on rye with your special mustard."

"Well, I couldn't disappoint the lovely Anna Goldstein, now could I?"

Zellie laughed. "No, you couldn't. And it's just like you to pretend to forget that she's been Anna Morgan for almost fifty years."

"I didn't forget, sweetie," he replied. "Maybe just a little wishful thinking, that's all. Now, what can this good-for-nothing make for you," he said, gesturing to a boy who waited patiently for his boss to finish being...well... Jake.

"Turkey club for me," Zellie said to him with a smile. "And Mom's doing great. I'll let her know you asked about her."

"Reuben for me, thanks," I said.

The boy nodded to both of us and said, "Coming right up, guys."

Jake looked over at him. "Muriel and Stan's boy, Nathan. He's a good kid."

I smiled. "He must be, to put up with the likes of you."

We retrieved our sandwiches from Nathan and sat down at a booth near the back. Before she dug in, Zellie sat for a moment, deep in thought. I asked her what was up, and she said, "Does Jake look okay to you?"

"Yes, I think so." I looked over at him. "Pretty much the same as always. He acted the same way as he always does, overtly hostile to his employees, while having the greatest affection for them. Reminiscing about his professed unrequited love for your Mom, while we know full well he was crazy about only one woman in his life."

"Bessie."

"Yes. His late wife of fifty-five years, Elizabeth Rothberg. 'Bessie' to all of us."

"She was such a wonderful lady. I bet he misses her a lot."

"She was sick for a long time."

"Yes. A great deal of strain on them both. We all went to the funeral. My goodness, what a turnout. Both for her and for Jake. Is that it? Or is there something else?"

"I don't know," she said. "It's just a feeling. Could be nothing. Let's eat." And she took a big bite out of her sandwich. "Wow." It was all she could say as she devoured her turkey club. I did the same. Nothing matched Jake's sandwiches anywhere.

We finished our meal and rose to our feet to leave for our appointment with Patsy Bruder, but sat back down when Jake came over and joined us. He wasted no time speaking his mind.

"Word around town is that you guys discovered another body."

"Word travels fast," I said.

"Well, maybe just in here. You know most of Monmouth County comes in here. Anyway, I knew the dead guy. Sort of."

"Ferdinand Darrow?" Zellie asked.

"Yeah, him. And I didn't like him."

"You like everyone, Jake," I said. "What was different about this guy?"

"He was just a little too polite. You know the type. All congenial on the outside, but will stick a knife into you the moment you're not looking. He gave me the creeps."

"How did you know him?"

"Well, I didn't know him. He came in here a couple of times, and I kind of just engaged him in conversation. Or at least tried to. I gave up after the first few attempts."

"What did he say?"

"Not much. He was pretty close-mouthed. Almost secretive acting. But spooky just the same."

"Hard to imagine you not being able to strike up a conversation," Zellie said.

"I know. Strange. I take great pride in my conversing skills. It's almost a religion with me. Anyway, I thought you might like to know, you guys being big time investigators and all. You looking into this?"

"Yes," Zellie said. "It's our latest case."

"Thanks for the information," I added. "And the great sandwiches."

"Anytime. I'll be here."

Zellie grabbed her purse, and we headed out of Jake's and hoisted ourselves into the Suburban.

CHAPTER THIRTEEN

We arrived on time for our appointment with Ms. Bruder. She was all business. You could see it in her face. And oh, what a face. She was only about sixty, but her visage cried out octogenarian, at least. Lots of lines, whether from age, weather or worry, who could tell? Maybe all three. A kind of elliptical skull, but not the way you'd think. Turned on its side so that her giant almost frog-like cheeks gave the impression of a head greater in width than height. Her stringy, poorly dyed brown hair hung down in bangs, which almost obscured her forehead, completing the sideways oval.

A tool belt hung from her hips, with many building manager utensils hanging at odd angles in the pockets, including a hammer that looked at least as old as the person carrying it. I couldn't help thinking it a little odd to hire an elderly looking woman as the all-purpose handyman, fixer and building manager, but she looked competent. And she greeted us in a businesslike manner.

"They told me to cooperate with you," she said, skipping the usual formalities of handshakes, greetings, and pleasantries. Her tone was one of a very busy person speaking to us only because ordered to do so. But I sensed that the reluctance was rooted in her long list of things to do, and spending time with us would put her behind schedule.

"Kind of unusual," she added drily. "Jayne the Pain rarely cooperates with anyone." She looked us over. "I shouldn't have said that," she added. "Oops."

"We won't repeat it," I hastened to assure her. I intended to gain her trust, so that she wouldn't hesitate to say other unscripted things, but it turned out that this was unnecessary.

"Nah, repeat it if you want. I've never met her in person, as she's a big-ass executive in a cushy office, and I'm a lowly worker bee out in the field, but I talk to her plenty, and know she's an A-hole. You can write that down and repeat it. Write it fifty times on a blackboard. Notify the press. Big headline: 'Jayne Merriweather is an A-Hole.' She wanted cooperation, she'll get cooperation. Whaddya want to know?" She paused, looking us over, her eyes narrowing "Why did she tell me to cooperate? Are you friends of hers? As if she has any friends. But still, why did she send you here? That is not in her character to do that. She's almost legendary in her secretiveness."

"We're not sure," Zellie offered. "She started out being kind of close-mouthed like you said, but then she seemed to relax a bit."

"I bet she did a threat assessment and concluded that you posed no danger. Interesting," she added, the suspicious look fading. "I suppose she told you nothing of value, in that supercilious way of hers?"

"That's an accurate analysis," I said. "You know what we're looking into, right?"

"Ferdinand Darrow."

"Yup. What can you tell us about him?"

"Silent. Thoughtful. And I don't mean considerate. I mean lost in thought, as if something weighed on his mind. Pre-oc-cupied, every time I saw him."

"Did you see him a lot?"

"No. How often do you see a building manager? A couple of things need maintenance, minor repairs, things like that. And I handle all the buildings we own. Not just that little cot-tage. Tenants pay their rent to the main office, and it's not like I do the cleaning – that's handled by 'Genuinely Clean.' Some-one from that outfit probably saw him every weekday. Talk to them. A fellow named Russell Devereaux. Russ is a good guy. He can tell you who did the regular visits to the cottage. Tell him that Patsy sent you."

"Did you ever talk to Mr. Darrow?"

"Well, sure. Several times on the phone, to hear what prob-lem he had, and to make appointments to visit. He didn't want me there while he met with clients, which I understood. So, we coordinated our schedules. I'm very scheduled. I like order, and I hate to be late." She made a show of looking at her watch. "And I saw him on the half-dozen or so times he had an issue to address."

I ignored the attempt to hurry us along. "What were the issues?"

"Oh, I don't remember. A leaky faucet, that was one. The window wouldn't open. Too hot in the office, then too cold. A quiet guy, for sure, but kind of picky, if you ask me."

"Did you ever see any of his clients?" Zellie inquired.

"I told you he never wanted me there when he met with clients... but... there was one time." She paused, as if deep in thought. "It was a dark-haired lady who was just leaving as I ar-rived. And Mr. Darrow seemed a little flushed, like they'd been arguing, or maybe they'd just had sex. Could have been either, I guess."

"She didn't say anything?"

"Nope. Not a word. Kept her head down and didn't even look at me."

"What did she look like?"

"Well, she had dark hair." She looked at Zellie. "Much darker than yours. Taller than you, and definitely not as pretty."

Zellie ignored the compliment. "Did you notice anything else about her? Her clothes, anything? And I suppose you didn't hear her name?"

"She wore a smart outfit. Not like me," she added ruefully, looking down at her tool belt. "Business dress. And no, I didn't hear her name. Is that all?"

"Not quite." I said. "Did you happen to notice anything in the office with anyone's name on it?"

"I don't snoop," she said, a hard edge in her voice.

"I'm sure you don't," I said, my voice dropping to a near whisper to soothe her rising temper. "I didn't mean that. Only, when doing your job, you notice things sometimes."

"I didn't notice anything."

Time to leave well enough alone. She was shutting down. And we could always come back. "Well thank you, Ms. Bruder."

She nodded. "You're welcome." But she didn't mean it, and I wondered what nerve I had touched.

As we walked out to the car, I looked over at Zellie, and could see she wondered about it, too.

"What made her clam up like that?"

"I don't know. I asked a routine question. But she's a terrible liar, and she noticed something. And she's a snoop."

"No doubt about it," Zellie agreed. "It's almost three-thirty," she said, glancing at her wrist. Where to next?"

"Why don't you give Melissa a call and see if she received the autopsy report yet. If so, we can swing by and pick it up."

"Okay, will do. While you drive, I'll also call that Russ guy and see when he might be available to talk to us."

"Good idea."

Zellie called, and Melissa told her we could pick up the autopsy report anytime, and that it was a piece of cake getting it. She also told Zellie that Chester acted like a little puppy eager to please.

"That doesn't sound like him," I said. "She must have an incredible massage technique."

"Maybe," she said, an element of doubt creeping into her voice. "I wonder." She didn't elaborate, and I let her think about it. Zellie has great instincts, and interrupting her thought process wouldn't help. She'd tell me when she was ready.

She called the offices of Genuinely Clean and asked for Russ. He was out on a job, and she left a message on his voice mail. "I like a boss who helps with the actual work. It shows he cares about his business."

I nodded agreement, while paying attention to my driving, and we soon arrived at Melissa's real estate massage parlor.

Melissa got up from behind the entry desk, and greeted us with overt warmth, again acting like we were her best buddies. She gave each of us hugs. I wondered a little at the familiarity of it all, and could see that it surprised Zellie as well. I decided to let it go, and chalked it up to our bonding at the shared experience of discovering a body.

"The autopsy file is right here," she said, almost breathlessly. "I feel like a detective. It's so exciting." She looked at us for a moment. "It must be old hat to the two of you, but I'm just beside myself."

"Did you read it?" I asked, more to calm her down than because I was interested in her answer. She obviously had read it. It was open on the desk and I saw her close it the moment we entered.

"Well, I might have peeked."

"It's okay," Zellie said. "You're the one who got it for us. Nothing wrong with curiosity."

"It was poison," she blurted. "A high concentration of zinc phosphide, it says. Murder, no doubt about it. Here. Read it for yourselves."

She thrust the file in our direction and Zellie took it from her. We huddled our heads together and read it in silence. Melissa's summary was correct. Zinc phosphide poisoning. Whatever that was. But it was deadly, and most assuredly murder. I tried to make out the name of the pathologist who performed the autopsy, but it was just a signature without a corresponding typed name. And an indecipherable signature. The report bore the letterhead of the Office of the Medical Examiner for the State of New Jersey, County of Monmouth. It contained nothing else of value to us.

"Does this help us figure out who did it?" Melissa asked.

"Us?" I asked, an eyebrow raised.

"Well, I know you two are the detectives, but I hoped... I mean, I discovered the body, too. I was hoping to help you solve the case." She leaned forward and lowered her voice in a conspiratorial whisper. "You may think the life of a real estate broker massage therapist is exciting and glamorous, but it's not that way at all. It's boring, to tell the truth. A murder, now that's exciting."

"Well, you've helped a lot already," I said. "And we intend to call on you for further assistance as the investigation progresses. Don't we, Zellie?"

"Yes, for sure."

"Oh, I'll be ready. No question about it. Call me anytime. In the meantime, I'll keep my ear to the ground and let you know if any more useful information comes my way."

"Great, thanks," I said, and Zellie nodded agreement as we turned to leave.

With that, we left the office and went out to my behemoth, I mean car.

"Shall we call it a day?" I asked. "There are things I need to do tomorrow morning in Eatontown and I want to get an early start."

"I have errands to run that I never seem to get to. Why don't you drop me off at my house, and we'll meet up tomorrow afternoon at...," she paused. "I started to say the office, but we don't have one. We need to take care of that."

"We tried. But that darn Ferdinand Darrow had the nerve to die in our new office."

Zellie giggled. "Very inconsiderate of him, I'd say."

"Very."

"Why don't you pick me up at my house at say... one o'clock tomorrow, and we'll get lunch and get started again. And no discovering any bodies while we're separated."

"And no getting kidnapped," I added.

"Right. Not that either."

I kissed Zellie, and dropped her off at home and drove down the street to my house. We have to stop this two-house business, I thought. We needed an office, sure. But we needed a home for the two of us even more. And one other thing we needed, and that was the nature of my business the next day. And I wanted to keep it from Zellie. I hated to sneak around behind her back, but it couldn't be helped. I required counsel on this though, and I knew just the attorney from whom to seek assistance.

CHAPTER FOURTEEN

Hi Marla. It's Arnie. I need some help, and I think you're the best person to ask. No, it's nothing like that, thank goodness." I explained what I needed, and she agreed. "When can we meet?" I asked.

"Today, if that works for you. I have only two morning appointments. I'll finish up here by ten o'clock. Why don't you stop by the office and we can talk about it?"

"Okay, but for obvious reasons, Zellie can't know we met at all, or she'll get suspicious. And you know how persistent she can be. She won't stop until she gets answers."

"I know. But maybe we should have a good cover story in case she finds out - like you have a legal problem, or something."

"What problem could I have? You're a criminal lawyer."

"How about keeping you out of jail for the Mort disaster?"

"Marla, that's ridiculous. Zellie and I helped put the bad guys away. She'd never believe I was worried about going to jail for that."

"Oh, I know. How did you find time alone to call me, anyway? You two are inseparable."

"She's at the gym and then running errands. We do spend time apart, you know."

"I assumed so. But I rarely see it these days. And there is no way you'll keep this a secret from her for long. What's your timetable?"

"I'm hoping for next weekend. That is if we can conclude our business successfully before then."

"Maybe we won't need a cover story if it's that soon, but let's just say that you wanted a referral for a securities lawyer to help deal with the fallout from your prior employment."

"That's a better idea, but it won't explain our sneaking around together."

"How about we're having an affair?"

We both laughed at that, but in hindsight, maybe we shouldn't have. We agreed to meet at ten o'clock and left our cover story to be concocted at that time. Before I hung up, I cautioned her against disclosing to anyone about the nature of our business, including Ted.

"He has a big mouth, you know."

"I know. The big sweet lug can't keep a secret. But it's no problem. Mum's the word. I'm an attorney, remember? Client confidences are my business."

***

Zellie finished her food shopping and, as none of her groceries required immediate freezing or refrigeration, she decided to pop in at Marla's nearby office and attempt to drag her out for a coffee break. Arnie had said something about going to Eatontown on an errand, so it was a good time for some girl talk.

She drove over to Marla's office, and was about to turn into the small client parking lot when she spotted Arnie and Marla coming out the front door with their heads together, laughing as if sharing a private joke. Zellie made the instant decision to just keep driving.

She didn't know why, but somehow, it seemed not a good idea to interrupt their private reverie. A whole host of unwanted feelings washed over her. She wondered if she was jealous, but didn't think so. She trusted both of them.

So she headed home and put her groceries away.

CHAPTER FIFTEEN

I pulled up in Zellie's driveway and checked the clock on the dashboard. 12:58. Right on time. I fought traffic all the way and went about 100 miles an hour the rest of the time, but I made it. Before I got out of the car, I sniffed all around my body. Nope. No sign of Marla's perfume. Luckily, she doesn't wear a powerful scent. I can't believe I'm doing this. Sneaking around on Zellie. But I have to do it, at least for a little while. Okay, time to go in. Act natural, I reminded myself.

As is my custom, I knocked a few times, and let myself in. Before I could even enter, the hand of an unseen person grabbed my arm, and dragged me inside, straight into a warm, inviting embrace. And my goodness, a terrific one. The hug faded into a passionate kiss, and before I knew it, Zellie had pulled me into the bedroom. Not that I needed dragging, mind you. Zellie is incredibly sexy, and I love everything about her. I forgot to act natural. There was no need to act. She never asked me what I did this morning. And I didn't ask her, either.

***

We were sitting in Zellie's kitchen, having a little snack.

"What's next?" I asked. "Should we interview Russ at Genuinely Clean?"

"Yes," she said, taking her time to speak. "We still need to cover that base. But I've been thinking. Ever since Melissa gave us that file and was so anxious to tag along on our investigation, I've wondered about her."

"Melissa?" I asked, doubt creeping into my voice. "She seems harmless. And given she discovered the body with us, it seems natural she would want to come along for the ride. Doesn't it?"

"I suppose. But maybe I'm just jaded from our last case, where an invisible hand led us around by the nose, and pointed in whatever direction the unseen force wanted to explore."

"How could I forget? Do you think Melissa led us to that particular office on purpose?"

"I don't know what to think, but it's worth looking into. Think about it. She offers us the Buckles Building, which it's at least possible she knew would be a non-starter for us. She later expressed surprise at us being detectives, but our first case and our names were big local news. Then she told us that the only other available office space is the cottage. It's possible, but I don't think so."

"You know, I don't see you as the suspicious type."

Zellie smiled. "You'd be surprised. We're investigators. I'm learning the skill."

For a moment I flashed on my morning activities, but it passed. "Well, I agree that we should check out why Melissa showed us that office space. But how?"

"I have no clue why. But I have an idea on how."

It was my turn to smile. "Of course you do."

"She had to get those listings from somewhere, didn't she? Most brokers use the Multiple Listing Service, or MLS. Melissa even referred to it when she talked with the police. Let's face it, she is not the most advanced real estate broker in the world. She must use it, too. Were they the only available office buildings? We should look at the MLS ourselves, and see. And use every other search engine to check as well. Let's see what was available at the time, or at least what's out there now."

"Makes sense. And it seems so...competent. Do you think we're getting good at this?"

"It doesn't seem possible, does it?"

"For me, maybe. But for you, sweetheart, the sky's the limit."

CHAPTER SIXTEEN

Y ou're kidding, right?" Ted looked outraged. It was a cultivated look. It isn't easy to offend Ted. He took most things in stride, and this didn't rile him up. We were sitting at our usual table at Audacious Bagel, and Zellie and I had just asked him to do us a favor.

"We're serious, Ted," I said. "I think you can handle it. Or is our simple request too hard for you?" I played along with his feigned distress.

"You want me to access the MLS. The Multiple Listing Service? That MLS? Me? The impresario of unauthorized access? The sultan of sneakiness? Wasted on something mundane as that? I'm insulted. Nay, aggrieved."

"We know it's beneath you, Ted." I said. "And to answer your question, your majesty, yes. You. But to assuage your injured sensibilities, what we really want is for you to access the MLS as it existed when Melissa first showed us the office building."

Ted looked mollified. "Well, that's different. Easy, but at least not a job for a simpleton. But there are many public applications and databases that can search property listings. And Zellie, you could do that in your sleep."

"I know, and I'll do that myself," Zellie said, unruffled by Ted's ministrations. "But I can't do what we asked you to do.

Those databases only look at what's available now. They're not as good for telling what was available at a fixed point in time in the past."

"Okay. I can do that. No problem. I'll get right on it."

He didn't move. We looked at him expectantly.

"I didn't mean right away. I meant after breakfast. Anyway, Marla should be here any minute." I shifted a few times in my seat, drew my fingers across my brow, and rubbed my neck as he continued. "I called her and as luck would have it, a client canceled this morning."

It wasn't that I didn't want to see Marla. I just feared that one of us might slip and say something about our clandestine meeting. And I didn't want Zellie to find out. Or Ted. And Marla didn't worry me. As a criminal attorney, she could keep a secret. She had confidences so locked away, Houdini couldn't unlock them.

No, it was me I worried about. I tell Zellie everything. I always have. And I hated keeping a secret from her. Absolutely hated it. She was so smart and perceptive, she'd know in a second that something was amiss. And I'd blurt it out and ruin everything.

I glanced over at Zellie. If I wasn't mistaken, she looked a little uncomfortable herself. I wondered what that was all about? My musings were interrupted by the appearance of our intrepid waitress, the one and only Delilah. She wore a T-shirt that read "Sample My Luscious" on the front. I resolved not to say a word, even though all eyes were upon me, waiting. I refused to walk into this one. I wondered whether she saw us sit down and changed into another one of these provocative shirts just to get a response from me. But that's kind of self-centered of me. Of course she didn't do that. The world doesn't revolve around me, now does it?

"Hi guys," Delilah said, with a sunny smile. "What'll it be today? We have a special – an herb crusted red snapper bagel sandwich. How about it, Arnie? And no comment about my T-shirt? You know you want to say something. I saw you sit down, and I put this one on just for you." She twirled around, showing us the words "Bagel Infusions" on the back. Then she laughed, and we joined in.

How does she do that? It's almost like she read my mind. Then I saw Zellie giggling. Zellie. She put Delilah up to it, telling her I had vowed not to say a word about Delilah's sexually charged attire next time we went to AB. Once more, I had walked into it. This time skewered for not saying anything. I can't win.

At that moment Marla walked in and sat down. She took one look at Delilah's T-shirt and burst into laughter. She looked at me. "They got you again, didn't they?"

I hung my head and nodded. "Yes, they did. This time for keeping my mouth shut."

"You said nothing about a T-shirt that says 'Sample My Luscious?'"

"I know. The shame of it all."

We gave Delilah our orders and she hustled off to fill them.

"What did I miss? Other than watching Arnie's befuddlement."

Marla. She is so great. Not a shred of tension in her voice, and launching right into safe territory. I don't know why I worried.

"We asked Ted to do some of his patented electronic research," Zellie offered. "And he engaged in his customary histrionics about how demeaning our research projects are to someone of his sublime skill set." She looked at Ted. "Does that about cover it?"

"Pretty much. But you left out the sultan stuff. Royalty. It's very important to include that in assessing my inflated ego."

Marla chuckled and leaned over to give Ted a soft kiss on the cheek. "That's my little prince. Big-headed, but with an enormous heart."

I glanced over at Zellie and thought I caught a brief wrinkle in her brow and a pursing of her lips, but she caught my look and smiled, so I figured I was mistaken.

After eating our breakfast, and engaging in amiable conversation, Marla rose to leave for an appointment back at the office. Ted followed suit, after telling us he would have our results later in the day. We left a tip for Delilah and paid the bill on our way out. I took Zellie's hand, and as we walked to the car, we decided to make an appointment to see Russ at Genuinely Clean, then get down to some serious research about Ferdinand Darrow. Our day thus planned, we jumped into my SUV. While we sat there, Zellie confirmed that we could go right over. As long as we could talk while he was working, he was "all ours." We sped over to the address he gave us, which turned out to be the vacant office in the Buckles Building. It was on the second floor, with Buckles on the first. Before we ascended the stairway, I spotted Buckles' secretary, Belinda, with her unmistakable big puffy bottle blonde hair, and waved. She came right over and gave us hugs.

"Still working for Buckles, I see."

"Yeah, and he's still a weasel. But I guess he's my weasel. And he's treating me nice. He's acting almost like a human. I wonder what that's all about. But I guess you two showed him. He hates you, you know."

"Oh, we figured as much. He's blessed, that one. Somehow stayed out of jail. If he gives you a hard time again, you should leave."

"I know. But the pay is... well, lousy, but it almost pays the bills."

We nodded in sympathy.

"And it's a job. Anyway, gotta run. He gets antsy, you know. And if he sees me talking to you, whoo boy, I'm in big trouble. But good to see you guys. I mean it." And she headed back to Buckles' office.

"Poor kid," I said.

We trudged upstairs to meet with Russ, who was sweeping the floor as we entered. I studied him for a moment. I guessed his age as forty or so, five-eight, with a stocky build, and a shock of wavy brown hair. He had a wide, friendly face, which sported what looked like a perpetual smile, showing gleaming white teeth. He hummed a Beatles tune in a low voice. I could just make out *Let it Be*. We introduced ourselves and shook hands.

CHAPTER SEVENTEEN

M ind if I keep working? I have to keep to a schedule, or I don't get done. And if I don't finish, I don't get paid. And I like getting paid." That electric grin again. I couldn't help smiling, too.

"No problem. Mind if we ask you a few questions while you work?"

"Nope. Fire away."

"You know why we're here, right?" I asked, as a preamble.

"Sure. It's about the dead guy. Clarence Darrow."

"His actual name was Ferdinand."

"I guess I knew that. But he was a lawyer, right? So I called him Clarence, and he didn't seem to mind. Anyway, he never told me to stop."

"Did you talk to him much?"

"Sure. Pretty much every evening. He insisted on the cleaning and maintenance and any other visit to occur when he was there. That's not unusual, though. Some people are like that. As a lawyer, he could have kept confidential client stuff hanging around. Top secret, you know. Not for the eyes of a mere custodial type like me." Again, the broad smile.

"What did you talk about?" Zellie asked.

"Oh, this and that. Mostly sports, I guess."

"Big football fan?"

"Well, yes, I suppose. But not the football you're thinking about. Soccer. He called it football. I like all sports, although I'm an American football guy. Baseball, basketball, hockey, that sort of thing. But he loved soccer. Knew all the teams in Europe and was a rabid World Cup fan. So, I got to know the teams and players, too. It's good business to talk the same language as the customers. Mind if I turn the vacuum on for a couple minutes?"

"Of course not. You have a job to do, and we don't want to interfere."

We watched as he vacuumed the office, taking the hose out of the side to get in the corners. He turned it off and turned back to us.

"Anything else you talked about?"

"Nothing I can think of offhand. The weather, the news, that sort of thing. Pretty much just chitchat. I'm kind of fast moving, anyway. I don't dawdle, and unless clients have issues to discuss, like the quality of the maintenance, I say a few things and move on. Like I told you, I have a schedule to keep. Friendly is one thing. But clients don't want you hanging around. And this guy was less forthcoming than most. Kind of secretive, if you ask me. But I chalked that up to the type of business he did."

"Did you ever see any of his clients?"

"No, never. I come at the end of the day, after clients are gone. But wait a minute, yes. There was one. A woman. A couple of weeks ago."

"What did she look like?"

"Oh, gee, I'm not sure. White, with dark hair for sure. I don't know, maybe taller than me, or maybe the same height, but definitely not as heavy." He patted his stomach and smiled. "You get the idea."

We did. A medium height, medium weight, dark haired white woman. Not real helpful.

"Did you hear them talking?" Zellie asked.

"Not really. As soon as I came in, I could hear voices, and could tell that he had company. I figured it was a client with a late appointment, and I didn't want to disturb them."

"But you listened anyway," I said in as conspiratorial voice as I could muster.

"Not exactly. His militancy about privacy and the sanctity of the attorney-client relationship made me kind of reluctant to get him worked up."

"But you heard something, right?"

"Only a few words, I swear. I heard her call him a liar. It was pretty loud. I couldn't have ignored it even if I tried."

"She was angry?"

"I guess so. I just stood in the doorway, and they sat in his private office, but you don't shout at someone unless you're kind of mad at them, right?"

"Sure," I said. "Did you hear anything else?"

"I don't think so."

"What did you do next?"

"I made a little noise, so he thought I just entered, and went about emptying the trash and doing my usual stuff."

"Did they say anything to you?"

"Not really. She hurried out without a word. He said hello, and not much else. I figured this client had upset him, and he wasn't in the mood for the usual few minutes of small talk, and I left it at that."

"Do you know the exact date this happened?" I asked.

"Um. The week before last, I think. I'll check. He pulled out his smartphone and looked at his calendar. "Yes. two weeks ago today. I made a note I needed to order that liquid soap because I had just enough to fill the dispenser in his bathroom that day."

"Thanks. If you think of anything else, please call. We appreciate you taking the time for us. We know you're busy."

I handed him a card, and he glanced at it and put it in his pocket. "Sure, no problem."

When we got outside, Zellie grabbed me by the arm. "Okay, let's see it."

I feigned innocence. "See what?"

"We don't have business cards. We barely have a business. And we don't even have an address." She paused for a millisecond. "Yet," she added. "But you handed him a card. Let's see it, buster."

"Okay, okay." I held up my hands, palms facing her, and chuckled. I pulled out a little plastic card case and showed her a card.

"A to Z Investigations," she read. "In raised, gold, embossed print. Very snazzy. And a phone number. Minimalist. I like it. When did you have these printed?"

"I went to a one-hour print shop in Eatontown. A place Marla recommended. I wanted to surprise you." It wasn't the only reason I went to Eatontown, or the sole purpose for meeting Marla, but I conveniently left that out.

"I just had a few made, because we want to put our business address on there. When we have one."

"Well, it would be presumptuous of us to put it in before we sign a lease. Or solve the murder."

"Right. So, for the time being, no address or business phone number. Only a cell phone number."

"Not even our names?"

"I didn't want to go there. It's the A to Z Agency. Not the Z to A Agency. If I put the names on there, it would necessitate putting my name first. And egalitarian that I am, I left the names out."

"At some point, we have to put our names on there. And just because it's the A to Z Agency, it doesn't mean that your name goes first."

"It's not Zellie and Arnie, it's Arnie and Zellie. Zellie and Arnie sounds dumb."

"I like the sound of Zellie and Arnie. It has a nice ring to it." Zellie was giggling.

"You see why I didn't put our names on there? I didn't want to get into an argument about who should be on top. Um. Maybe that didn't come out right." I was laughing, too. Neither of us cared whose name was first. The important thing was that we were together.

"Okay, enough of this. What did we learn?" I asked.

"Someone argued with Darrow two weeks ago."

"And it was a dark haired, white woman."

"That matches the basic description of the woman Patsy Bruder saw, but with no other distinguishing characteristics, it could be almost anyone."

"Right. Of course, Jayne has dark hair."

"So do a lot of other women. Anyway, we learned that he was alive two weeks ago. That was your point in asking that question, right?"

"Yes. And that's new information. The medical examiner's report didn't specify that."

"No, and that's a funny thing. That coroner's report was skimpy. What kind of report doesn't even give the approximate time of death?" Zellie asked.

"We should look into that further. Maybe there is a supplemental report Melissa didn't receive."

"Yes, we should. And just maybe we weren't given the full report."

"That's a possibility. It's not like the Middletown police want to do us any favors."

"But we didn't ask for the report, Melissa did."

"Dunston had to know she requested it for us and wanted to keep us in the dark."

"We'll have to do a little digging to find out if we have the same information as the police."

Let's go home and continue our discussion there. And maybe take a break before we conduct further research."

I smiled. "A break sounds like a good idea." It seemed like we were taking a lot of "breaks" during this investigation. Another one of the advantages of working together.

CHAPTER EIGHTEEN

We walked Lazlow when we returned home. After sniffing almost everything outside and doing his business, we gave him some water and he settled into his bed for a doggie nap.

A couple of hours later, Zellie and I sat together in front of the computer, trying to find more information on Ferdinand Darrow, an attorney in Middletown, New Jersey. But he had no attorney profile online. No address, no website for his office, and no phone listing. Strange. A local lawyer with a prominent name having no online presence. There had to be a trail, and we were confident we'd find it.

"This is hopeless," I said.

"Totally," Zellie agreed. "There's nothing here. There just doesn't seem to be a Middletown attorney named Ferdinand Darrow. We need a different approach. Maybe we should visit Mrs. Minniefield. She's good at helping us order our thoughts. Making sure we're going about this right."

"Okay, we haven't seen her in a while. I miss her. And we can bring Lazlow over for a play date with Fideaux."

"I'll call her."

She readily agreed, and we headed right over to the little white house with the black shutters where Mrs. Minniefield had resided for decades. It sat on the corner of the street where Zellie and I grew up, and lived our entire lives. Mrs. Minniefield was an old friend, confidant, and sensible adult advisor for both of us for as long as we both could remember. We trusted her without reservation.

When we arrived, she hugged us, and ushered Lazlow into her big, fenced-in backyard, where her dog Fideaux waited. The three of us watched their doggie greeting ceremony, which consisted of lots of sniffing.

When they both ran off, we returned to the living room, where Zellie and I sat down on the little loveseat. Mrs. M. sat on the delicate looking armchair that we knew from long experience was her favorite. It painted an incongruous picture, with her broad shoulders and large body almost consuming the chair, and the two adjacent overstuffed easy chairs remaining empty. She fills a room with her commanding presence just like she fills that chair.

She looked at us with those razor sharp, intelligent gray eyes, and said, without preamble, "How are you doing with the Ferdinand Darrow investigation?"

Zellie and I exchanged a look. How does she do that? We hadn't even spoken to her since we discovered Darrow's body, or more accurately, Darrow's body discovered us. I figured she read it in the paper and guessed. Mrs. M disabused me of that notion. Almost as if she read my mind, and before either one of us could answer her, she continued.

"I know your inquiries are preliminary and are a necessary part of the investigative process. I couldn't agree more with your choices of initial interview subjects. As you know, when I ask how it's going, I'm looking for your overall impressions at this early stage."

Typical Mrs. Minniefield, cut right to the crux of the matter. Don't tell her stuff she already knows. And don't try to figure out how she knows it. She's a marvel. And I wouldn't put it past her to know what they told us.

But I guess she didn't know, showing real interest when we told her our impressions from our various interviews. Our decision to look into Melissa's candor intrigued her.

"Interesting," she said. "A real estate broker directing clients to a particular listing, without showing them all available office space is unethical, but is sadly not uncommon. But still...," she paused for a moment as if pondering something, then almost imperceptibly shook her head. "It's worth checking out. You asked Ted to work on that, I assume?"

"Yes," Zellie answered. "I can do basic computer searches, but that one requires his expertise. We've tried to find more information about Darrow, but know little about him. No lawyer has such a tiny public footprint. And not one with a prominent name."

"Why don't you keep at it for a while," Mrs. Minniefield suggested. "You won't be able to find any background on him if he's in the Witness Protection Program, for example, but you might not have explored all avenues available to you. And Arnie, don't look at me like I can access WITSEC records. I may have good law enforcement contacts, but not that good."

I had private doubts that Mrs. M. couldn't get access to pretty much anything, but kept my mouth shut.

"Have you looked at birth records? Was he born in the United States? Have you considered the possibility that Ferdinand Darrow is not his original name? Name changes are public records. Also, have you considered looking at immigration records? They're pretty searchable now. You might find something there."

"We considered the possibility that Ferdinand Darrow was not his real name, but have found nothing yet. But we hadn't thought about immigration records. That's a good idea. Thanks."

"It won't be that easy," Mrs. M. warned. "You're comparing a general description and age, but you may not have the right name, time frame, or country of origin for his emigration."

I have an idea about that," Zellie replied.

Mrs. Minniefield smiled. "I'm certain you do."

We exchanged pleasantries with Mrs. M, retrieved Lazlow, and departed. I always loved seeing her. She could move from direct and forceful to warm and loving in a second. A rock-solid personality with a fondness for dogs and of course, us.

***

"What's your idea?" I asked as soon as we returned home. I couldn't wait to hear what she had in mind.

Zellie fired up the computer and went online. "Let's assume that the name Darrow is bogus," she said. "A lawyer named Darrow? A little too coincidental, don't you think? It's like he chose the name to fit his desired profession, or his training, perhaps in a different country."

"He could have seen *Inherit the Wind* overseas.

"Right. So, I thought, where did the name Ferdinand come from? Clarence would have been overkill, so maybe he chose something more familiar. Mrs. Minniefield suggested we check immigration records. And look at this!" She held two thumbs up.

I looked over her shoulder, inhaling her sweet fragrance as I did so.

"You smell nice."

"Eau de Ivory soap. And thank you. But look." She pointed at the screen.

I looked at the web page she indicated and saw that Ferdinand was a Spanish version of a Germanic term comprising the terms for journey, brave and daring. "So we look first at emigration from Spain and Germany," I said. "Brilliant."

"Maybe not so much. That's a lot of immigration records to look at. How far back do we go? Our dead guy could have come over as a child a half century ago, or even be the son or grandson of someone who came over a hundred years ago."

"It's a lot to look at, sure, but you've narrowed it way down. And I'm guessing post-1960 anyway, because that's the year *Inherit the Wind* came out."

"Oh, good thinking."

Zellie didn't ask me how I knew the year. I'm a movie trivia buff.

"I have to come up with something. It seems you're the one who always has an idea."

"Now that's not true. I can tell you have another idea right now." Zellie said, stroking my thigh.

"We've been getting distracted a lot, haven't we?"

"It's about time we had fun. But I think we should keep at this right now."

"No question. We have a business to run."

"And with luck, one that pays the bills someday."

"A minor detail."

Zellie continued to study the computer monitor. I watched for a while, then announced my intention to pop out and get the mail. She nodded absently, and I went out. I retrieved a few bills and advertisements from the box, and one long, official-looking envelope bearing the seal of the State of New Jersey.

"Jury duty," I muttered under my breath as I returned to the house. I opened it while Zellie continued working.

"Crap," I blurted out.

Zellie looked up. "What's the matter?"

I brought the letter over and handed it to her.

"Crap," she said. "How did they know?"

"Somebody finked on us. The cops, or Jack Buckles. Had to be one of them."

It was a letter from the New Jersey Attorney General's office, telling us we were violating the Private Detective Act of 1939, and to cease and desist acting as private investigators without a license. We had ten days to get a license, or demonstrate that we were working for a licensed private detective, or someone with the requisite background and experience. Failure to comply could result in arrest by the State Police and being charged with a misdemeanor. Also, conviction of the offense would cause a permanent bar to becoming licensed.

"What can we do about it? We can't just get five years of experience overnight."

"We'll think of something. And don't worry, the solution won't involve Mike Mullen. Anyway, I'm not sure we've even violated the law in this case. The last one, I suppose, but not this one."

"How do you figure?"

"We just finished saying we don't have a paying client. We don't even have a client, he being dead and all. I'm not a lawyer, but I'm pretty sure you have to be doing it for money to be a professional detective."

"Hey, that's right. As long as we have no clients, we're good to go."

"A terrible business model, to be sure, but that's the idea."

"We should communicate our promise to the Attorney General that we won't take any money until we're licensed, or otherwise work it out."

"Sure. I wonder if they'll buy it?"

"Sure they will. It's only fair."

***

They didn't buy it. I tested the theory with the New Jersey Attorney General's office. Doing so required navigating five different voice menus transferring me from one place to another. Kind of like the bureaucratic version of a pentathlon, and enough to drive the sanest person bonkers. At last I reached someone, who I swear only knew the word no. He never met an issue he could say yes to. And an advisory opinion? Forget it.

"It doesn't matter whether you're getting paid. If you hold yourself out to be a private investigator, you must have a license. Period. And what is your name, sir?"

"Bruce Wayne," I replied.

"Well, Mr. Wayne, I am noting that you must get a license right away."

I thanked him for his time and rang off.

"That went well. Not."

"What are we going to do? I don't want us arrested."

"We could hire a lawyer. I think the state guy I talked to is wrong. We're not taking any money, so we're only private citizens asking a lot of nosy questions. We couldn't have been clearer about that with the people we interviewed."

"If we have no paying clients, how can we pay for a lawyer? There's Marla, I suppose, but she's a criminal lawyer. We can call her if they arrest us. But we don't want it to get that far."

"No, we don't. And what we want is to get licensed, so we can keep our business going. The only thing a lawyer could do is maybe let us continue to not receive money. We just need to get licensed. Which means finding someone to be our nominal supervisor, without telling us what to do."

"We'll figure out something. In the meantime, the letter says we have ten days. That's plenty of time to solve the case,"

Zellie pronounced, with a firm rap on the desk. "It's time to get back to work. And look at this." She pointed at the screen.

"What am I looking at?"

"Right there. Only one hundred eighty-seven names meet our search criteria."

"Only?"

"You must admit, that's not many, given the sheer number of immigrants coming to the United States from Spain and Germany since 1960."

I nodded. "You're right. But how do we cull the list down to something we can manage in less than ten days?"

"I think we can narrow the search criteria. It was important to get the full universe of names first, then to work from there." She looked at her watch. "It's getting late. We can sleep on it and think about ways to limit our inquiry."

"What do you want for dinner?" I asked. "We have a choice of Chinese from Chow Chow Ming's, pizza from the takeout window at D'Agostinos, or my famous homemade spaghetti and meatballs."

"Let's go with the famous pasta," Zellie said, laughing. "Then we don't even have to leave the house. I'll even make my not so famous garlic bread."

"It would be famous, if anyone knew about it." I said loyally.

"That's kind of what makes fame, isn't it? That people know about it?"

So, we had spaghetti and meatballs, with garlic bread and salad, watched a little television, and went to bed early. I drifted off to sleep with Zellie nestled under my arm.

CHAPTER NINETEEN

When I woke up the next morning, Zellie had already risen. I wandered into the kitchen and stood in the doorway. She didn't notice me at first, which gave me a moment to study her profile. She stood over the stove, stirring some scrambled eggs, and softly singing Simon & Garfunkel's *Sound of Silence*. I looked toward her right ear for signs of ear buds, but saw none.

I continued to look at her with unabashed admiration. She was clad in her customary sweatshirt, with her brownish blonde hair draping her shoulders. Her nose, ever so slightly *retroussé*, accentuated her clear complexion and pretty face. She wore not a shred of makeup at this hour of the morning, and oh my goodness, was she beautiful. Okay, okay, I know I'm prejudiced, but if genetics had anything to do with it, Zellie would keep those good looks for a long time. Her mom, now in her late seventies, was still a knockout.

Something stirred at my feet, and I noticed Lazlow, lounging in his usual place just inside the door jamb. He eyed the food Zellie was preparing with more interest than his usual lugubrious demeanor might otherwise dictate. At his movement, Zellie noticed me. She turned that thousand-watt smile and dark brown eyes on me.

"Well, good morning, sleepyhead," she exclaimed. She looked down at the pan. "These should be ready in a moment."

I moved up behind her, reached around her waist and pulled her close. I felt her warmth radiate over my entire body.

"How long have you been up?"

"About an hour. I took Lazlow for a walk. He pooped on Mrs. Carey's front lawn. I thought about hightailing it out of there before she noticed us and brought out the shotgun, but seeing as how I had the pooper-scooper with me, I decided to pick it up and dispose of it properly."

"Put it in the wooded area behind the house, I'm guessing."

"You'd be guessing right." She took another look down at the pan, turned the burner off and turned her body so we were hugging face to face. She kissed me on the lips. "Breakfast's ready," she said with a smile.

Just then, my cell phone rang. I sighed, disentangled myself from Zellie, and answered. I listened for a few moments. "Are you sure? Well, that's interesting, and not altogether surprising. Thanks Ted. Talk to you later. Okay, sure, will do." I ended the call.

"Ted found out something?" Zellie raised an eyebrow.

"Just what we expected. At least a dozen places that could meet our needs were available on the day Melissa showed us the one where we found the body."

"So, she was lying."

"We can't jump to that conclusion," I intoned. "She could just be a lousy real estate broker. But it is suspicious. There had to be more than just Buckles' place and the one she showed us, and you would think a real estate broker would know that."

"And if she only told us about those two for some insidious reason, she already knew the Buckles Building would be unacceptable to us."

"Ensuring that we would only visit the other one – with a dead body in the attic.

"She's not your ordinary real estate broker. It's not even her training. She's a massage therapist."

"Do we even know whether she has a real estate license?"

"We didn't ask. So, no, we don't know even that. But I for one wouldn't hold it against her if she doesn't. We're not licensed either," Zellie said with a smile. "And we're great at our job."

"Yes, we are," I said. "And I think we're getting somewhere with this case, although I can't say the pieces are falling into place. More like suspicions to check out."

"Maybe we should wait on confronting her, and just watch what develops. We can do it later if it serves a purpose. I think we should assume that she has an ulterior motive in expressing a desire to tag along on our investigation. In the meantime, we can try to figure out why she's interested, and why she manipulated us into finding the body."

"Okay, we'll put Melissa off. What about Jayne? Given what we know now, it seems unlikely that she ran into Darrow at a charity function. We know he guarded his privacy, and no one even reported him missing. Not someone relishing the public eye, rubbing noses with the beautiful people. He seems more like a recluse."

So, we made a plan. We'd revisit Jayne Merriweather, believing she hadn't told the truth about Darrow when we first met.

As soon as we made that plan, we saw its flaws.

"It's not a good plan," Zellie said.

"No. It's not. No way is she going to just confess that she lied, apologize, and tell us the full story. And she might even have told the truth. We don't know."

"No. Bad plan. Very bad plan," Zellie said, as if scolding it. "What should we do?"

"You're the one who says this, but I have an idea."

I told her what I had in mind, and she agreed that it could yield more useful information. It had two parts. First, we'd find out who else attended the society charity functions Jayne frequented. If anyone seemed like a good candidate for us to interview, we'd do so, with our focus on anyone who might have known Darrow. Second, we'd attend the next such charity function.

"And how do you figure we'd get an invitation?" Zellie asked. "It's not like we're society types."

"No, but we have a secret weapon who fits the description."

"Rupert Cavendish, III."

"The very same. And come to think of it, we should ask Rupe whether he knew Darrow. I'm guessing not, because the whole thing seems like a figment of Jayne's imagination. But attending one of Jayne's pet events might yield important information about her, and her potential motives for lying to us. She could have just said she didn't know him other than as his landlord."

Rupert Cavendish, "Rupe" to his friends, was a fellow with whom we attended grade school. After that, he went to the finest preparatory schools, and then Harvard, but we stayed friends. You never quite let go of guys with whom you once rode bikes and played touch football. He was more or less a trust fund baby, but he never acted uppity and was embarrassed by his so-called station in life. It was never clear to us why he attended any public school at all. Years later, he explained that his parents believed in their kids getting better socialized by exposure to lots of other children from all walks of life. It was a nice thought, but our elementary school was not exactly filled with inner-city kids. Monmouth County is an affluent, I guess you would call it an upper middle- class area if such a term exists. Rupert's family was downright rich, though, so his parents must have considered our school a step down. Anyway, Rupe was and still is a great guy. We see him and his lovely wife Sarah on occasion and always have a good time with them.

"No time like the present," I said, as I picked up my phone, and dialed his number. Rupe answered on the first ring.

"Arnie, old boy," he said in that affected British aristocracy accent he used just for me. "To what to I owe this prodigious bestowal of transatlantic communication? And interruption of a fine polo match to boot."

"Rupe, you bloviating blowhard of a snob. You're not overseas. You're right here in Monmouth County. And you wouldn't know a polo pony from a Holstein. You are, however, an expert on manure, which is what you're slinging right now."

Rupe laughed. "Guilty on all counts. What's up?"

"Zellie and I are embroiled in another investigation, and we need your particular brand of socio-economic superiority."

"That unfortunately is my most marketable area of expertise. What do you need? I mean, what does Zellie need? I wouldn't do a thing for you after insulting me like that."

"Are there any society type benefit functions coming up soon?"

"There always are. And I happen to know the next one is a benefit for the Barton Springs salamander. *Eurycea sosorum.* It's endangered, you know."

"Um. Sure. I knew that." There was a pause on the other end of the line. "Okay, okay. I didn't know that. What is the Barton Springs salamander, and why do you know all about it?"

"Why, I read it just now off the invitation I am holding. The Barton Springs salamander, which is an endangered lungless salamander, only lives in the habitat of Barton Springs, which of course you know is in Austin, Texas."

"And there's a benefit for it? That all the local *glitterati*, including you and Sarah are going to?"

"Heck no. We're going to the Knicks game."

"Can we have the tickets to the benefit?"

"Sure. And I'm not even going to ask why you want them. I assume it's not a burning desire to rescue a respiratorily challenged amphibian?"

"No, definitely not. But a donation preceding our arrival might smooth the way for our asking nosy questions of the attendees."

"Consider it done. And when are you and Zellie coming over for dinner? Sarah mentioned you just the other day."

"Soon, Rupe. I'll call you after we conclude this case. For reasons I can't explain, we only have ten days to finish it. Give her our love."

"Will do. Love to Zellie. And good luck."

I turned to Zellie after I hung up. "We're in."

"Great. I'll need a new dress. I can't very well wear a sweatshirt and jeans to Oak Hill Country Club. That's where it is, right?"

"Yup. And I'll dust off my tuxedo. We're joining high society."

We needed to formulate an action plan. The tickets to the benefit would no doubt arrive later that morning. Rupe wouldn't wait for us to pick them up. Addicted to alacrity, he'd send a courier to traverse the three miles to my house. Rupe did nothing in a conventional way, and he enjoyed carrying on the pretense of a supercilious rich guy. Zellie and I knew better, and Rupe would never perform the charade with those who didn't know him well. He was humble and good-natured, and kind and respectful to rich and poor alike. And I knew for a fact he detested the self-important demeanor of others having similar backgrounds.

We continued researching Ferdinand Darrow's history, planning to redouble our efforts to identify his country of birth. It now seemed that the paucity of historical information meant that he was not born in the United States. There were many areas we could search, however, and it seemed necessary to get a full picture of the decedent before we could identify his killer. So we tried to find out where he received his education.

The search gave only a scant picture about his education, but yielded a new fact - a bar identification number for a Frederick Darrow. Similar name. Maybe an alias. We figured that searching the bar identification number might give different results and we were right. It gave us the district in which he was admitted to the bar. And it turned out to be in Hudson County, about thirty miles north. As New Jersey court records are only partially online, and attorney admission information is not part of their internet database, a trip to Hudson County was in order.

I volunteered to go visit the courthouse, pointing out that Zellie was immersed in her immigration search, and it made more sense to split up, given our time constraints. She hesitated, but agreed. We both knew the real reason I wanted to go, but we avoided verbalizing it, whether out of superstition or delicacy, I'm sure neither of us could say. During our last investigation, Zellie visited a courthouse and obtained invaluable information, but, well, let's just say bad things happened after she left. So it was my turn.

Zellie also figured that when she became tired of staring at the computer, she'd go shopping for a new dress. Although I told Zellie in general that I intended to run a few errands after I finished, I had a special, super-secret project in mind.

***

Zellie studied the monitor, wondering how to narrow down the hundreds of possibilities in the immigration database. Limiting the results to the nineteen-sixties or later helped, but it still left decades and hundreds of potential identities for Ferdinand Darrow. She hoped Arnie visiting the Hudson County Courthouse yielded further information. It might ease her task. But the database contained little detail other than name, gender, height and weight and year of birth if available. It omitted even that meager information in many entries.

She thought about it for a while and downloaded the entire search onto a Word document and then reordered all the names and information into alphabetic order. She brushed a few strands of hair out of her eyes and looked at the list again. Something clicked in her brain. She looked again at the derivation of the name Ferdinand. As she remembered, it had both Germanic and Spanish roots, combining concepts of voyage and bravery. But more to the point, she spotted the information she expected. A list of nicknames for Ferdinand, which included Ferd, Ferdy, Fred and Freddy. She reordered her list, which had reflected last names first, into an alphabetized listing of first names. And there it was. Friedrich Abogado. Freddy the lawyer.

CHAPTER TWENTY

Excited by her discovery, Zellie phoned Arnie, but the call went into voice mail.

***

I was on the phone with Marla, setting up our second assignation, as we jokingly called it, for after I completed my business at the courthouse. Satisfied with our plans to meet at the Eatontown mall, I concentrated on the road to Jersey City, the site of the Hudson County main courthouse. Before I did, however, I looked at my phone and saw I'd missed Zellie's call. I called her back, getting her voice mail.

***

After getting Arnie's voice mail, Zellie called Marla, to check her availability to go dress shopping later that day.

Marla answered on the first ring, but told Zellie that she was meeting someone in the afternoon. "We can go tomorrow," Marla said. "I'll clear my calendar and we'll go shopping and have lunch afterwards."

Zellie agreed, but told her she might do a preliminary survey and return the next day to get Marla's opinion.

"Where would you go looking," Marla asked, in a voice which Zellie thought sounded a lot like studied nonchalance. A lawyer's voice. Zellie wondered about it for a moment, then decided her imagination was getting the better of her. She guessed that Marla switched between personal voice and lawyer voice all the time and sometimes interchanged them.

"Maybe some department stores along Route 35," she said. "I'll see if something pops out at me there, before I visit the more expensive places at the mall."

"Okay, Marla said. "We can go to the Eatontown mall to-morrow," and have a nice lunch at someplace nearby."

Their plans made, Zellie said goodbye and ended the call. Then she thought about Freddy the Lawyer, and what it meant. It doesn't mean anything, she lamented. It's just another alias. A bogus name inside another bogus name. It made no differ-ence whether the murderer had killed Ferdinand Darrow or Friedrich Abogado. Or John Smith, for that matter.

Back to square one. They knew nothing. Not even the real identity of the victim, much less the murderer. And given the paucity of the medical examiner's report, they even suspected that they didn't know the actual cause of death. And they had only ten days to complete their inquiries, before the State of New Jersey charged them with asking pesky questions with-out a license, or something like that. Zellie hoped Arnie found something out at the Hudson County Courthouse to move the investigation forward, because at present, everything seemed to move sideways.

She thought about it for a minute more, then shrugged and headed out to go shopping.

* * *

I pulled into the parking lot next to the Hudson County Courthouse and took a ticket from the machine, which caused the gate to open. Eight bucks an hour, I groused to myself. New Jersey courts must need money. I found a parking space and pulled in. Stepping out of my car, I surveyed the area for the main entrance, and headed in that direction.

Knowing the courthouse drill, I had deposited my firearm in the gun safe at home, as I needed to remove all of my metal belongings and place them in a tray as I showed the security officers my driver's license on the way through the metal scanners situated inside the doorway. After navigating that gauntlet, I examined the sign on the wall for the room number for attorney admissions information. Not locating such a listing, I walked down the hall to the clerks' office. In my experience with courthouses, that office contained the people most knowledgeable about the various administrative functions performed by the Court. Deductive reasoning at work.

I entered the clerks' office and encountered a wall of bulletproof glass. It presented a formidable obstacle to communicating to the people sitting at the desks far beyond the transparent barrier. I peered through the glass to get their attention, to no avail. Then I noticed a buzzer next to a grating into which you spoke, much the same as placing an order at a drive-through fast food joint.

I pressed the button and spoke in a halting voice.

"Um, hello? Anyone available to help me?" A garbled voice greeted me. The clerks didn't even need to stand up and move to where I stood. They could just respond from their desks. But I couldn't understand the voice. It resembled a fast food lane even more. Rather than just guess at what the person (and I had no idea which person) said, and forsaking my instinct to place a glib order for a burger and fries, I spread my hands, palms up, in the universal signal of abject confusion. Kind of a physical rendering of "Huh?"

"She asked how she could help you," a friendly voice said behind me. I turned around to see a smiling fellow in the standard lawyer uniform of a pinstripe suit, white shirt and red paisley tie.

"How could you understand that?" I asked in amazement.

"Years of practice. Believe it or not, this place once exuded old world charm. No impenetrable wall. Just a simple oak counter with real people exchanging pleasantries before conducting business. Now it more resembles a glass fortress than a clerks' office. But we must adapt," he added in a practiced automaton voice. Then he waved to a pretty brunette sitting at a desk far away from the glass. She waved back, and left her desk to approach us.

"This is Debbie," he told me. "She'll help you." He turned back to the window and spoke into the speaker. "Debs, this is my friend...?" His eyes cut to me.

"Arnie," I replied. "Arnie Fischer."

"Arnie Fischer," he said into the speaker. "He's new here and doesn't know our mysterious procedures. Could you give him a hand?"

He turned back. "Debbie is the best. I keep trying to steal her away from here, but she has an undying loyalty to public service."

Debbie could hear everything. "Don't listen to Josh, Mr. Fischer. This idiot wants to pay minimum wage for maximum work." She said it with a smile and obvious affection. "How can I help you?"

"Maybe you should help Josh first," I said. "He might have to get back to Court or something."

"Nonsense, Arnie. You were here first. And I have no pressing appointments. He eyed Debbie. "Not law firm appointments, at least. I'll just wait over here." He gestured at two chairs flanking a small table bearing assorted law journals.

"Thanks," I said, extending my hand. He shook it and sat down.

"I'm looking for bar admission records for a particular attorney," I told Debbie. "Is this the right place?"

"If this is the correct department of admission, yes. We can retrieve that information, including a certificate of good standing. We just need the name, date of admission to the bar and the customary gratuity."

"The customary gratuity?"

"She's kidding, Arnie," Josh said from his perch right behind me. "She's referring to the appropriate fee from the judicial schedule of fees. There's a fee for everything. Have you tried to park here?"

"Yes."

"See what I mean?"

I turned back to Debbie, who smiled at me. "It's a $50.00 fee for the information you want. A hundred dollars if you want the certificate of good standing in a form suitable for framing."

"I think the regular one will do, thank you."

"What's the name and admission date of the party you wish me to search?"

"Frederick Darrow." I gave her the admission date Zellie pulled from the web.

"Freddy Darrow?" Josh again.

I turned to him. "Yes. Did you know him?"

"Everyone knew him. Freddy the Lawyer. He changed it from Friedrich Abogado. Father was Spanish, mother German. Freddy the Lawyer. He got his legal training overseas. In Spain or Germany, I don't remember which. He came from a long line of attorneys in Europe. He changed his name to Friedrich Darrow. You know, after the Scopes Trial attorney. And Freddy sounded more American to him. A terrible tragedy. His death, I mean. Anyway, why are you looking for his admission records?"

"My partner and I are looking into Friedrich Darrow's death," I said. I handed him a card.

"A to Z" Agency? Private detectives?"

"Not licensed. Yet. It's a long story," I added.

"But I don't understand. There's no mystery about Freddy's death. The auto accident was terrible for sure, but hardly worth the time and effort of even unlicensed detectives investigating."

I gaped at him in amazement. "Auto accident?" I asked.

"Of course. What did you think?"

I found the picture on my phone I'd taken of the dead body and showed it to Josh. "Is this him?" I asked.

"Not even close," Josh replied. "Who's this guy?"

"Are you sure?"

"A hundred percent. Freddy was thin as a rail. He ate salads for lunch." Josh said this with obvious distaste. "He could fit through a mail slot. This guy," he gestured at the picture, "could serve as the poster boy for Weight Watchers. The 'before' picture."

Josh patted his protruding stomach. "All this talk about food is making me hungry. Want to go get lunch? I'll fill you in more."

"Sure. If you don't already have plans," I added, looking at Debbie.

"Please go with him," Debbie said with a smile. "I always bring my lunch. Or at least that's what I tell him," she added.

"Hey, wait a minute. You don't bring your lunch?" Josh assumed a hurt expression, but followed it up with a chuckle. "She's just messing with me."

Debbie just assumed a "just Josh being Josh" indulgent expression. She turned to me. "Let me get you that file. I'll just be a few minutes. She printed something out on her computer and returned with two pages stapled together.

"Freddy Darrow's registration information and the certificate of good standing. And he was a good one, wasn't he Josh?"

"The best," he assured her. "A great lawyer, and decent person."

Debbie looked at me. "Find out who impersonated him."

"That's what my partner and I intend to do. Thanks Debbie."

Josh and I headed out of the clerks' office. I asked him to wait for me while I made a call, and we agreed to meet out front. I ducked into a corner and called Zellie. She answered right away.

CHAPTER TWENTY-ONE

Arnie! I found out the original identity of our dead guy."
She told me about her discovery and how she used
deductive reasoning to find the information that our
client was Friedrich Abogado, or Freddy the Lawyer.

I listened with great affection to Zellie's account, not wanting to spoil her moment. And my heart filled with pride and
admiration for Zellie's intelligence in working it out. I had just
stumbled onto the same information by the sheer luck of running into people who knew the mystery man. I explained this
to Zellie when imparting what I'd gleaned at the courthouse.
My concern it might deflate her enthusiasm for her discovery
did not materialize.

"Oh, forget about that. We both agreed that we needed to
visit the courthouse. And it was a good idea. And now we know
our client stole Friedrich Darrow's identity. Ask Josh as much
as you can about the real Freddy Darrow. In particular, ask
about his accidental death, if it even was an accident. It might
tell us why our client impersonated him. And don't forget to
give Josh our card. We might get referrals from him. Lawyers
need investigators, don't they?"

I smiled at Zellie's entrepreneurial spirit, and agreed with her approach, then reminded her I had a few errands to run after lunch.

"Okay, I'm going to look for a dress on my own. Marla's tied up today, but will go with me tomorrow if I can't find anything."

I knew why Marla was unavailable today, but for obvious reasons did not share this information with Zellie. I just said I'd meet her back home later that evening.

"We can go out to dinner so neither one of us has to fix anything," I said, and she agreed and rang off.

I caught up with Josh outside in front of the courthouse. He suggested a local diner, and we walked the few blocks to a small restaurant with a big neon sign on top with a missing "N" and "R" so it blinked "DI E."

"Kind of unfortunate that those two letters went out. I bet the owner is scrambling to get that fixed."

"Nah. It's looked that way for so long, we call it the Death Star. Death for the sign, star for the food quality and service. It's a surprisingly excellent restaurant."

A hostess showed us to our table and we sat down and gave a pleasant, middle aged waitress our orders. She called us each "honey" and told us to call her Doris. This settled, I asked Josh about Freddy Darrow.

"Did he tell you anything about his life? It might give us a starting point on figuring out why and how someone stole his identity."

Josh paused and considered for a moment. "Well, you know Fred," he began. "Oh geez, of course you don't know him. And now, I guess I don't either. I started to say he was a private person. Didn't talk about himself much. Quick to ask others about their lives, though. A natural at it. I think I told him my entire life story before I even realized it."

I smiled. "And knowing you for all of an hour, I'm guessing it's one heck of a story."

"No, it's boring. Born and raised in New Jersey...hey, wait a minute – you're good at finding out about people's lives, too."

I laughed. "Not as good as Fred Darrow, I guess. He would have had your biography written by now. I only heard you've lived in New Jersey your whole life."

"Ha! You didn't even learn that. I only said I was born and raised here, not that I've lived here my whole life. I went to college in Massachusetts and law school in Chicago... oops, I just gave you more information, didn't I?"

"Yup. But interesting as your life is, I'd kind of like to hear as much as I can about Mr. Darrow."

Josh rubbed his chin as if feeling for a beard that no longer existed. He must have once had facial hair, and felt his beard while thinking, much as some people steeple their fingers or touch their foreheads. I smiled to myself. He just told me more about himself, but I doubted at this point that Josh was involved in our case. But you never know.

"Maybe we should start with the basics," I prompted. "What did he look like?"

"He was shorter than us. Probably about 5'7" or so. Brown hair parted in the middle. Brown eyes, I think, but I'm not sure."

"How did he dress?"

"Grey suit, red tie, just like the rest of us." Josh laughed. "The lawyer dress code."

"Off the rack or tailored?"

"You know, I think tailored. They fit better than mine, for sure."

"Did he wear expensive clothes?" I didn't know where I was going with any of this, but had to start somewhere, and getting a sense of his economic situation, considering his recent emigration to this country, seemed sensible.

"You could say that, although look at me. You're not talking to the best judge of it." Josh looked down at his rumpled suit.

I chuckled. "Better than me, I can assure you."

"Why are you so interested in Freddy's looks and dress, anyway? Aren't you trying to find out about his imposter, not him?"

"It's a good question. But I figure the more I know about the person being impersonated, the better I can determine why the imposter chose him. To wit, what's the connection between the two men?"

"I guess that makes sense," Josh allowed. "But I kind of feel like I'm helping you sully the name of a guy we all loved."

"I don't intend to besmirch his reputation," I hastened to assure Josh. "But I fear that someone else did not like Freddy much, or didn't care at all, because he used Freddy's name to advance his own ends. And it's possible the identity theft and the murder are intertwined."

"I guess that makes sense. And I'm willing to help you find the killer. I'd say my primary motivation in helping you would be to find out who impersonated Freddy, but I suppose he already received more than enough punishment for that, because he's dead."

"Thanks Josh. You've been a big help already. I wonder about something else. Why do you think Freddy's death was an accident?"

"That's what the coroner ruled. After hearing you today, I have to wonder. Are you going to look into that as well?"

"I'd like to, but we have no standing, considering our lack of even a license as private investigators. But we'll do an informal review as part of the overall inquiry. How well did you know

Freddy? I know that's a hard question to answer, but can you give a general assessment?"

Josh paused for a moment. "I knew him pretty well as an attorney. Not much as a human being."

I smiled at that. "I take it your opinion of lawyers, of which you are one, is not great?"

"Oh, it's not that. Shakespeare's view notwithstanding, most of us are good people trying hard to do the right thing, consistent with representing the interests of clients. Some aren't, but I think they're the exception. What I meant was that we behave differently in our jobs than we do in 'real life.'" Josh fingered quotation marks after his comment. "It's a *persona*," he continued. "Oh, we can talk about sports and family in general ways between cases, but we reserve the deeper stuff for private life."

"What about Freddy?" I pressed.

"An enigma. Oh, we all loved the *persona*," he added. "But we knew nothing about his private life. At least I didn't."

"Did anyone else?"

"I don't think so. As you can no doubt ascertain, I'm the gregarious type. Talk to everyone and all that."

"I hadn't noticed." I said with a grin.

"No wonder you're not licensed," he shot back.

I laughed at his zinger. "Point well taken. Never overlook the obvious. So, I guess you're saying that if anyone knew the real Freddy, at least in the legal community, you'd be the guy."

"Yup. That's me. Courthouse *yenta*."

"Is there anything else you can tell me about Freddy? Was he a good lawyer? Honest? Quiet? Aggressive? Effective? Well-regarded by the Court?"

"I don't think so. Yes. Yes. Yes. No. Yes. Yes. And objection to the compound question, Your Honor."

"Wow." It was all I could manage.

"It's a skill honed with care after years of representing clients. And having three siblings."

"Ah. That would do it."

"But there is one more thing I just remembered. Freddy gave me a book once. Kind of out of the blue. And he inscribed it."

"That could help," I said eagerly. "Do you remember the name of the book and the inscription?"

CHAPTER TWENTY-TWO

Zellie made an impulsive decision. Nothing like a direct approach, she thought. It's lunchtime during a workday. Arnie's at a business lunch. I could call a friend and have lunch and congenial conversation, or I could work the case with a luncheon meeting of my own. Let's get this case solved, she decided. She'd call Melissa and try the subtle approach. Ply her with food and innocuous gossip about the case and get her reactions. It might yield important information.

That resolved, she called Melissa, who expressed delight at the impromptu invitation. She had no customers for either business, and could spare an hour for lunch. She could spare a few weeks, she had added under her breath.

Zellie heard the second part of Melissa's response, but made no comment. She'd leave that to luncheon conversation. They made plans to go to a restaurant near Melissa's office.

* * *

"Freddy gave me a copy of *The Brothers Karamazov*, by Fyodor Dostoyevsky. Such an esoteric type book does not often grace the hallowed halls of the state court, where conversation runs more to the star of yesterday's game, pick a sport, any sport."

"Did he explain why he gave it to you? You said you didn't know him that well on a personal level. And can you think of any reason he chose that book?"

"Well, I can think of two possible explanations for your second question, and none for the first. I don't know why he gave me the book. But he inscribed it. It said 'To my friend Josh: Does art imitate life, or does life imitate art?' Not explanatory, but I think you would call that a clue. The second, more generic explanation for the book choice, is that it has legal issues and a big criminal trial. This is just paraphrasing, mind you, but it includes a kind of sardonic reference to the overspecialization of professionals, by referring to a doctor in Paris who only fixes left nostril injuries, and a doctor in Vienna who specializes in injuries to the right nostril. I'm just speculating, mind you, but maybe he was referring to the same thing with us."

I laughed. "Did you talk about it?"

"No, he died soon after. And I hadn't yet read the book, so we couldn't discuss it."

"You've read it since. Any more revelations?" I asked, almost like a dog looking for another treat.

"It's a good book. Well worth reading. And I think I'll leave it to you to read it and draw your own conclusions. I think a little Russian literature might benefit you," he said with a smile. He got up and dropped a five on the table for the tip. "I have to get back to court. Nice talking to you, Arnie."

"You too," I said, pulling the check from his hand. "And I'll take care of this up front. Thanks for your help."

"Happy to oblige," he said with a slight wave. "Take it easy." And he left.

After paying the check and leaving the diner, I had just a few moments to call Zellie before going to the mall to meet Marla, but my call went to voice mail. I left a message giving her a quick summary of my conversation with Josh, and told her I'd fill her in later, after my errand.

***

Spotting Marla waiting at our agreed upon location in front of Benny's Sporting Goods in the Eatontown mall, I walked over and greeted her with a kiss. I cast a furtive glance in all directions. Satisfied I saw no familiar faces, I draped my arm around Marla's waist and we strode together to a store across the way.

CHAPTER TWENTY-THREE

Zellie rubbed her chin with her left hand while gripping the steering wheel with her right. Her luncheon with Melissa yielded little information. When confronted with Ted's information that many other office options existed, Melissa sheepishly acknowledged that she didn't use the MLS. She already knew about the offices she showed them, and she hadn't done any further work. "That's why my real estate business is lousy," she told Zellie. As for any knowledge about a dead body in the attic, she professed to know nothing. Zellie thought about that, and tried to remember Melissa's reaction. No question, she thought, it surprised her as much as them. The luncheon was otherwise pleasant, and Zellie steered clear of talk about the case, despite Melissa's insistent pressing her for details.

"You know I want to stay involved in the investigation," she had told Zellie. "I discovered the body, too. And anyway, it's much more interesting than real estate massage."

"Real Estate Massage" was now a profession all its own, Zellie thought with a chuckle, and headed for the first of the stores she intended to check out for a new dress.

She became frustrated with the local offerings, and decided not to wait to the next day to continue her search at the mall with Marla. She headed to Eatontown to scope out the mall's offerings, reasoning she could identify possibilities, and get Marla's opinion the next day. Arriving at the mall, she entered at one of the main entrances and ambled down the long hallway, looking at both sides at the various stores without going into any of them. She intended to walk the length of this part of the mall until she reached one of the various anchor department stores, but thinking if one or more of the various boutique clothing stores that lined the mall appealed to her, she'd go inside. As she did so, she saw someone who looked like Arnie from behind, and she laughed to herself that she must have him on her mind.

It seemed like all she thought about these days was Arnie and the murder investigation. The charity event, although part of the job, seemed like a nice change of pace. They could dress up and go to a fancy formal event as a proper couple, something they'd never done before. Sure, they'd gone to parties, even formal ones, but always as friends and almost always with dates. Their relationship looked and felt different now, and Zellie wouldn't change it for the world. It still amazed her they spent so much energy avoiding their inevitable romance. She knew their reasoning. Why take the chance on destroying their lifelong friendship for sex. But they both knew they had much more than sex as lovers. They had an unbreakable relationship before redefining it, but it seemed like the existing warmth, built over a lifetime, had multiplied. She wasn't discounting the sex. She liked that, too. She resolved to declare a rest and recreation period as soon as she and Arnie returned home.

Zellie looked again at the man up ahead. He had his arm around a woman's waist. A woman bearing a strong resemblance to Marla. Wait a minute. It **was** Marla. And the man with his arm around her was...Arnie! A wave of disbelief, shock, hurt, nausea and, yes, anger washed over Zellie. She tried to remember what Arnie had told her. He had an errand he needed to run. Well, this was an errand. And Marla, couldn't go to the mall with Zellie because she was meeting someone, but would go with her tomorrow. Well, she is meeting someone today. Arnie.

Zelllie paused a moment to collect herself. She tried to quell the hurt she felt and approach it with a rational mind. Number one, Arnie loved her. She knew that. He never, ever would do anything to hurt her. Marla's was her best girlfriend. Zellie hadn't known her as long as Arnie. She had known no one other than her parents as long as Arnie. But there was no more steadfast friend than Marla. So, in an unemotional Spock-like assessment, a logical and innocent explanation existed for Arnie and Marla walking arm-in-arm in a place neither one wanted to tell her about. Oh, screw rationality, she thought. She'd just confront them. But she thought better of it. So, what to do? Surprise them? Demand an explanation? Just casually run into them? Zellie decided that she either trusted Arnie and Marla, or she didn't. And she trusted them. Well, she trusted Arnie. Marla was a lawyer. They'd do anything to get what they wanted. Oh, no they wouldn't, Zellie corrected herself. Not Marla, anyway. If those two were together, they had a good reason. And it had better be a great one, she thought.

Zellie headed home, hoping Arnie told her soon about his and Marla's togetherness. She knew she wouldn't wait too long before just coming right out and asking.

Arriving home, Zellie sat on her living room couch. Now what was she supposed to do? She used to talk about these things with Arnie. His male perspective on relationships served as an ideal sounding board. She could also talk to Marla, who listened with a sympathetic ear to Zellie's ruminations about her burgeoning romantic relationship with Arnie.

With neither option available at present, Zellie had one thought. Mom. Unlike many mothers, Arnie's included, Zellie's mom had a calm and reasoned disposition. She answered Zellie's phone call, and lent a patient ear as her daughter recounted spotting Arnie with his arm around Marla at the mall, when neither one had told her anything about intending to meet there.

"What did they say when you asked them?"

"Um, nothing. I high-tailed it out of there. I'm sure they didn't see me."

"How do you know they intended to meet? Maybe it happened by chance."

"I don't think so. Marla told me she couldn't go shopping with me at the mall, because she was meeting someone. And Arnie just said he had an errand to run in the afternoon."

"Hmm. Interesting. If they intended to meet at the mall without telling you, and without lying to you either, that's pretty much what they'd say. They met for some joint purpose they don't want to tell you about, but also don't want to lie to you about either.

"Mom! You're not helping. That's what I'm afraid of. A secret tryst."

"At the mall? Be serious, honey. You have a birthday coming up. A more likely scenario is that Marla is helping Arnie pick out a present for you. Or something just as innocuous. One thing I know for sure, and you know it too. Arnie worships the ground you walk on. He loves you, and would never ever do anything to hurt you. The two of you have a bond like no other. The last thing in the world Arnie would do is jeopardize his lifelong friendship with you. And not when you two, thank God, made your romance official, like your father and I wanted since forever."

Zellie smiled. "I know you're right, Mom. And I don't know why I didn't just go up to them and greet them. If Arnie and I hadn't changed our relationship, I would have done that. But I guess I'm just not accustomed to how to act as a girlfriend, not just a best friend."

"The same way as always, Zellie. You're still best friends. Just a few more outstanding benefits, that's all."

"Well, thanks. This helped. I think I'll just leave it alone, and see what happens. How's Dad?"

"He's fine, dear. Your loveable moron of a father is out on the golf course."

"I didn't know he even played golf."

"He doesn't. At 88 years old, he decides he needs to take up a sport. He's taking his first lesson now."

"What's wrong with that?"

"Zellie, it's 100 degrees out there today. And he goes anyway, without so much as putting on suntan lotion."

"Ouch."

"Right. At least they cover those golf carts now. I'm just hoping he has a little fun and gives it up without serious injury. Like hitting himself in the head with a golf club, or something like that."

"One can only hope. And Mom?"

"What is it, honey?"

"You said Dad and you always wanted Arnie and me to get together."

"You knew that."

"Yes, I did. What about Arnie's folks?"

"Oh, they always wanted it, too. They're just, shall we say, a little less demonstrative than your father and me."

"That's for sure."

"They love you both just as much, you know."

"I know."

Zellie hung up feeling a lot better. Her mother was right. Arnie and Marla must have a good reason for meeting at the mall, and she'd let it go. If they were planning to surprise her for her birthday, she didn't want to ruin the surprise, or force them into having to lie to her to protect the surprise. She'd just pretend she never saw them.

CHAPTER TWENTY-FOUR

W hen I returned home, Zellie was sitting at the computer. She turned in her chair and asked about my visit to the courthouse. I told her the whole story, including my discussion and luncheon with Josh. The breadth of the information gleaned from a simple visit to a county courthouse amazed both of us. We now knew a real Ferdinand, Friedrich or Freddy Darrow existed, and that our client had impersonated him. We'd also learned about the deaths of two Darrows having variants of the same first name.

"Let's look into the circumstances of that car accident," Zellie said.

"Agreed. We also need to start reading Russian literature."

"Come again?" Zellie looked at me like I had just proposed dropping everything to climb Mount Kilimanjaro.

I explained about the book Freddy Darrow gave Josh, and the inscription on its front flyleaf.

"Does life imitate art or does art imitate life? He must have been referring to something in *The Brothers Karamazov* as descriptive of his personal situation, but what? And what did Josh think he meant?"

"He didn't say, and I didn't get the feeling that Josh knew Darrow all that well."

"Then why give him the book in the first place?"

"Josh said it's common for lawyers to give each other interesting books. Although the inscription doesn't fall within what anyone would call ordinary course."

"Had Josh read the book?"

"Yes, but he wouldn't tell me much about it."

"I think we have a book to read."

"Yup. Although in my case, I think I have Cliff's Notes to read."

"Once a math major, always a math major," she said. "But I admit, it might give us a quicker start on what Darrow meant."

"How did it go for you today?" I asked, between bites of a sandwich serving as a makeshift dinner.

"I had lunch with Melissa. And she doesn't seem like a cold-blooded killer. Also, I kind of believe she didn't use the MLS system. I think there is a fee for realtors using that, and her real estate business is pathetic. It can't generate much income. Independent realtors are rare, anyway. They all seem to be part of big national outfits now."

I sensed a little tension in Zellie's responses, but left it alone. I had a secret, so I didn't want to explore too much about today's events, other than to acknowledge my visit to the mall.

Zellie yawned and stretched. "Why don't we sleep on all of this until tomorrow morning. We're both tired, we've had long days, and we can talk about it all with clearer heads after a good night's sleep."

That's the problem, I thought. She's just tired. "Sure, Zellie. Good idea. We'll talk about it all in the morning. And maybe I can get a look at your new dress tomorrow afternoon."

Zellie's eyes twinkled for the first time. "Not a chance, buster. You'll see it on the night of the benefit."

"Okay, okay," I said laughing, and with some relief I'd elicited a smile from her. "I'm looking forward to it, but I can wait."

***

The next day, Zellie wanted to show me something on the computer. I pulled up a chair, and we sat side by side as she pointed to a spreadsheet.

"Look what I did. I went back over all of our notes..."

"We took notes?"

"Yes, we wrote summaries of all of our interviews and investigatory material as we went along."

"Oh right. We did that. When did we do that?"

"All along. How can we expect to know where we are in an investigation if we don't' keep notes?"

"Fantastic memories?"

"Sure, that's it, Sherlock. Anyway, we have a lot of notes. We know quite a bit. Your trip to the courthouse yesterday added a great deal to our store of knowledge."

"I would have said we don't' know much at all, other than we have two dead Darrows."

"Well, look for yourself." She gestured at the spreadsheet, which set forth all of our interviews, including a summary of yesterday's events.

"When did you do this last one?" I asked, raising my eyebrows.

"Got up early this morning."

I viewed the summaries with interest, and frank admiration for Zellie's industriousness.

We decided that while she went to the mall with Marla, I would get a copy of *The Brothers Karamazov* and an accompanying study guide at the local library. While there, I could take advantage of their massive electronic and paper newspaper collection and look into any news reports of Freddy Darrow's car accident. We figured that getting a copy of the police report would be next to impossible, but thought it plausible that the local newspaper might provide something useful.

I drove over there and asked the librarian for help finding the book. She perked up, and began a long soliloquy about her love for Russian literature, Tolstoy in particular, but Dostoyevsky, too, and how she had written her masters' thesis on Pushkin. And oh, what a joy to come across a lover of true literature, as everyone else wanted a best-seller, or help with a research project for school.

I enjoyed her enthusiasm, but it made me uneasy. I wondered if I should keep up the pretense of my literary acumen, or just charge ahead and tell her I wanted a study guide, which we all know is code for someone else reading the book and telling us about it so we don't have to be bothered with the tiresome task of reading.

I chickened out. I decided to go to another library, or at least get the study guide at one of the big box bookstores. I know, I know, it was silly. But I didn't want to disappoint her. I did tell her I needed to look at the newspaper database, and with good cheer she pointed me in the right direction. My copy of *The Brothers Karamazov* in hand, I walked over to the first in a row of computer terminals and sat down.

It took only a few minutes before I found the right local newspaper, and armed with Josh's rough approximation of the accident date, I found a one paragraph reference to the incident. A car driven by one Frederick Darrow, a local attorney, stalled in the middle of a busy intersection, and was struck on the driver's side by a car driven by Herman Octavius Garrett, a New Jersey resident, occupation unknown. The collision killed Mr. Darrow. Mr. Garrett sustained a few scratches, but otherwise escaped unharmed. The police issued no citations, although a witness, Flora Richmond, the owner of the local flower shop, Flora's Florals, speculated that Mr. Garrett ran a red light.

The article gave no further details, and it amazed me to find that much in such a short time. A few further attempts to find additional news reports proved unsuccessful, so I decided to follow up by calling Ms. Richmond. I looked up Flora's Florals on the computer, which rewarded me with an address and phone number, both of which I jotted down.

Waving goodbye to the librarian, I headed out to my car, and called Flora's Florals. A friendly sounding female voice answered on the first ring. I asked to speak to Flora Richmond, and she told me I was already speaking to her. I identified myself and told her of my interest in the accident, and before I could even give her my long disclaimer about my lack of formal qualifications, licensing or authority of any kind, she launched into a detailed account of the events of that "fateful day" as she called it. It no doubt had made a strong impression on her.

Without my prompting, she told me of her certainty that the man who crashed into that "nice Mr. Darrow" ran a red light, but that the police refused to give her account serious consideration. They assumed that because Mr. Darrow's car stalled in the middle of the intersection, he was at fault. She derided the explanation as an easy way to close the case without further effort on their part.

I asked Flora (she told me to call her that) how she knew Mr. Darrow, and she told me that he visited her shop every month to order flowers. For whom did he order flowers, I asked, and she told me it was always for his mother. In response to my request, she rummaged around while I waited on the phone, and gave me a name and address in Middletown, New Jersey. Eureka, as Zellie likes to say.

Before finishing my conversation with Flora, I ordered three bouquets of flowers – red roses for Zellie and a nice anonymous bouquet for a certain clerk of the court, I figured Josh would either be ticked off at me, or appreciative. Either way, he'd call tomorrow. And anyway, he could just deny that the flowers were from him. I swore Flora to secrecy about that one. She asked me who the third bouquet was for and I told her it was for her, and that she should put on the card – "For Flora, a truly lovely person. Arnie." I'm pretty sure I could feel her smile right through the phone before I hung up.

I gave Zellie a call before proceeding further. She might prefer a joint visit to Freddy Darrow's mother. Zellie picked up right away.

"I'm sitting in a dressing room," she told me.

I filled her in on the morning's events, and she let out a low whistle when I told her about the name and address Flora gave me.

"Should I follow up on it now, or wait to do it together?" I asked, to which she responded that I might as well check it out, as the shopping would tie her up for a while. Then I heard Marla's voice asking Zellie what she thought about the "strapless one," to which I offered my opinion that it sounded good. I received something approaching a "no one's asking your opinion," in reply, but with a slight giggle. She wished me luck, and I did the same. We made plans to meet later that afternoon, and I disconnected.

CHAPTER TWENTY-FIVE

The address turned out to be a retirement community. And a nice one, from the look of it. As I entered the gates to the complex, I viewed multiple ponds, a swimming pool and tennis courts. Multiple buildings, comprising eight one-story units attached to each other, dotted the community. I pulled up to a building bearing a sign reading "Gatehouse. Visitors Please Check-In Here." Because a metal bar prevented my proceeding further without a code or key card or something like that, I complied by ringing the designated buzzer. A tall, burly man wearing a crew cut, and a crisp white uniform appeared by the side of my car with a terse, but polite inquiry regarding my business.

I advised him I intended to visit Greta Abogado, to which he inquired if the party to whom I intended to visit expected me. He accomplished this without ever stating if Ms. Abogado even existed, much less lived in the complex. Good training. And something told me that our usual truthful statement of lack of a license or other legal authority would have no effect on this man at all. And I figured he'd shoot me, or at least crush my spleen or something, if I lied to him. So, I told him the unvarnished truth. That I had no appointment, and she didn't expect me. But I was looking into her son's death and had come hoping she'd agree to talk.

To my surprise, he nodded, and went into the gatehouse and picked up a phone. He exchanged a few words with someone, and returned to the side of my car. "Her caretaker said it's okay, but to please wait fifteen or twenty minutes. She'll call me when they're ready to receive visitors. You can wait over there." He pointed to a parking area just inside the gate. I thanked him and parked as directed.

About twenty-five minutes later, he came over and gave me directions.

"Drive straight down this row and make the first right. Her building is the first one on the left. Do you have the address?"

I nodded yes, thanked him, and followed his directions, pulling into a visitor parking spot a few yards away from her building. I walked up to the front door and knocked. A competent looking middle-aged woman answered the door.

"Ms. Abogado?" I asked.

"I'm Helga. Her executive assistant." She smiled. "Greta is in the living room. You're Mr. Fischer, I presume?"

"Yes, ma'am."

"Please do not upset her. She just lost her son, and is distraught. But she wants visitors."

I followed her into the living room, in which an elderly, but sharp looking woman sat in a wheelchair.

"Good afternoon, Mr. Fischer. I'm Greta Abogado. Please sit down. And forgive Helga her little joke. She's my home health aide. I have no more use for an executive assistant than I do for a basketball coach."

She spoke perfect English, although with a heavy German accent. At least I thought it was German. I'm not a linguist. I explained the reason for my visit and expressed my condolences, and she looked at me with tired eyes.

"So much tragedy. So much death. We came to this country seeking a better life, not so much for me, I'm an old woman. But for my family. For those that follow. What is the saying? So they could stand on the shoulders of their parents and grandparents, to make a better life for themselves. The old country was cruel to our family. But America - it seemed so promising. But tragedy is not absent in America, either. I won't say we've had poor treatment. Look around you – this is a beautiful place to live. But only for an old woman. My family is gone."

I leaned forward. "Ms. Abogado," I began.

"Please call me Greta. I don't feel like a Mrs., and I can't get used to Ms. Everyone calls me Greta, so you should, too."

"Okay. Greta it is. I hope this isn't too hard for you, but can you tell me a little about your son, Friedrich Darrow?"

Greta looked surprised. "I will, but don't you want to hear about Ferdinand, too? Both of my sons were murdered."

I guess this didn't shock me. It made sense. They were lawyers sharing an iconic surname, with almost identical first names. Although that last part seemed odd.

"I'd appreciate your perspective on these murders," I said. "One took place here in Middletown, and the police ruled the one up north as an accident."

"Accident, feh. It was no accident. He was murdered. But those dummkopfs called it an accident. And the police here, they don't seem to think there's any connection, either. 'That one was just an accident, ma'am. It happens,' they say in those superior voices they use. I'm not a fool. Calling that one a murder means more paperwork. Re-opening a case, and all that. And I don't think they'll spend much time on poor Heinrich's murder, either."

"Your son's given name was Heinrich?" I asked. "And your other son?"

"Friedrich and Heinrich Abogado. Abogado is a name we took upon coming to the new world. It means 'lawyer' in Spanish." I nodded. We knew that, courtesy of Zellie's deductions.

"Why did they take the same new American names, instead of Abogado? I asked.

"They watched *Inherit the Wind* together." And neither one wanted the name Clarence. Friedrich adopted the name Freddy. His little brother took the name Ferdinand, because in the old country the name is associated with courage and bravery. And because he didn't want the name Henry. They liked being Freddy and Ferdy Darrow."

"Why do you think someone murdered them?"

Greta sighed. "The police asked me that. I don't know. In the past few years, I saw little of them. Friedrich sent my favorite lilies from time to time, but almost never visited. Heinrich lived in the same town as me, but came here only twice – and one of those times to help me move in. I'm sure they split the cost of my unit. But they lived separate lives."

"What makes you so sure that the car crash was not an accident?" I agreed with her, but was curious to hear her perspective.

She shrugged, exhaustion washing over her face.

"I suppose a mother's intuition isn't enough for you. It didn't impress the police. That nice flower shop lady doesn't think so, either. Have you spoken to her?"

I nodded. "This morning."

"Then you know she saw it happen. And she's sure that car ran the red light. But the police didn't listen to her."

"That's what she told me, too." I said. "Can you think of a reason Ferdinand, um, Heinrich was murdered?"

"No," she said with some hesitation.

"What is it?" I prompted.

"Well, Friedrich was a sweet boy. Quiet, purposeful. An avid reader. Hard to believe he offended anyone, much less to the point of murder. But his brother, well, that's a different story. Heinrich was not a bad person, quite the contrary. He was a good boy. Just not as successful as his brother. And he had a personality that might offend people, at least sometimes. But again, to the point of murder? I don't believe that."

CHAPTER TWENTY-SIX

I don't know," Zellie said. "It sounds kind of crazy."

We were sitting in Zellie's kitchen, sipping our coffee, while I recounted my visit to Ms. Abogado. "Unusual," I agreed.

At that moment, the doorbell rang, and Zellie rose to answer it. "A guy with flowers," she said, peering through the peephole. She opened the door and a skinny kid, no older than seventeen, and just licensed to drive, proffered a bouquet to Zellie, with a snappy "Flowers for Ms. Zellie Morgan."

Zellie smiled and thanked him, and took the flowers, while I hastened over to give the lad a tip. He left while Zellie searched for a vase to hold the two dozen red roses I sent her. She located a pretty glass vase and arranged them while speculating "I wonder who sent them?"

"Maybe there's a card," I offered.

"Well, look here. There is a card. And it says 'To my gorgeous sweetheart and best friend. Love, Arnie.' They're from you?" Zellie feigned shock and amazement.

"Don't sound so surprised. Hey, wait a minute. Is there someone else you were expecting flowers from?"

"Oh of course not. Thank you, this is sweet. What possessed you to order these? I hope you're not feeling guilty about anything."

I hesitated, but just for a nanosecond, and charged ahead.

"Not a chance. You know I spoke to that florist yesterday, and I wanted to do something nice for you because I love you, and I know you like flowers, so it seemed like the thing to do at that moment."

If Zellie caught my brief pause, she revealed nothing.

"Ooh. Spontaneous affection. Very sexy. Thank you, they're beautiful. And so is the thought." She gave me a long kiss, and I resolved to send flowers more often.

Both of us wanted to engage in some rest and recreation, but we had a job to do, so we sat back down at the table and talked more about the case.

"We're agreed that something is wrong with that whole story, right?" Zellie looked at me for affirmation, and I nodded.

"So, our next step is to look into that further. Try to poke holes in it if we can."

"We also have the Russian literature thing," I pointed out.

"Our reading assignment," Zellie said.

"Yes, and as far as I'm concerned, my first step in that regard is to find a study guide for the book. I'd like to read it," I said, convincing neither of us, "but the thing is like 850 pages. We don't have the time for that."

"I agree with you. We don't have the time to read it. And we'll get a study guide. I'll also do an online search and get a summary that way. But I might know someone who's read it."

"Who do you have in mind?"

"I bet Marla read it. I'm guessing it's a lawyer thing."

"Josh referred to legal issues and a big criminal trial in it, but that doesn't make it a lawyer book any more than the fact that one attorney gave it to another. Lawyers must exchange books about Willie Mays or Michael Jordan, too."

"They must. But given a choice between speed reading a 850 page book translated from its original Russian...."

"Or making a wild unsubstantiated assumption? I choose that," I said, almost tripping over my words in my haste. "Anyway, it doesn't hurt to ask her."

"Just what I was thinking," Zellie said. "I'll call her now."

She took out her phone and speed dialed Marla. They spoke for a few minutes, then Zellie put down her phone, turned and gave a gleeful, "She said, and I quote: 'Sure. I read it. Great book. Want to borrow my copy?' I told her we had taken one out from the library, but hadn't read it yet, and needed a quick synopsis for our case. She's meeting a client in just a few minutes, but will sit down with us at AB in an hour, and give us at least a running start on a summary."

"Good news. And we haven't had breakfast yet, anyway."

Zellie reached over and patted my stomach. "We can't have you going hungry, now can we?"

**

We sat at our regular table at AB, and Marla joined us right away.

"Do you want the short version, the book report version, or in-depth analysis?" Marla asked, with a touch of patronizing humor in her voice.

"Short," I said.

"Short to start," Zellie amended.

"What she said," I agreed.

"Okay. Short version, with my posthumous apology to a great author. A greedy, philandering, not nice guy has three sons with his wife, and one with someone else. Someone murders the father, there's a big dramatic trial of one of the sons for the killing, and it turns out that the son on trial is innocent, because his half-brother did it. The end."

"Wow," I said. "The guy took 850 pages to say that?"

"Oh sure, Arnie. He was just very wordy, that's all. Although there might be a little more to it."

At that moment, Delilah came over to take our order. She wore a T-shirt reading "A Beautiful Pair" on the front. I resolved to keep my mouth shut. For about two seconds.

"Okay, okay, I'm prepared. Let's see the back."

"Whatever could you mean, Arnie?" She laughed and turned around, and the back read "Our Newest Creation and a Smoothie."

"That's a lot of words to fit back there," I observed. "And what's the new creation?"

"Hence the small print. And the new creation is a barbecued chicken infusion. You'd love it."

"Um, I don't think I'll have that for breakfast, Delilah, thanks. Maybe another time."

We placed our orders, but she paused before leaving. "I overheard you talking about *The Brothers Karamazov*. Great book."

"You read it?" Zellie and I asked at the same time.

"Sure. I love to read."

We knew Delilah took post-graduate marketing courses at night and worked as a waitress by day. That's what the whole T-shirt business was about. Real-life marketing to a friendly audience. "When do you have time to read?" I asked.

"During breaks, vacations, at night before going to sleep, pretty much any chance I get. Life is more than work and school. Anyway, it's a great book. The movie was okay, but the book is much better." With that, she bounded off to put in our breakfast orders.

We looked at each other. "There's a movie?" I said hoping against hope it might obviate having to read the book, or even a summary.

"Yup. Starring Yul Brynner, Lee J. Cobb, and a young William Shatner before his Star Trek days. Not great. But maybe just good enough for your purposes." Marla laughed.

"I wonder how we can get hold of a DVD?"

"Try the library. They have lots of movies. You can check them out for free."

"Given our office budget is zero, free seems like a good price. But that might mean going back to the library and admitting to that nice librarian I'm an idiot who doesn't want to read the book."

"Now, now. You are an idiot who doesn't want to read the book," Zellie said. "No shame admitting it." Zellie and Marla were both doubled over laughing.

"What about you?" I asked. "You don't want to read the book, either."

"Me? I'm not about to go to my public library and tell a librarian I don't want to read. Not a chance."

I sighed. "Leaving the tough jobs to me. I get it. Somebody has to take on the big, important responsibilities. I'll do it. But I will wait for the librarian to go out to lunch, and then ask her assistant to help me."

"Your bravery is duly noted, soldier." Zellie smiled at me.

"Do you guys want to wait to watch the movie, or do you want something more than the half-assed summary I gave you?"

"I vote for that half-witted thing." I said.

"She didn't say half-witted. And maybe she has insight we won't get from the movie."

"I don't know about that. It sounds like Delilah might have more to say about it than I do, but I can tell you I took away the idea that Dostoyevsky seemed fixated on conflict. He placed lots of things and people at war – whether ideas, philosophies, religion, it almost didn't matter. Opposites were in huge supply, and always in conflict." That's my take, anyway." With that, Marla stood up, pushed her chair in, and walked out.

We stewed over that for a while, and any possible relation to our case.

"Doesn't it raise more questions than it answers?"

"It does." She sat for a few moments, and I left her alone, figuring she was considering a course of action.

"I think we should view the scene where Freddy died. It might give us some perspective. We can also visit Flora. A personal interview is always different from a phone call. She can show us what she saw that day, and we can gauge her veracity. For all we know, she may have a hidden motive for her story."

CHAPTER TWENTY-SEVEN

I think we can assume that not all police are as moronic as Officers Dunston and Madison," Zellie stated, as we drove north.

"They set the gold standard for dopiness," I allowed. "Where are you going with this?"

"Let's stop and accept that the police and prosecutors up there are not complete idiots. They can't all be like those two. So we can assume a modicum of honesty and competence. They have an accident at a major intersection in town. One driver's car stalls in the intersection." Zellie paused and looked at me. "Sound familiar?"

I nodded, but refused to disparage Matilda. I gave a backhanded wave showing my impatience. "Go on."

"Another car collides with the stalled vehicle and kills its driver."

"Right, so far as stated in the newspapers."

"But it's not a hit and run. The driver stays and cooperates with the police."

"Okay," I said. "What about it?"

"Does that sound like a premeditated, cold-blooded killing?"

"No, but maybe it was more opportunistic. The killer saw his chance, and took it."

"And stayed to talk to the police?"

"Maybe he had no choice. Maybe he couldn't get away, so tried to just talk his way out."

Zellie looked unconvinced. "It seems strange, that's all," she said.

"Do you think it wasn't a murder?"

"I'm questioning everything."

"Point taken," I said. "But remember, not only Flora thought so. Josh sounded like he questioned the whole thing. And I spent a lot of time with Josh. I doubt he made all of that stuff up."

"I know. He sounds decent. But he was only speculating, and as I understand it, didn't say he thought someone murdered Darrow. He just wondered about it. But I'm interested in what the florist says. She's the only one who witnessed the crash."

"Agreed. Remember, I only spoke to her on the phone. And no one referred me to her. I found her name in a newspaper account. It never occurred to me that she might not tell the truth."

"Well, she might well be telling the truth about what she saw, or at least what she thought she saw. She said she told the police the same story."

"We have to wonder about the statement about a car running a red light? As you said, she might have thought she saw that. Those things are bang, bang, done in an instant. Hard to know what you saw. The police might have thought the same thing, and just discounted her story as not provable."

"True, "Zellie agreed. "One more thing to press her about."

We drove the rest of the way without discussing the case further, other than to speculate about what the charity benefit would be like, and what we intended to do there.

"Dance?" I offered.

"Eat lots of fancy *hors d'oeuvres*?" Zellie added.

"People watch?"

"Try to gather information about the case," Zellie said. "We're working that night. Although I've never gone to a fancy, rich people charity event. Have you?"

"Nope. And I'm guessing that this one is about a thousand dollars a plate. If Rupe wasn't so filthy rich, and contributing way more to that charity already, I'd feel bad about taking the tickets. But he assured me it cost him nothing for the tickets. They were complimentary to him."

"I hope my dress is fancy enough," Zellie said. "Marla helped me pick it out, and she's attended a few of these kinds of events."

"I bet the donors at those events were murderers, jewel thieves and other unsavory people she defends," I said.

"No doubt." Zellie laughed. "I think you're wrong, you know."

"Oh, I know. I'm just joking." I said. "And I'm sure your dress is beautiful. Anything would look great with you wearing it."

"You're sweet. Thank you."

I pulled into the parking lot for Flora's Florals. The lot also provided parking for several other small shops attached to each other, forming a right angle. We strolled to the entrance. Peering in the window, we saw copious hanging plants surrounding several display cases, which I assumed were refrigerated. They contained various kinds of flowers. Plant and flower arrangements surrounded us as we walked into the store and approached a small counter at the rear. We saw no one, neither customers, nor anyone working in the store.

We looked at each other for a moment, and Zellie pointed to a small bell on the counter, which I pressed. As if conjured by the magic bell, a small woman with a round face and snow-white hair, and wearing granny glasses materialized from a side door I hadn't noticed.

"Can I help you?" she asked with a tight-lipped smile.

I introduced us, and she produced a broad smile. "Oh, you dear boy. Thank you for the flowers. I sell them, as you know, but no one ever sends them to me. Until you did, yesterday. And this is your beautiful sweetheart you sent the roses to." She looked Zellie over with approval. "She's a looker, no question about it." Her voice turned anxious. "Um, but why are you here? Was there something wrong with the flowers?"

Zellie spoke up, having stood there with obvious amusement. She knew about the flowers I'd sent to Flora, as I'd told her about it yesterday, causing her to say with a smile that it was a new part of our investigative method – bribing suspects with flowers to get them to talk to us.

"They were gorgeous," Zellie said. "How were yours?"

"Oh, your wonderful young man here told me to pick out something beautiful for myself, and that's just what I did. But I gave him a wholesale price on my flowers," she added in a whisper. "May I give him a hug?"

"Go right ahead," Zellie said, and Flora did just that.

After letting go of me, she looked us both over, and asked again why we came if there was no problem with the flowers. We paused, because we hadn't planned a course of action. Who should speak first? What order to ask the questions? No plan. Oops.

Into the breach jumped Zellie.

"We'd hoped to get a look at one or more of the sales slips, or whatever you use to reflect flower orders. For Mr. Darrow," she added.

"Well, I don't know, that's kind of personal for some people," Flora hedged. "And I regretted giving you his mother's address on the phone. I shouldn't have done that."

"He won't object, Flora. Mr. Darrow is no longer with us," I said in a soothing voice, bowing my head for emphasis. "And we're looking into the circumstances of his unfortunate passing."

Flora crossed herself. "No, he isn't in the earthly world anymore. I guess it's okay." She motioned to the side door. I keep the slips in the office. My nephew keeps telling me he'll put them in the computer, and back them up in the clouds somehow, but he never gets around to it, and, I'd rather deal with paper. You can feel it in in your hands. How can you do that if it's up there in the sky?"

I nodded my sympathy. "I like paper, too."

She shook her head, and we followed her into the office, which turned out to be a small room with several filing cabinets, no windows, and a big antique wood desk. On a side table sat an aging desktop computer, much like my own. The place was immaculate, with not a scrap of paper on the desk, nor a speck of dust anywhere. The place could double as an electronics lab's "clean room." It was that tidy.

"Nice little office you have here," Zellie ventured. "Very, um, orderly."

Flora looked around. "I like everything in its proper place. She moved briskly to one of the file cabinets and retrieved a folder marked "Darrow."

"I keep a file for every client. That way, I can provide the proper customer experience for each person, and remind them not to send the same thing twice to the same person. I have a file on you, too, dear," she added, looking at me.

We couldn't believe our luck. Written order forms for all of Darrow's flower requests. Flora handed me the file, and Zellie and I pored over it. There were seven in there, all to Greta Abogado, and all to the same address, the one we'd visited in Middletown. The last one was dated three months ago. The order was always the same, a dozen lilies. I looked up at Flora.

"Always lilies?"

"Yes," she said. "I tried to talk him into something different. Ladies like variety, I told him. He always shook his head and said it had to be lilies."

"Shook his head?" Zellie asked. "He came in person?"

Flora looked surprised. "Yes, always. A nice man. Quiet, but talkative at the same time. Do you know what I mean?"

We nodded, and Flora continued. "I came to very much enjoy his company," she said, pausing to take in the memory.

"What did you talk about?" Zellie asked.

"Oh, nothing in particular. Plants and flowers. That's my business, so I'll talk about that with anyone."

"Did he ever tell you why he always ordered lilies?"

"No. I know that because I asked him one time. He looked a little sentimental for a moment, and then told me that his preference was tulips, but his mother didn't share his fondness for the colorful bulbs."

"Did you ever talk about anything else?" I asked.

"Well, this and that. Weather, soccer - football he called it. I know very little about football, but he seemed fond of chatting about it. I can't think of anything else. But he had the nicest voice. A slight accent, and don't ask me what country, I'm not good at that, but mellifluous, I think that's the word for it. Sweet on the ears, like a violin."

"Did he stay long, when he placed orders?" I pressed.

"No. A few minutes of chit-chat, that's all. I'm pretty lonely here, so I appreciated even a small amount of talk. I guess that sounds sad."

"Not at all," Zellie said. "A little break from a long day."

Flora trained her eyes on Zellie. "You understand."

Zellie murmured assent. "What can you tell us about his accident?"

"It was no accident," Flora said, with considerable force. "That man ran the red light and bashed right into Mr. Darrow."

"How can you be sure?" I asked.

"It happened right at that intersection over there." She pointed at the wall and then chuckled. "Let's go out into the shop, and I'll show you."

She took the file back, and with great care, deposited it into the file cabinet. I watched, but said nothing. All the orders were in the same tidy script, which I assumed was Flora's, and contained no information other than Greta Abogado's name, address and phone number, which I committed to memory. It also contained the types of flowers – always lilies, and the eighth of each month for seven months, without variation. I made a mental note to ask Flora about that, as we followed her out the door to the main part of the store.

She opened the front door and motioned us outside. "It happened over there, right at that intersection."

I asked the obvious question. "Were you outside?"

Flora looked at me for a millisecond and then said "Of course. It happened at precisely 12:40 p.m., as I walked back from Sigmund's with my egg salad sandwich. I go there every day at 12:30 to pick up my sandwich and walk back to the shop."

After viewing the orderliness of her office, and the fastidi-ous manner in which she executed her lunch routine, the precision of the time she witnessed the accident caused little more than a ripple of doubt in my mind. I could see that Zellie felt the same way. We believed she saw the accident and believed the timing.

"Tell us what happened, right from the beginning," Zellie urged.

"Not much to tell," she said. "As I walked back to my shop, I spotted Mr. Darrow's car stopped at the intersection. I know his car because he parked right in front of the shop whenever he visited. At the time, I couldn't be certain it was his car." she amended. "It looked like it, and it looked like him in the driver's seat. But I didn't know for sure. It did turn out to be him," she said, her eyes filling with faint tears. "A terrible shame."

Zellie gave Flora a moment, followed by a gentle prod. "What happened next?"

Flora collected herself. "The light changed to green, and Mr. Darrow moved his car forward, but it stopped. He moved it forward a few feet, and it stopped again, this time in the middle of the intersection. The light was still green when a car came barreling from the left and crashed into Mr. Darrow's car. As you know, it killed him. That other driver murdered him," she amended.

We looked at the intersection in silence for a few moments, showing both respect for the deceased, and for Flora's benefit, but also to study the scene. You had a clear view of the light from the spot on which we stood. And of greater importance, you could see the light in both directions, at least from one side. You couldn't see the light from the side which the other driver crashed into Darrow, nor could you see the light from the opposite side of the direction Darrow traveled. I pointed this out to Flora in the most benign way possible, and she bristled.

"I saw the green on Mr. Darrow's side, and the yellow switch to red on this side right before the collision. Why would the light be different on the other side? It makes no sense. You sound like the police," she said, casting suspicious eyes on us. "They looked for reasons to call it an accident. It was no accident," she said, with rising fury. "I went to them to do my civic duty, and all they could do was patronize me by saying that these things happen fast, and that they were looking into it. Then nothing," she said with disgust. "Nothing at all, and poor Mr. Darrow gone from this Earth. I even told the newspaper my story, and at least they printed it, but nothing happened. And now, you're doing the same thing."

I held up my hand. "Flora, please listen. I believe you. But we need to explore all avenues, even the ones that might seem unpleasant or inaccurate."

"We can't just ignore possibilities that are inconvenient, or don't fit a preconceived notion," Zellie added.

Flora seemed mollified. Zellie and I looked at each other and made a silent agreement that our interview had ended. We thanked Flora for her time and assistance, and took our leave.

"Awfully unconvincing criminal mastermind," Zellie said as soon as we left the store.

I nodded. "She believes her story, that's for sure. And she's as detail oriented as they come. So where to now, pretty lady?" I asked as I pulled into traffic.

Zellie smiled. "Straight to the movies, handsome. And step on it."

"Yes, ma'am. Stepping on it."

We headed for home for an exclusive viewing of Yul Brynner and Lee J. Cobb in a Russian extravaganza. As I drove, we discussed where we were in figuring out who killed our client.

"Nowhere," I said.

"Pretty far along," Zellie replied.

"How do you figure that?"

Zellie ticked off the reasons. "We know his name, where he came from, his profession, his brother's original name and profession, and that he had a mother living in Middletown. Also, that someone poisoned him."

I stopped at a traffic light just before we reached Middletown.

"Your place or mine?" I asked with a smile.

Zellie had no chance to answer, as something smacked into us with vicious force. I heard a terrible crunching sound, and blacked out.

CHAPTER TWENTY-EIGHT

I woke up in Riverview Hospital in Red Bank, with Zelie hovering over me.

"You're okay," I said with relief. "Um, how am I?" I looked down at myself on the hospital bed.

"In one piece, thank God." Zellie said. "But a terrible concussion. A real humdinger, our irreverent doctor called it. Aside from some cuts and bruises, that's the only problem. But don't get any ideas," she said, as I struggled to get up. "You're staying put, at least overnight. I'd say you could get some sleep, but we both know they'll wake you up every few minutes to check to see if you're okay."

"Where are the doctor and the nurses?" I asked. "Shouldn't someone be here, waiting for me to wake up for the first time?"

Zellie looked at me with anxious eyes. "For the first time? You were awake in the ambulance, and in the emergency room. The doctor spoke to you already. He told you to stay overnight for observation. Do you remember any of that?" Zellie looked worried. "I better find a nurse," she said.

Before she could do so, I held up my hand. "I remember," I said, and I did. It all flowed back, but in a confused sort of way. "The accident shook me up, I guess. But I remember. I suppose the doctor is right I should stay overnight, so my head clears up."

"Darn right you're staying. And I'm staying right here with you."

"You can't sleep in the chair, Zellie," I said.

"Who said anything about sleeping?"

"I'm thinking the staff will frown on us making love in here."

Zellie giggled. "You're sounding like yourself already. No, silly. I'll stay awake with you. The doctor told me I could. Said if I was up to it, that having a friendly person here would be good for you. And I am very, very friendly," Zellie said, with a few exaggerated winks.

"You were in the accident, too. Aren't they worried about a concussion for you?"

"They checked me out, did a concussion protocol and everything. I'm okay."

"Well, that's a relief, anyway." I peered at her. "You have a cut on your arm."

"It's nothing. A couple of stitches. If you look, you have a few of those, too."

I felt my arm, and discovered small bandages on my arm and thigh. "Yup, me, too." I said. "Zellie, I appreciate your willingness to stay here, but you need your sleep. I can't ask you to stay."

"You didn't ask. I declared it as fact. I'm staying," she said. "That's all there is to it. We'll both get sleep tomorrow."

I smiled. "Well then, welcome aboard. I suspect we're in for a bumpy ride," I managed, in a weaker voice than I intended.

"Arnie," Zellie started. "It wasn't an accident."

"What?" The details swirled in my mind. The stop at the intersection, the crunching impact, the air bags. Flashing lights, medics. I didn't remember more than that about the accident itself. I remembered the aftermath, albeit in a vague, fuzzy way. But the accident itself, nothing. It happened too fast.

"I don't remember much, either," Zellie said, in a soothing voice. "We were stopped at the intersection, and a car came out of nowhere and smashed into the front right fender of the car. Then it took off, without stopping."

"A hit and run?"

"Yes. I told the police all I could, but the only thing I saw was that it was a dark blue Ford Explorer. The rest is a blur for me, too. It happened in a flash. That's it. All I know. Not very helpful, and the police, although they were nice, they didn't seem too optimistic that they'd find the person that hit us."

"Wow," I said. "The same thing as Darrow. Except a hit and run this time."

"You remember the case," Zellie said with relief in her voice.

"I remember." I looked down at myself. "Oh. Right. I haven't shown an acute command of today's events."

Zellie leaned over and kissed me. "No, you haven't. And we can talk about it tomorrow. I just thought you should know."

"Thanks," I said. "Sweetheart," I added. "I love you."

"I love you, too. Now lean back and try to rest. The nurses and I will make sure you don't sleep for too long."

"Great. Rest, but don't sleep."

I fell asleep in about one second. A tremendous exhaustion overtook me, and I couldn't keep my eyes open. But it didn't last long, as a nurse tapped me, ostensibly to take my temperature. But a part of me knew they didn't want me to sleep long. I struggled to sit up, and glimpsed a sleeping Zellie in a chair next to my bed. I smiled in her direction, but she didn't stir, and I put a finger to my lips. The nurse glanced at Zellie, nodded agreement, and took my temperature in silence. She wrote something on her clipboard and left. Zellie slept through the whole thing.

I stretched out and tried to sleep, but my mind roiled, and I fidgeted in bed. I looked over at Zellie, whose eyes popped open.

"Who, what, where?" she said, and I had to laugh, although it hurt to do so.

"That about covers it, but you left out how and why."

Zellie smiled at me. "Good morning, good-looking."

"It's not morning," I said. "It's two a.m."

She looked at the clock. "So it is. I kind of fell down on my keeping you awake job, didn't I?"

"No, you didn't. It's about time for a wake-up call now. The nurses just took the first couple of shifts, that's all."

"How are you feeling?"

"Achy," I admitted.

"Yeah, me too." Zellie felt her side. "And this chair isn't helping."

I motioned to a spot next to me. "Why don't you get in for a while. There's plenty of room."

Zellie looked around. "Is the nurse due to check on you?"

"Just did. You slept right through it."

"Then I think I will for a little while. Move over."

I moved over and Zellie slipped under the covers with me. I felt better already from the warmth of her body next to mine. We both dozed off, only to have a nurse wake us up with loud taps on the bed.

"Out." she said to Zellie. "My patient needs to rest."

Zellie mumbled an apology. "I'm getting out. We were resting together in quiet, that's it."

I looked at the clock. Five a.m. They let us sleep together for three hours. Must have thought it good for me, and they were right. I gave a silent thank you to the good and caring nursing staff of Riverview Hospital.

They discharged me at 8:00 a.m., with a warning. Concussions can be tricky, they told me. I should go to the doctor if I experienced any continuing effects. They told Zellie to keep an eye out, too, but I noticed her different treatment, not being a relative. They only relented a little when I told them I had no one on Earth closer than her. Still, I hated their attitude.

We took a taxi to my house. The accident had resulted in a huge dent in the front left panel of my SUV, with possible engine damage. The insurance adjuster would assess whether it was a total loss, or if someone could fix it. A complete loss would force me to use my old car, my favored result. It's irrational, and it doesn't provide reliable transportation. But I didn't care. My heart belonged to Matilda, and I wanted to drive only her. No way I wanted to continue to forsake her for a young, glamourous model.

Once home, we had a brief discussion, and proceeded straight to bed. To sleep. Despite the few hours respite afforded by the nurses, hospitals are a terrible place to sleep. And we were exhausted. So we slept. Until noon, when we got up, ate a little lunch, made a huge tub of popcorn, and cued up the movie.

Zellie and I have a long tradition of movie watching, and local theaters barred us for talking too much. At home, we have no such restrictions, so we gab through entire movies. As watching this movie was business-related, Zellie asked if we should abstain from our usual chatter.

"No way," I said. "That's just plain wrong."

Zellie chuckled. "I was hoping you'd say that." As the movie started, she snuggled close on the sofa, and I leaned over and whispered sweet nothings into her ear. Um, no I didn't. What I said was, "Can we deduct this popcorn as a business expense?"

"We'll ask the accountant we never got around to hiring."

"The A to Z Agency has no income," I pointed out.

"We've been much too busy growing the business," Zellie replied.

"So that's what we've been doing. I thought this was flailing around, talking to a bunch of people, and almost getting killed."

"Well, that's our investigative method."

"And you can't argue with an investigative method," I agreed.

So we watched the movie, yakking the whole time about how there seemed to be a lot of Russians in the movie, that Yul Brynner got all the girls, and none of his brothers seemed to get any, and useful things like that. We did glean from the movie that Marla's description seemed on the mark. There were lots of conflicts between brother and brother, father and son, religion or no religion, love interest and love interest. And money at the center of the whole thing.

"What do you think Darrow meant?" I asked Zellie after the movie concluded.

"There were so many conflicts in that thing, it's too hard to tell," she answered. "But we'll figure it out," she added, and with a sly grin, she took my hand.

"Meanwhile, I think a little rest and recreation is in order. It could clear our heads and help us solve the case."

I needed no convincing.

CHAPTER TWENTY-NINE

L inkage must exist somewhere," I mused out loud.

"Between what?"

"The book and the murders. A book about brothers, not at war with each other, but in competition."

"And a terrible father," Zellie pointed out. "Where's the father in this little vignette of ours, and the other two brothers? The movie had three brothers and a half- brother."

"We don't know," I admitted. "But I think it would be a terrible mistake to believe the book and inscription mean that Darrow's situation somehow is an exact duplicate of the novel. My guess is that something in the book reminded him of his life, nothing more than that."

"I agree with you. But where does that leave us? We have to figure out which part of the book he meant? I don't think we should do that. We should just follow the facts where they lead us. And the book fits in somewhere. We just don't know where yet."

"You have any ideas on our next step?" I asked.

"I do. We should go back and look at our office."

"At the Moo-Mart?"

"That's not our office anymore, remember?"

"Oh, I remember, all right, I just miss the place, that's all. So, we're back to the place we still intend to rent. What do you expect to find there?"

"I'm thinking we missed something. Signs of a struggle, maybe. I don't know, something. Darrow died in the attic? How did he get there? And why did he die there? Why didn't he just leave the attic and get help?"

"All good questions."

"I think knowing how he died may help us figure out who did it."

"He was poisoned. We already know that."

"Let's find out more about the poison, then. And let's redouble our efforts to find out who visited Darrow in his office other than the vague references to an angry woman, and a mysterious dark-haired lady."

"We've sort of neglected basic stuff, haven't we?"

"Oh no, I don't think so. The facts led one way, and we followed those leads. I think we should file that information away and go in a different direction for the time being."

"Makes sense. Let's go. We still have a little bit of the afternoon left."

Zellie called Melissa and told her we wanted to view the office again. Melissa readily agreed, and we met her there. She opened the door for us, pointed to the removal of the crime scene tape, and noted her restored freedom to rent the place to us, or anyone else.

"Are other people looking?" Zellie asked.

"Well, not that I know. You've already figured out I might not be the most active broker in the world. Okay, you're my only clients. But other brokers may have people looking. If you like it, you should grab it."

"We like it," I said, and Zellie gleamed.

"Yes, we do. Very much," she said.

"Great, I'll take care of everything. I know how to close a deal," she added.

"I'm sure you do," I said. "May we look around now?"

"Go right in and make yourself at home." She looked around. "As at home in an empty space as you can," she said with a little laugh. "I'll just get out of your way."

We thanked her and looked around. At least I did. Zellie stared at the trap door leading to the attic.

"Do you see something?" I asked.

"Look up there. See those tiny indentations? What do you think they are?"

"I saw what she meant. One big indentation, with a second long one, almost scraped, and with a faint line running from it, like an exclamation point. "Could be anything," I said. "What's bothering you?"

"Give me a boost," she replied. "I want a closer look."

I obliged by clasping my hands to make a foothold and lifting her up.

"It looks like something pressed against this and made these marks," she concluded. "Okay, you can let me down."

"What do you think pressed against it," I asked. "And second, why would it matter?"

"You know, I think it might matter a lot," she said. "Aren't we wondering how the killer got Darrow up there, and then how he or she kept him there?"

"Yup. That's the question." I agreed. "What about it?"

"I don't know how Darrow got up there, but I think I know how someone trapped him up there."

"How?"

"Someone wedged something between the floor and the attic trap door."

"Like a ladder?" I asked.

"Maybe. But would a ladder make those marks? I suppose it doesn't matter, unless we find something around here that matches those indentations, which I doubt, because the place is pretty empty."

"Maybe there's a shed, or something."

I called out for Melissa to come inside, and she put that notion to rest.

"No shed. No outbuildings at all." She pulled aside the curtains on the big windows and pointed through the grime to the vacant back of the building. See? Nothing but parking spaces back there. Tenants use the attic for storage, and an outside service does the cleaning."

"Did you ever see anything in here tall enough to reach the ceiling, like a ladder, or scaffolding, or something like that?" I asked Melissa.

"No, it's always been empty when I've come here to show it."

"How many times have you shown it?" Zellie asked, a trifle mischievously.

"Okay, okay. You got me. The same number of times you've been here." She looked around. "There's nothing like that here, and unless it's in a closet or the attic. Oh..." She looked up.

"The attic," Zellie said. "We need to go up there and take a look."

Melissa recoiled. "I'm not going up there. And I'm not standing here while you open the folding stairs. Remember the last time I did that?"

"We do," I assured her. "And you don't have to go up there, or pull down the folding stairs." I reached up to grab the rope, and Melissa backed away, her palms facing out, like she was defending against an unseen force. Zellie stood back a little, too, although I think it fair to say none of us expected a second body to fall down, after the police had concluded their examination of the premises. I pulled the rope, and the folding stairs to the attic lowered on a creaking spring. Nothing fell on my head, except maybe a smattering of dust. I wiped it off my hair and looked up into the dark space. With a glance at Zellie and Melissa, I headed up the ladder, which groaned on its springs with each step.

Upon reaching the top, I whipped out my Dad's knife/penlight, and illuminated an area larger than a crawl space, but insufficient for anyone to stand up in. Several loose nails secured a board covering rows of cross beams. I assumed it served as a storage space at one time, but it was empty at present. Emptied by the police, in all likelihood. A thin layer of dust covered the struts next to the board, and on the edges of the board itself. Something had disturbed the detritus in the center – boxes, equipment, a body, I couldn't tell by a cursory inspection. I tried to figure out how the body got so far out on the folding stairs it could fall down when the trap door opened. No way someone could have moved the body out there. There was only enough room for one person, so it was impossible that someone had hidden in the attic and shoved the body down when we pulled on the string.

I hated to do this. I wasn't claustrophobic, but I don't like cramped spaces, much less one serving as a dead man's tomb, but I had my penlight, so I could keep the place lit up. I looked down at Zellie, who peered up.

"Close the stairway door and let the stairs go back up into the attic," I said.

"While you're up there?" An apprehensive Zellie didn't like the suggestion.

"I'm not thrilled at the prospect, but I have this." I held up my source of illumination. Let's see if someone can push the stairs down from the inside. And while the door is closed, I'll look at whatever Darrow saw when he was up here."

"Another crazy idea for the A to Z Agency," Zellie muttered, but complied. "Here goes. I'll give you five minutes, and then I'm pulling it down again. Time will be hard to gauge, so for the most part, stay off the trap door."

"Don't worry, I have no intention of doing so, I said. I may check right away to see if my weight is enough to force the door down. You noticed that it moseyed down on the springs anyway, but I won't be dumb about it."

"I think the dumbness scale is already approaching critical, but I am curious to see what you find out."

"Me too," I said, and she closed me in.

CHAPTER THIRTY

I examined the inside of the trap door. We'd already looked at it from down below, but I wondered about how the door fit the opening from this side. Nothing struck me. I tried to push the door down from a prone position on the board, and found it impossible. The angle and accompanying physics were all wrong for it to work. Next, I crept out on the door itself, with some not so inconsiderable trepidation that the door would crumble under me, and I'd tumble to the ground. I needn't have worried. While it bent a little, it remained shut. I supposed that a panicked and trapped person might exert more force, and maybe even opened the door, but it wouldn't be easy. I scurried back to the safety of the board, and rapped a few times on the trap door. The door swung open, and Zellie and Melissa looked up at me.

"Coming down," was all I said, and I climbed slowly down the stairs, and told them what I'd found.

"One thing of note – there was dust everywhere, except on the board sitting on the cross beams."

"Meaning that someone, or something sat up there," Zellie said. "But we already know that. Darrow was up there."

"I'm thinking about what wasn't there. The cross beams formed a perfect place to store a ladder or any other long equipment, but the dust tells us that there was nothing there, either for Darrow or the maintenance people to use for work around the office. I gestured at the windows. Like hanging those tall drapes for example."

"Or propping the door closed from downstairs." Although opening the door from the inside would have been almost impossible anyway. Someone wanted certainty, and they found whatever made those marks in the door somewhere else."

"Yes."

"But the only two people with access from the outside were the landlord, Jayne Merriweather and Patsy Bruder, the building manager. Also, Russ Devereaux, the office cleaner, who claimed he only came when Darrow was present. I wonder whether he had a key, just in case Darrow wasn't here."

"And those were only the people we know who were authorized to come in here. Jayne could have given permission to any number of people. We also don't know who Darrow let in himself," I pointed out.

"We need to snoop around to see what equipment Bruder and Russ carry with them on the job. A ladder, or maybe something else that could serve as a prop to wedge in between the floor and the attic door."

We thanked Melissa and headed back home, but only after resolving to get moving on renting the office. We needed a place to work without distractions.

On the way, I told Zellie an idea I had. I figured we should look into who owned and/or managed the retirement community where I met Greta Abogado. Then we could talk to someone in management about whether the perpetrators had any connections to the place. Oh man, I used the word perpetrators, even to myself. Get a grip, I thought. I sound like a bad movie, even in my thoughts. Zellie laughed when I told her.

"We need a righteous collar of the alleged perps, Sam," she mimicked in her best police procedural voice. She laughed again, and so did I. And once again, I marveled at how Zellie's laugh could engender such warmth of spirit. I reached over and placed my hand on her thigh, and she rewarded me with a smile. But I resolved that we'd work when we returned home, and that's what we did.

"It's a long shot, I know, but Greta said she thought her two sons shared the cost of her place. Maybe someone in management knew them both, or knows something of value."

"It's worth a try. Any lead could help."

Zellie trudged over to my aging desktop computer to begin her research on the ownership of the Sunny Ponds Retirement Community, or SPRC – Middletown. I looked over her shoulder as she typed in the information.

"You remembered the name? I'm impressed."

She looked back at me. "I cheated. I knew about it already. Looked into a lot of these places last year when Dad had his health scare."

I nodded. Not a great time for Zellie and her parents.

Zellie studied the monitor, clicking on various links, and pointed at the screen. "Well, looky here," she said. "Check out the parent company of SPRC - Middletown."

I peered at the name on the screen. Many Counties Properties. Jayne's company. The same outfit that owned our new office, or as we gumshoes call it – the crime scene.

"I'm pretty sure this is an important piece of information," I said.

"No question, but what does it mean?"

We put our heads together and came up with a plan. We'd try to find a link between Many Counties Properties and the two Darrows, other than the fact that their mom lived there, and Ferdinand rented an office from the same company. We'd also try to track down as much information as we could about Greta Abogado.

"We're getting somewhere now," Zellie exulted.

I was not so sure about that, but kept my thoughts to myself. No sense in tempering Zellie's enthusiasm.

"Have you tried on your tux?" Zellie asked, jarring me out of my reverie.

Her question seemed like a *non sequitur* at first, but then I realized its full import. The benefit was tomorrow, and we expected Jayne to show up. A perfect opportunity to press her for information.

Zellie saw momentary confusion in my eyes and tittered. "You forgot, didn't you?"

I admitted it, and Zellie turned serious. "You're not having memory problems, are you? I never should have let you crawl around in that attic after your concussion."

After assuring her I felt no ill effects from the crash, I offered to try on my tux, which to my great pleasure, fit like a well-worn pair of shoes.

"You look terrific," Zellie said, "I only hope I look half as good as you."

"You'll be the belle of the ball," I assured her. "And a dream to have on my arm," I added, reaching out to give her a warm embrace. She held up her hand. "Stop right there, mister. No mussing up the clothing before the big dance."

I settled for grasping her hand, and holding on to it, while leaning over to give her a gentle kiss.

"How do you propose to find a link between the Darrows and Many Counties Properties?" I asked, still holding Zellie's hand, and adding a kiss on her neck just under her ear.

"I haven't figured out those details yet... you'd better stop that if we want to get anything done," she said, moving me away, with a soft, but firm push.

"We also need to follow up on everyone who had access to the office, and their corresponding access to a ladder, or other prop that made those marks," I pointed out. "That information might obviate the need for anything else. Because that person is the killer."

CHAPTER THIRTY-ONE

Zellie nodded, but remained quiet. I knew this look. She was figuring something out, and it was always best to just let her think. But she looked up.

"We need to go get a sandwich."

Of all the things I expected from Zellie as a result of her thought process, I didn't expect hunger.

"Um, are you okay? I asked. "You were in the crash, too."

"Oh, I'm fine," she said, and chuckled. "That sounded crazy, didn't it? I mean we need to go talk to Jake. There's something he said I think we should get clarified before we do anything else."

"Well, I'm famished anyway," I said. "So, you can explain on the way."

"You better watch your diet," she teased. "You want to still fit into that tux tomorrow night. And you're overdressed for Jake's."

Looking down, I saw I still wore the tux. After I changed back into my usual khakis and collared shirt, we headed out.

Walking to the garage to retrieve Matilda, Zellie stopped me.

"Let's take my Honda," she said. "If it would make you feel better, you can drive," she added, handing me the keys.

I shrugged, but took the keys and got in the driver's seat with little grace.

"Oh, I didn't want to upset you," Zellie said, placing her hand on my shoulder. "I know you're dying to drive Matilda again. And I wouldn't mind riding in her. Just not today, okay?"

"Okay," I muttered assent. "But I'll need to drive her at some point, given that my Suburban's in the shop."

"What's the status of that?" she asked. "Have you heard from the insurance adjuster?"

"Not yet," I replied, giving a silent prayer for irreparable damage.

"You're hoping they can't fix it, aren't you?" Zellie asked this as a question, but it was more a declaration than anything else. What can I do? She knows me too well.

"Kind of, yes," I said. "Anyway, enough about that. What's your idea about Jake?"

Zellie looked down at the notebook she held in her lap. "Jake looked troubled about something when we saw him. I hope we can get him to tell us a little more about his encounters with Darrow. If Jake only knew Darrow from the few times he came into the deli, and he didn't talk much, how did Jake even know his name?

"What did he say in that minimal conversation that gave Jake the creeps? And what is troubling him? Shouldn't we press Jake on all that?"

"His information could be useful," I agreed. "But Jake sometimes talks a lot without saying much."

"True enough," Zellie said. "Let's see if we can pin him down."

We walked into Jake's Sandwich Shop to the usual hearty greeting from Jake.

"Look what we have here, Nathan! Arnie and Zellie. Again. Second time this week. You know what that is, Nathan? Loyalty, that is," Jake answered his own question while his young employee stood by wearing a stoic expression. I figured that by now, he was used to Jake's customary histrionics.

"Hi Jake," Zellie said. "We're back for two sandwiches and some conversation."

We ordered our sandwiches, and Jake told Nathan to bring them over to our table when he finished preparing them. Then we all walked to a nearby table, and Jake sat down with us.

"Conversation is my stock-in-trade, kids. What do you want to talk about? The old days? I hope it's the old days. Reminiscing, I seem to be good at that," he said with a touch of regret in his voice. "How about sports? That's better. But I know you two, you have something on your minds, so out with it."

Zellie and I glanced at each other. Jake stopping long enough to ask us what we wanted to talk about? Very unusual. But Zellie didn't wait to figure it out. She jumped right in.

"We were hoping to talk a little more about your encounters with Ferdinand Darrow," she said.

"That guy? What about him? Didn't we talk about this last time you were here? I'm pretty sure I told you everything already."

For a guy that jabbered about just about anything, Jake's reaction was out of character. I wondered what was going on, and I could see Zellie recoil. She didn't expect that response, which bordered on, but didn't quite reach, outright vitriol.

To Zellie's credit, she plunged ahead, asking Jake to go over the times he had seen Darrow, and giving a smooth explanation that, as detectives, we had an occasional need to go over old ground to move the investigation forward. Jake seemed appeased by Zellie's matter-of-fact tone.

He recounted the three times, to his memory, he added, that Darrow had entered the shop, that his manner was over-polite, almost as an affectation, and not true solicitude. Despite what Jake referred to as the guy's creepy demeanor, he had attempted in his customary way to engage the man in conversation, but the man rebuffed him. And that lady he came in with once. She wasn't much better. Kind of stern looking. I didn't even try to talk to her. The guy he met here once seemed nicer, though. I chatted with him before Darrow arrived to meet him, and he seemed normal, at least until Darrow arrived. They didn't seem like friends, I'll tell you that."

"Can you tell us anything else about the people Darrow met with?"

"No, I don't think so. They weren't very talkative, and I have a shop to run," he added. "And before you ask, I don't eavesdrop. Unless it's necessary, of course," he added with a slight smile. "Maybe someone needs an extra pickle, or something like that. Listening in on customers' conversations is bad for business."

"What did these people look like?" I persisted, not giving Jake a chance to leave.

"Man was about 5' 7" with a medium build, graying hair, and blue eyes. Woman was tall and dark-haired. I don't remember anything else. Is that it?" Jake looked restless, anxious to get back to the counter.

"One more thing," Zellie said, "And then we'll let you go. How did you know his name, if he wasn't talkative, and you'd never met him before?"

Jake looked a little startled, although maybe from Zellie's tone, which, contrary to her earlier gentle prodding, approached brusqueness.

"I don't know, he managed after a long pause. "Must have heard it somehow. Maybe he told me? Maybe I heard it on TV? I don't know. Anyway, I've got to get back. Nathan is helpless without me." Jake had returned to his customary banal chatter, and we knew the interview was over.

"Whoa, you really put it to him back there, Zellie. All gentle and sweet, then bam, hit him with the big question," I said as soon as we were outside.

Zellie put her head in her hands. "I know, I know. I think I overdid it. Jake's mad at me. And I didn't mean to upset him. But he's holding something back."

"No question about it," I agreed. "But what? He runs a sandwich shop. He can't have any interest in all of this, other than as an observer. And he was the one who told us he had met Darrow. We didn't ask."

"I know. And my dramatic 'how did you know his name' thing was silly, if you think about it."

"Why?"

"He could have heard the name from almost anywhere. Someone mentioning it in the shop, Darrow telling him, even TV like he said. I overdid it. And ignored our investigative method, too." Zellie kept her head down, shaking it side to side. She rubbed her forehead with her fingertips. I tried to console her.

"Maybe that's part of our investigative method," I said. "And anyway, he didn't see it on television, because I don't think it even ran on television. The local papers, yes, but TV, I don't think so. At least as far as I'm aware. No, he was holding something back. Not lying to us, but not telling us everything."

Zellie popped up her head. "I wonder. Maybe they met somewhere else, or didn't meet, but Jake knew about him somehow."

"I suppose it's possible, but how do we figure that out?"

"We don't, I guess," she said. "But we make a note and file it away. It might fit the puzzle later."

"Okay, we'll do that. What next?"

"You have any ideas?"

"I think this would be a good time to stalk either Bruder the building manager, or Russ the office cleaner."

"We'll do Bruder. Where do you think we'll find her?"

"Let's park outside our new landlord's headquarters and see what develops."

So we parked. And waited. We watched and waited some more. I looked over at Zellie. "How long have we been at this?"

She looked at her watch. "Eight minutes. I've had enough. How about you?"

"Let's get out of here. Maybe we'll try again tomorrow."

"Yeah, tomorrow. Good idea."

I put the car in gear and drove away.

* * *

After our ridiculous attempt to mimic television detectives by going on a stakeout, we put our heads together to come up with better ways to gather information.

"Darrow's client list would be useful, wouldn't it?" I mused.

"It sure would. It might tell us who came in contact with him other than the people we already know."

"I wonder how we can get our hands on it," I said, but Zellie had already made a beeline for the computer, and was clicking away before I even finished my sentence.

"We can't get his client list, because the police presumably took his files. But court records are public," she said over her shoulder as she kept working. "I'm just checking to see if Darrow appeared in court in any cases. And it's not that easy. It looks like a million different courts in a million different locations. I don't know where to begin. This is going to take a while," she said. "And we don't have that much time."

"Try any court in Monmouth County first," I advised. "And I assume you're searching by attorney name?"

"Checking Monmouth County now. He was a wills and estates lawyer, right?"

"That's what people told us. Try the Surrogates Court," I said, and Zellie looked back at me with raised eyebrows. "How do know that?"

"I know stuff," I said. "And in my previous life, I dealt with securities, remember? Lots of testamentary transfers. Hence, knowledge about the Surrogates' Court."

Zellie typed in a few characters and clicked her mouse. "Bingo!"

"What did you find?"

She pointed to the screen. "Look."

She gestured at a list of cases under the name Ferdinand Darrow. It wasn't a long list, and one name popped out in glaring neon lights. In the Matter of the Estate of Elizabeth Rothberg. Zellie clicked on the link, which revealed a banner telling us we need to review the records in person, as the Court did not permit online viewing.

"Next stop, Monmouth County Courthouse," I said, and Zellie nodded. But I detected a little hesitation in her movements, then remembered. This was the exact courthouse she'd visited before her kidnapping. At about the same time of day as today.

"Don't worry, we're going together this time." I assured her. "And tomorrow morning is soon enough."

Zellie took my hand in a signal I took as gratitude for my quick grasp of her predicament, and I leaned down and kissed her.

CHAPTER THIRTY-TWO

We don't think Jake killed Darrow, do we?" I asked Zellie as we drove to the courthouse the next morning. I was still driving Zellie's car, not wishing to add to her anxiety by enlisting Matilda for the ride.

"I can't believe it. It's Jake, for goodness sake."

"I don't either," I said. "But he's not telling us something. And it's not just that he knew Darrow through his involvement with Bessie's estate."

"That's what's bothering me the most. Why not just tell us that part? It's public record. And there's nothing to hide. Why the cloak and dagger bit about saying he only met him at the deli, and thought he seemed creepy. He just made all that up."

"And volunteered all of it." I added.

"Maybe he figured we'd already found that out, and that's why we were there the first time. He was just gauging how much we knew. Anyway, we're here. And look, there's plenty of parking. I pulled into a space right in front, to assuage Zellie's obvious nervousness.

We entered the building and went to the clerks' office. All such offices seemed the same, right down to the bulletproof glass separating the clerks from the riff-raff outside the window.

"I seem to be living in clerks' offices," I said to Zellie, who smiled at me and pointed to a row of computers next to the window.

"No need to bother the clerks this time," she said. "All case files are retrievable right there."

I pulled a chair from in front of an adjacent computer, and sat down next to Zellie, who had planted herself in front of the first terminal. She made a quick search to bring up the same limited information we'd seen at home and then clicked a link unavailable from home. Presto, the case docket appeared. We peered at the first page, which listed parties appearing in the case, and saw in bold print the name Ferdinand Darrow, Esq., representing himself. It listed Jacob Rothberg as administrator of the estate, represented by David R. Smedley, a well-known local lawyer. No will existed, and Ferdinand Darrow had some sort of dispute not explained on the case docket. To find out more, we needed to look at the actual documents filed in the case. As the Court was still converting all of its paper documents to digital form, not all documents were available online, including the ones we wanted. So we'd need to bother the clerks, and headed back to the window.

We requested the case file for the estate of Elizabeth Rothberg, and when the clerk delivered it, she directed us to a small table at which we could review the documents. She cautioned us not to remove anything, and it was plain she intended to monitor our actions to insure compliance. Copies were twenty-five cents a page, and copying was awkward. Two prongs held each document to the file, and were required to stay down, so that we had to make each copy by holding the entire file against the glass. The fourteen-inch legal size completed the irrationality of the process. I started to say something about it, but Zellie stopped me.

"They hate it, too," she said. "It's one reason they want it all digitized. But the size and age of many of the documents makes the scanning process extra difficult. We'll just go along with it and hope that either our next case doesn't require court documents, or they'll have finished the process. Anyway, let's look at what we have here, and figure out if there is anything to copy."

My curiosity trumping my desire to gripe, I agreed. Zellie took the file to the table and I sat down next to her, looking over her shoulder as she paged through the documents. Most of them appeared routine – the application to administer the estate, together with a death certificate for Elizabeth Rothberg, paying a fee (there's always a fee), assigning a judge, appointing Jake as the administrator, and the appearance of David Smedley as his and the estate's lawyer.

There was nothing unusual in any of that. An accounting of Elizabeth and Jake's property reflected their ownership of a house in Red Bank. Interesting, but none of our business, and not pertinent to our case, in that there appeared to be no dispute about it reverting to Jake as the joint owner.

What jumped out at us, though, was a one-half interest in a parcel of real estate in northern New Jersey, stated as an asset of Elizabeth Abogado. A document filed by Ferdinand Darrow contained an assertion that because Jake had no ownership interest in the property that Elizabeth owned, he had no claim to it. The objection further stated that Elizabeth had given Darrow an interest in the property in a phone call. The purported value of the disputed asset stated in Darrow's objection – a cool million dollars.

We looked at each other. Bessie's maiden name was Aboga-do. And she'd received an interest in some valuable real estate in that name, which I guessed she owned before she married Jake.

"Bessie's an Abogado. And it looks like she had money," I observed.

"And a heck of a family squabble. Look at this," Zellie said, placing her index finger on a paragraph in the next document in the file, titled Estate's Response to the Fraudulent, Slanderous and Conniving Allegations of a Greedy Relative. It described in legal terms that the claims had no merit. It disputed Darrow's claim that Bessie had given him any property interest, pointing out he had produced no evidence to support his position, that giving real estate as Darrow alleged, must be in writing under New Jersey law, and arguing that his claim wouldn't take precedence over Bessie's husband.

"Powerful stuff," I said. "And look at the end, where it states that the sole purpose of the fraudulent claim is to get the estate to pay him money just to go away, and rejecting any such payment as giving in to extortion."

Zellie flipped to the last document in the file.

"But they did," she said. "Look at this."

I leaned over and read the brief text of a Stipulation of Settlement, in which Jacob Rothberg agreed to pay Ferdinand Darrow the sum of $100,000 to waive forever any further claim of any kind against the estate. The document contained no further explanation of any kind. The judge had entered an order approving the stipulation, and the estate administration had been closed.

"Well, that's all very interesting," I said. "Jake had an obvious reason to hate Ferdinand Darrow."

"He did," Zellie said. "Jake's all upset about losing Bessie, and he has to deal with that. Must have devastated him. But don't you wonder something else?"

"What?"

"Who owned the other half interest in the property with Bessie? There's nothing in the file about it."

"Some other relative or friend, I suppose. But we should find out. You know, there's one thing we haven't done."

Zellie arched one eyebrow. "Only one thing?"

"One of about a zillion things we haven't done," I amended. "We haven't checked to see if our client is a lawyer in good standing in this Court, like I did upstate for the other Darrow. We're here now, let's perform our due diligence on that."

"Good idea."

We returned the file and asked the clerk to check Darrow's status. She returned in a minute.

"No record found," she said. "We have no listing for Ferdinand Darrow in our attorney database. Is there anything else I can do for you?"

Upon assuring her we had no further business, we took our leave.

"Well, that threw us for a loop," Zellie said, as we walked out. "All this time we assumed our client was a real lawyer."

"Josh told me that no one checks unless there's an issue. So, it turns out you can have an office, call yourself an attorney, and just start lawyering, or whatever it's called."

"Representing clients."

"Yeah, representing clients. And without a license. It's outrageous, that's what it is. Oops. Sensing any irony here?"

"It had occurred to me, yes," Zellie said. "And we should figure out a way to do something about our um, lack of authority. But more to the point, we need to look into Bessie's background. It never occurred to us to do it before, because who'd of figured that her family tree would have any importance to our case. But we need to do it now."

"We need to check Jake's background, too. Including a credit check," I said, with a deep sigh. "Sometimes I hate what we do."

"Me, too. But it can't be helped."

We arrived back home and went right to work. We had only a few hours before we needed to get ready to go to the benefit. Zellie jumped on the computer and clicked away. I made a few calls, to conduct telephone interviews of people who knew the Rothbergs, and might have information about their family tree. I also called Ted, to see whether he could start a background check, using his own methods, the details of which I preferred not to know. He agreed, with something approaching gusto.

"We should also go see Mrs. Minniefield tomorrow. She's lived here longer than us, and probably knows more about Jake and Bessie than we ever could."

"Good idea," Zellie said over her shoulder. "And maybe she has ideas on how we can get licensed. That thing about Darrow made me feel a little dirty, doing the same thing as he did."

"We're not the same. We take great pains to tell everyone we're not licensed. And we're trying to get the truth and help people. Darrow was a scam artist."

"I know. But just the same, I hope Mrs. M has ideas to get us on the right side of the law."

"From your lips to Mrs. Minniefield's ears," I said. "Finding anything?"

"A few things. This is not that straightforward. I have records seeming to reflect multiple relatives of Jake and Bessie, but they all need verification through other sources. I have various names and addresses, but no clear sign of relationships, or even that the names are their relatives."

"So it will take a little time," I said.

"That's about the size of it. Maybe Ted will have information, and we can compare and contrast."

"I hope so," I said. "Now let's get a look at you wearing that new dress," I added, affecting a leer.

Zellie laughed. "Not so fast. The dress is at my house, and I'm dressing there while you put on your tux here. Then you can pick me up for our evening event."

I put up my hand with a smile. "Okay, okay, have it your way. I'll see you at seven-thirty."

CHAPTER THIRTY-THREE

Zellie took her car and headed home, while I retrieved my formal attire from the closet, and laid it on the bed. Then I undressed and took a shower, donned my tuxedo and made sure I had put nothing on backwards.

All of a sudden, I came to a shocking revelation. I was nervous about our date. I'm not sure I had ever been anxious around Zellie in the half century I'd known her, but there you have it. No arguing with how you feel. I wondered if she felt nervous too. She'd made a big deal out of us having a proper date. I'd assumed that she was just having fun with it all, but maybe I'd missed something.

I looked at my watch. 7:20. Time to get moving for the two second drive to her house up the street. I went out, and started up Matilda. She coughed a few times, sputtered, and died. Accustomed to Matilda's inscrutable start up idiosyncrasies, I waited a few moments and turned the key again. Showing her pleasure at my gentle ministrations, Matilda's ignition caught and I headed up the street.

I parked in the driveway and headed for the side door to let myself in as usual. For some reason, I thought better of it and went around front and rang the doorbell. Much to my surprise, Marla opened the door, and directed me to the living room, where Ted sat in studied silence. The two of them waited for me to speak, and I obliged.

"Um, Mr. and Mrs. Morgan, I'm here to pick Zellie up for our date."

"She's still getting ready, Arnold. Why don't you sit down and tell us a little about yourself?" Marla played her part with perfect pitch, and without a trace of humor.

Discarding the somber tone, Ted grinned and said "Yes, sit down Arnold. I must tell you I have a real problem with you dating my daughter. She's a precious flower, you know, and I think she deserves someone much better than you."

With that, we all laughed, but stopped at a noise coming from the top of the stairs. Zellie was making her way down, one step at a time. When she reached the landing, she stood there, holding the hem of her floor length evening gown. With the form of a ballerina, she released her grip, causing ripples up and down the shimmering dress. Zellie mesmerized me with the grace and beauty she presented in her monochrome royal blue strapless gown. She twirled, showing off her bare shoulders and her brownish blond hair, which covered the nape of her neck. She evidenced no difficulty maintaining her balance on three-inch heels. A tiny gold locket dangled from her neck on a thin gold chain. I recognized it as one her mother had handed down to her. It contained pictures of her grandparents when they still lived in Germany, the old country as they referred to it.

All I could say as I stood there was "Yowza. You're beautiful, Zellie."

"From where I stand, you cut a fine figure yourself, and look great in that tux. Are we ready for the benefit?"

"Ready if you are," I replied. "If these poor simulations of your wonderful parents say it's okay."

"Okay with us," Marla said. "You two look great, and perfect together as always, don't they Ted?"

"A perfect couple. I've always said that."

Zellie put her hand on my arm, and I escorted her out to my car. I kind of wished I'd rented a limousine or something fancy for the occasion, but I didn't think of it until this second. Anyway, I liked showing up at a fancy benefit in a classic Chevy. Nothing like a little iconoclasm to shake up the rich and beautiful people.

In any event, Matilda loves Zellie. I know that sounds crazy, a car loving someone, but Matilda always puts on a show for Zellie. And this was no exception. She started up right away, gave off an almost musical hum from the purring engine, and transported us with quiet efficiency to the Oak Hill County Club. I pulled up to the valet parking, and was almost disappointed that the fellow taking my keys not only didn't turn his nose up at having to lower himself by driving such a vehicle, he commented on what a great set of wheels I had.

"That have a 283 in it?" he asked.

"No, she has a 327," I said in a proud reference to the higher horsepower of Matilda's version of a 1966 Chevy Impala.

"Nice."

I rushed around to the passenger side and let Zellie out. She took my arm, and we headed inside, where a large banner announcing 'Welcome, Friends of the Barton Springs Salamander' greeted us in the vestibule.

I showed our tickets to the folks sitting at a table in front of the ballroom, and they pointed to a series of place cards on an adjacent credenza.

"You'll be sitting at the Cavendish Industries table," a woman told us, gesturing to her right. "The place cards for that table will be on the far left side."

We walked over and found our place cards, and in our usual nosy manner, surveyed the rest of the cards.

"Look over there," Zellie whispered in my ear. "Place cards for Many Counties Properties, LLC. They have a table here, too."

"And look at that," I whispered back. "There's a card for Jayne Merriweather. She's expected here, too."

We took our place cards and headed over to our table, where, in a pleasant surprise, we found none other than Rupert Cavendish, III and his lovely wife Sarah Cavendish, already seated. They stood as we arrived.

"Rupe, you pompous, blathering snot," I said, in the most genial manner I could muster, while extending my hand.

"Arnie, you four-flushing, pusillanimous weenie," Rupe responded, also affecting a pleasant tone.

We shook hands, and I turned to Sarah, with an affectionate kiss on the cheek, while Zellie received the same from Rupe.

"Have they always been like this?" Sarah asked Zellie.

Zellie sighed. "As long as I can remember. They were exchanging good-natured insults in grade school. But they were friends then, too."

"So what kind of cloak and dagger do you have planned for tonight, guys?" Rupe asked. "I told Sarah about it, and she insisted we come tonight. Right, honey?"

"At least one of us thought it would be a good idea, yes, dear." Sarah turned to us and said, "Oh, I was dying to come, but I wondered whether we'd be in the way."

"Nonsense," I said. "We're thrilled you're here. We don't get to see you enough."

Zellie echoed my statement. "We're very happy you came."

"So, did you know Ferdinand Darrow?" I asked Rupe.

"Never met the guy. Sarah?"

"Never heard of him until the murder."

"What about Jayne Merriweather?" Zellie asked.

"Jayne, we know," Rupe said. "She's active on the charity circuit. She's an executive at Many Counties Properties. They own a lot of real estate and other enterprises around here."

"Yeah, we know. She will probably be our new landlord." I said.

"Arnie, I'd think about somewhere else. Those people swim with the sharks, if you know what I mean."

I knew what he meant. But I didn't know it about Many Counties Properties until that moment. I glanced at Zellie and saw her look of surprise as well.

Rupe continued. "And I'm sure the charity stuff is just good public relations to cover up some of the more unsavory parts of their operation. You know how that's done, Zellie. Not that you had unsavory clients."

"No, our firm represented musicians, and some athletes. We had a few bad-boy acting-out episodes to deal with, and we used charity work to put a better face on their brands. It was a win-win proposition. They'd get good publicity, and also benefit good causes. Like helping sick kids and wives of firemen killed in action." And with a twinkle in her eye, she added, "Not so much saving a cute lizard."

"It's a salamander, Zellie," Sarah corrected. "A cute salamander." And then she cracked up laughing, and we all chortled along with her.

"Sometimes I wonder if they come up with these bizarre charities just to entertain us all," she said after the laughter died down. "We support a lot of good causes, but sometimes I wonder what the organizers of these events are thinking."

We had a brief discussion about that, and chit-chatted about other things, more or less catching up.

Rupe then said, "Why don't you let me set you up with some nice Grade A office space in one of my buildings?"

"We can't afford your rents."

"Oh, never you mind about that. We'll work something out, like maybe you could serve as my personal valet to defray some of the rent, or maybe as my driver, that's it. Driving my car would be a big step-up for you from that pile of nuts and bolts you call a car."

"Two things. One, you don't have a valet or a driver, and don't need or want either. Two, you drive your own car, and the only difference between yours and mine is the year. And mine is a better year."

"1965 was a better year than 1966, everyone knows it."

"Was not!"

"Should we separate them before this devolves into fisti-cuffs, Zellie?" Sarah asked.

"Nah, it's fun to watch."

We calmed down, and Rupe said, "I'm serious. You guys should think about my offer. But no matter what you do, don't rent from MCP," he said, referring to the acronym associated with Many Counties Properties.

"We'll think about it, thanks. But I won't be your valet or driver. It's butler, or no deal."

"I think I can arrange that," Rupe said with a smile. He sprang to his feet. "Jayne, how nice to see you," he said.

I always marveled at Rupe's ability to pass with seamless skill between the two worlds he lived in – the high society in which Rupert Higginbottom Laramie Cavendish, III was born and bred, and the genuine, down-to-earth Rupe that Zellie and I knew and loved since childhood. He had a remarkable ability to sling the bull which, given his comments of just moments ago, was much in evidence here in his interaction with Jayne Merriweather.

"Jayne, you know Sarah, but let me introduce you to our friends, Arnie Fischer and Zellie Morgan."

Jayne eyed Rupe with obvious suspicion, but he showed no outward signs of guile. Sarah, too, bore the doe-eyed innocence of a newborn. She was as talented as Rupe in keeping up appearances.

"We've met," she said. "Mr. Fischer, Ms. Morgan." She nodded at us. "I believe they are thinking of renting the office space in which one of our tenants died." She added, in a disparaging tone, "You're also amateur detectives as I understand it."

Rupe remained stoic. "Good detectives, I'd say."

Jayne didn't argue the point. "Rupert, Sarah, I'm so glad you're here to support the Barton Springs salamander. It's a terrific cause. I don't know what those poor creatures would do without our help." She continued in that fashion for a few minutes, and then said she needed to circulate. "Networking, you know." She bid Rupe and Sarah goodbye, gave an almost imperceptible nod at us, and headed to another table.

"Networking," Rupe mimicked. "Hitting up the big spenders for an investment in one of their shady schemes, no doubt."

"Do you know of anything specific?" Zellie asked.

"Oh, I have no evidence, if that's what you're asking. But one hears things, such as about that retirement community they own. Word has it that there are issues over there."

"What kind of issues?" I pressed.

"Oh, it's an okay retirement community, as far as that goes. That's the legitimate part of the business. But my understanding is that it's not just elderly people, or typical retirees there. They operate a host of other businesses at that location, and they don't always follow the exact letter of the law. Just a rumor, mind you. I don't know much more than that. I know my friends should not do business with those people."

"Point taken," I said, and Zellie nodded. "We'll just have to find somewhere else." I saw Rupe starting to say something, and I held up my hand. "No doubt in one of your buildings," I added, and Rupe said nothing further on the issue.

We spent the next hour or so talking. We danced a little to the fine music blaring from the live band, switched partners a few times, and enjoyed ourselves. Before another song played, I rose, and announced, "Time to go to work. Wish me luck."

CHAPTER THIRTY-FOUR

Zellie and I discussed this on the ride over. We had no idea how it would play out, and our chances of success appeared doubtful, given Jayne's chilly reception.

I strode over to the table at which Jayne sat with a few other guests, introduced myself to the others, and asked Jayne to dance. She demurred at first, but her tablemates pushed her to take me up on it, with loud cheers and encouragement.

I had lucked out. Her colleagues, or friends, whoever they were, pushed a very reluctant Jayne into accepting my invitation to dance. She intended to reject me, maybe with a little nastiness thrown in, if not for that fortuitous turn of events. They peppered her with cries of "Show him how it's done, Jayne," and "Dust off those dancing shoes," and my personal favorite, "Don't forget to let him lead, we know it comes hard for you."

Jayne looked at them, looked at me, and got to her feet, to a chorus of cheers. Placing a hand on her waist, I guided her to the dance floor, while the band played a waltz. Saying nothing at first, I let her warm up a little. I sensed that she enjoyed dancing, although I hadn't seen her on the dance floor all evening. She'd focused so much on networking, she neglected to have fun. She made no comment in the beginning, but after a few seconds, she looked at me and said "You dance well, Mr. Fischer. Arthur Murray?"

To which I responded, "Mom." Jayne chuckled at that, and it broke the ice. I explained that at an early age, my mother insisted that I learn to dance, saying that one never knew when that ability might come in handy. I didn't tell her that my dance partner for those lessons was Zellie, whose mother also insisted that she learn to dance. No doubt another excuse to push us together, not that we needed any help in that regard.

But Jayne relaxed a little at my personal revelation, responding that she had learned to dance the same way. But she hardened a little after a few moments, when I took my time letting things play out. She broke the silence with a curt demand I tell her my real motivation for asking her to dance.

"You want something," she said. "Out with it."

I responded that we were still looking into Darrow's death, and thought she might have more to tell us, to which she answered that she'd already told us everything she knew about Darrow.

"There's nothing left to tell."

I took a chance. We'd talked about this gambit in the car, but I wasn't sure I'd do it. We didn't know if she knew Freddy, nor did we know what connection Greta Abogado had to all of this. She might just be what she portrayed. Or she might not. Heck, she might not even be the real Greta Abogado. I had just taken her word for it. I threw caution to the winds.

"You never told us about your connection to Freddy Darrow and Greta Abogado."

If this surprised Jayne, she didn't let on.

"You never asked me about Freddy Darrow and Greta Abogado, not that it's any of your business."

"Don't you want to help?"

To my surprise, Jayne softened, but offered nothing more.

"Isn't that the job of the police?" she asked, as the music abated. "Thank you for the dance, Mr. Fischer." That was it. She headed back to her table, and I returned to mine.

The three of them accosted me. "Did you find out anything?"

"She's a good dancer," I said. "Oh, about the case. She knew Freddy, for sure. Greta Abogado, too, and not just as a tenant in one of MCP's properties. I didn't find out anything else."

"Did she tell you more about our client?" Zellie asked.

"Nothing, other than to deny knowing him in any other capacity than what she already told us. I struck out," I added.

"No, you didn't," Zellie said, putting her hand on my shoulder. You found out she has a connection with both Freddy Darrow and Greta Abogado. We'll take it from there. And you had a nice dance with a pretty woman," she added, with no sign of jealousy.

"I had several dances with two beautiful women," I replied, looking at her and Sarah, "one of whom is my sweetheart."

When the festivities concluded, we said our goodbyes to Rupe and Sarah, and headed back to my place.

***

"So, where are we?" I asked, after we paused for a few minutes to let the evening's events settle in our thoughts.

"I think we have an outline of what's going on. We need to fill in a few details, for sure, but the general parameters are right in front of us."

"What do you mean?"

We have two guys murdered. I say two guys, because that Garrett guy killed Freddy Darrow. But we don't know whether it was premeditated, or even whether someone else was involved. And I think Garrett rammed into our car."

"Agreed."

"He must have followed us either to or from Flora's Florals."

"How do you figure that?"

"Otherwise he couldn't have known where we'd be to orchestrate the hit and run."

"You know, you're right."

"We've heard nothing to suggest that the northern Darrow was anything other than an upstanding attorney who sent flowers to his mother and gave a book suggesting family strife to a fellow lawyer. And we have our client, who seems more akin to a fraudster, masquerading as an attorney."

"Yup. On all counts." I agreed. "Go on."

"We have a well-known, well respected deli owner, who seems to have encountered our client in a hostile and personal manner."

"Right. And our client's mother living at a retirement community owned by the company at which Jayne Merriweather works." Zellie added. "If Greta is legitimate, and if her story is true, which we don't know."

"And we found out Jayne knows, or knew both Freddy Darrow and Greta Abogado, and that that company she works for is shady."

"What about Melissa?" I asked.

"I'm not sure. It makes sense she couldn't afford to pay the fee for the Multiple Listing Service. But it is odd she led us right to the place with the dead body."

"Could be just a coincidence," I said.

"Maybe it is, but how did she have just one listing?"

"She had the Buckles Building listing," I pointed out.

"It's possible she was unaware it was a non-starter for us." Zellie sounded doubtful.

I wondered about Melissa, too. There was something just a bit wrong with her, and not just her multi-dimensional business. A lack of authenticity maybe. A little too interested in the case – which wouldn't exist but for her leading us there.

CHAPTER THIRTY-FIVE

W hat do you think the police are doing about the murder?" I asked the next morning.

"Quiet on that front. We haven't run into them once, and it's their job to investigate."

"Maybe they're happy to pawn this one off on us," I said.

"Sure, that's it. But it's a good question. Even if we had a license, they'd be within their rights to tell us to cease and desist."

"They've not been shy about that in the past. Speaking of which, we only have a few days left on the state's ten-day ultimatum. What are we going to do to put ourselves on the road to actual authority?"

"I don't know. We need to get around to talking to Mrs. Minniefield. She might have an idea. Wasn't it a little strange that the state gave us ten days, instead of just telling us to shut it down until we got a license?"

"Strange, yes. Lucky break, double yes. It had the effect of authorizing us to continue investigating for ten days."

"I doubt that's what they meant, but it could be read that way, yes."

"Let's read it that way."

"Aren't we already?" Zellie said, with just the tiniest smirk on her pretty face. "So, what's next?"

"We know now that Darrow had few clients, from our court search."

"Few involved in local court proceedings. We don't know about any other courts, or clients that never involved the court."

"True," I acknowledged. "So how do we find the rest?"

"In particular, one dark-haired lady who Darrow argued with." Zellie supplied.

"Yup."

"They weren't actual clients, because he wasn't a real lawyer. They were just marks for Darrow's specific type of confidence game."

"Ooh. Good thinking. Let's look into reports of people being bilked by Darrow. A simple Darrow/fraud internet search might turn something up."

"My earlier web search might have revealed that stuff, although I didn't check in particular for fraud. I was just looking for an attorney profile. But I have another idea. Twitter."

"Um, sure. Twitter. I know what that is," I added when Zellie glanced at me with amusement.

"A regular web search wouldn't pull up tweets. I still have my account from my public relations days. Hmm, let's see...."

It didn't take long. The first search yielded like a million tweets. All about various schemes Darrow had perpetrated. Zellie ran a second web search for Darrow fraud, with the same result.

"Maybe we should have done this sooner," I said, stating the obvious.

Zellie grimaced. "You think?"

We now had confirmation he was a con man and a bad guy. The kind of person that gets murdered, we supposed. But somehow this case seemed more complicated than that. We still didn't know which of the many angry people killed him. But maybe we had a clue. I saw Zellie point at one entry, um, tweet.

"Candace Devereaux. She says Darrow bilked her out of five thousand dollars."

"How is she related to this case?"

"Could be the sister, mother or wife of Russ Devereaux, the cleaning guy."

"Maybe. It could also be someone with the same last name. How common is Devereaux? Can you check?"

I needn't have asked. Zellie clicked her mouse a few times, and presto. Confirmation that Candace was Russ' younger sister.

"Is five thousand dollars enough to kill for?" I asked.

"I don't know, but Russ didn't tell us the truth. He had a definite ax to grind with Darrow."

"Good grief, is everyone lying?"

We knew at that point that almost everything Jayne had told us was a load of something very smelly. Because no way was this guy a model tenant, or one who paid his rent on time. And we figured that she lied about the length of time Darrow rented that office from MCP. Our new office. Although I don't think either one of us believed we'd sign a lease at this point.

And it also begged the question – how much did Melissa know before leading us by the nose right to the whole mess.

"The cops must know all of this," Zellie said.

I hung my head. "Sure they do. They've left us alone because they can't be bothered trying to find someone who killed a guy who just caused people misery. And I have to wonder why we care, either."

"It's what we do," Zellie replied, in a soft voice.

"We try to find killers of boils on the butts of the world? To do what? Give them medals?"

"To bring them to justice."

"Okay, okay. Anyway, I had a thought about the sheer number of complaints about Darrow's so-called legal services. It doesn't matter how many people hated Darrow, or felt aggrieved by him. The mere fact of so many disenchanted people is significant, but not everyone is a possible suspect."

"I agree. But what's your reasoning?"

"Only a few people had the access to Darrow's office necessary to do the deed. A client at a late appointment couldn't have done it, because they would have had to pre-position a ladder or some other wedge in the office, then poison him, and lure him somehow up to the attic, to die up there. Very unlikely. It had to be someone he knew, and let into the office to work or something, or it had to be someone with full access to the building."

"Or someone who broke in and placed the ladder there."

"There doesn't seem to be any evidence of that," I pointed out. "And there's one other thing. Who in their right mind would post a complaint online, and then kill the guy?"

"People don't always think," Zellie said. "But I agree with you. It's not what most people would do. So, we're back to Jayne, or someone else at MCP; Patsy Bruder, the building manager; or Russ Devereaux, who we now know had a reason to hate Darrow. We don't know of anyone else who had access. Unless it was a friend or relative, or business associate who had access to the office. Melissa is out on that score because she didn't get the listing until after the office was vacant."

"We don't know that. MCP might have given her the listing before Darrow's lease ended. And we can't rule her out, anyway. She has dark hair, and Russ told us Darrow argued with someone with dark hair. She may have known Darrow before we even found his body. And how did she get that listing? Does she have a connection to MCP?"

My phone rang at that moment. I looked at the caller ID and didn't recognize the number. I started to ignore it, and let it go to voicemail, when something clicked. Josh. I answered.

He started right in without even saying hello.

"I just visited the clerks' office, and Debbie asked me if I'd sent her the beautiful bouquet that sat on her desk. Know anything about that, Arnie?"

"Um, kind of depends whether or not you're angry."

"Not."

"Well, then I might know something about it. What did you say?"

"I told her that whoever sent them must like her a lot."

"Quick on your feet, counselor. What did she say?"

"She said if it's who she thinks, she likes him a lot, too, but wishes he'd just come out and say so."

"What did you do?"

"I asked her to come outside for a moment, and explained, as best as I could, that a guy I just met was an incurable romantic, had seen in just a few minutes our strong connection, and had moved things along of his own volition. Then I hoped like hell it was the truth, because if I found out that some other guy had sent them, her dad, or a boyfriend or something, I was totally screwed."

"So, what was her response?"

"I don't think she believed one word, but she kissed me, and said I didn't need to come up with such an elaborate ruse, but she loved the imagination and effort that went into it."

"And?"

"And we have a date on Friday night."

"All's well that ends well."

"Ends justify the means?"

"Something like that. Hey Josh, I have another question about Freddy Darrow."

"I guess in a weird way, I owe you. Shoot."

"Did you ever meet or hear about Freddy's mother?"

"I met her. She came to court one day to watch Freddy in action. He was a little nervous about it, but he did just fine. She watched him from the gallery, which in our little courtroom is just a bunch of long benches, sort of like church pews."

"What was she like?"

"Nice old lady. Thick accent. Looked the part of an immigrant. Very proud of her son. She beamed when I told her he was a first-class lawyer."

"Nice of you to say."

"I'm a nice guy. Even bought a woman flowers, or so I'm told." Josh laughed. "It was easy to say. It was true, and it made an old lady happy."

"Did he seem affectionate toward her?"

"Seemed devoted, if that's what you're asking."

"Was Freddy the kind of guy who'd involve himself in anything shady?"

"Whoa. He was a good guy. I told you that. The man I knew wouldn't take a nickel if he found it on the ground. He'd try to find the rightful owner."

"Boy, he's a lot different from our Darrow," I muttered.

"What did you say?"

"Oh nothing. Our Darrow turns out to not be such a nice guy. Tough cookie."

"To be clear, I didn't say Freddy wasn't tough. He was a strong character. And people didn't mess with him. You kind of knew that about Freddy. Nice guy, but don't pick a fight with him. And that's more than one question. I gotta go. Thanks for what you did. We both appreciate it. You and your partner/girlfriend will get an invite to the wedding."

"Getting a little ahead of yourself, are you?" I chuckled, and rang off.

"Josh?"

"Yup. He has a date with Debbie."

"Is there anyone you didn't send flowers to?" Zellie asked, looking at the bouquet I'd sent her, and pretending, I think, to look a little hurt.

"Nope. I sent them to everyone. But the best bouquet went to you, my sweetheart."

"It is beautiful," she said. "So, from the one side of the conversation I heard, the Greta Abogado you met matches Josh's description."

"Well, I guess we thought that already. But we learned that while Freddy Darrow was meticulously honest and decent, he was no pushover."

"So, if his life, or maybe his mother's life was in danger, he'd be inclined to do something about it, even if it was his own brother who posed the threat?"

"Josh didn't say that. I don't think he even knows Freddy had a brother. But I get the impression that Freddy was not someone to mess with."

"So we're back to the theory he might have had something to do with our client's death."

"He might not have killed him, but he must have known what his brother was up to, and might have taken action that resulted in his death. But that's mere speculation, and Freddy was killed before our client. I can't figure out that piece."

"Maybe our client found out that his life was in danger, and took matters into his own hands." Zellie said, and then paused, her index finger stroking her forehead in thought. "But then we have the same problem. *Who killed our client?*"

CHAPTER THIRTY-SIX

I think we should verify Greta Abogado's information and maybe see what other family members are out there."

"Why the sudden interest? Her story seems to check out."

"Does it? Maybe the fact that she has a son named Friedrich, who changed his name to Frederick and called himself Freddy. That we verified independently. But the only way we know he had a brother was from Mrs. Abogado, who described him more or less as good boy who was not as successful as his brother."

"Isn't that what a mother might say about her son? She's not about to say 'my son is a criminal who maybe even killed his brother.'"

"Maybe." Zellie looked doubtful. "Name changes are available online, if you know how to look," she said, almost to herself. "And I know where to look."

"You know I'm standing here, right?"

Zellie laughed. "I guess I was thinking out loud. I think we should verify the two Darrows' original names. Let's not assume she told the truth about that."

"Makes sense"

At that moment, my phone rang. I picked it up, said "uh huh, uh huh. Totaled, you say? You've told the insurance people? The adjuster is right there? I'll get a check for the value within two weeks? Okay, thanks."

Zellie raised one eyebrow, and looked at me.

"Beyond repair." I couldn't keep a straight face, and Zellie knew it.

"You're not getting a new car with that money, are you?"

"Um, maybe not right away. Matilda is purring like a kitten, so why drive anything else, something impersonal, like a Chevy Suburban?"

"I like Matilda," Zellie said.

"And she adores you."

"But I'm sure she'd like a rest sometimes. She's getting a little older, and might enjoy a day off here and there. And I can't believe I'm talking like this. Arnie, get reliable transportation, and drive Matilda for fun. There, I said it."

I cracked up, doubling up with hysterics. When I caught my breath, I looked up at a giggling Zellie.

"That's what I'll do. Give the old girl a rest. She deserves it."

"Yes, she does."

"You know we're about the same age as she is," I said, and we had another round of laughter. "Maybe we need a rest, too."

"Not a chance. So, are we going car shopping?"

I grimaced. "Oh sure. That worked out well for us last time, didn't it?"

I was referring to our first case, which featured a car dealership, and not in a good way.

"It worked out pretty well, I'd say."

"You have a funny way of turning a nightmare into a pleasant dream, but okay, yes, it worked out well. But no car shopping for me right this minute. I have a car, and we have a case to solve." And another big thing I need to work out, I thought.

"Oh, okay. I'll leave you alone. Let me see," Zellie continued muttering to herself. "Name changes. How do I find name changes?"

"You could try complimenting the computer on its abilities," I offered.

As usual, Zellie ignored my *kibitzing*, and concentrated on the task at hand. She entered a few keystrokes, muttered something referring to cow manure, and made a few more keystrokes, with similar chatter. I left her alone, and wandered off, only to hear an exclamation from the other room.

"Yikes! Arnie, where are you? Check this out!"

"What's up?" I asked, hurrying over.

Zellie pointed at the screen. "I found Heinrich, and the name change to Ferdinand, that checks out. And just for the heck of it, I ran the names of everyone involved in the case. You'll be happy to know neither one of us ever changed our names."

"Very gratifying to know that about myself," I said.

"I didn't even do it when I got married," she continued. "But she did, it." Zellie pointed to the screen.

"Well, we knew that already from the Court documents." I said. "Jake married Elizabeth Abogado, and she changed her name to Rothberg."

"Agreed," Zellie said. "But what about this one?" She pointed to another name on the list.

"Helga Bruder Abogado." I read aloud. "Who's she?"

"I have a guess," Zellie ventured.

"The building manager, Patsy Bruder's relative?"

"Yes. And I'm guessing she married an Abogado."

"One of Bessie's relatives," I said. "And the name Helga is familiar, but I can't put my finger on it."

"Wasn't that the name of Greta Abogado's executive assistant, home health aide, or whatever role she assumed for the purpose?"

"Yeah, I think so. And she never gave her last name."

"Makes sense in a way - a family member as a caregiver."

"I think we need to talk to Patsy Bruder again. No question she's familiar with the Abogado family through her relative. She never told us any of that."

I called and struck out. Voice mail. I didn't expect a call back. I told Zellie, and she gave an absent nod.

"The book Freddy Darrow gave to Josh," she said after a momentary pause. "It had four brothers and a despicable father. Remember that one brother was always pious and decent, and another one a louse."

"I remember," I said

"So, we have one good brother and one bad brother in the book or movie, just like we have in real life."

"Yes."

"In the movie, two other brothers appeared, one of which was a half-brother. Should we be looking for more brothers?"

"I don't think so. I don't see how a literal comparison with the book gets us anywhere."

"Well, we haven't found other brothers. But we have found a hornet's nest of family discord."

"We have," I agreed. "Um, not to raise a delicate subject, but we need to talk to Jake again."

Zellie held her head in her hands. "I know, but the thought of it makes me sick."

"I understand. It's Jake, for goodness sake. We used to work for the guy."

"We never worked for him. That's a figment of his active imagination."

"Great, now he has me believing it."

"But we have to visit him again. And this won't be a friendly conversation. We know a lot more now, and his whole story is a lie."

"Maybe not all."

"What are you thinking?"

"If Jake comes clean on his relationship with our dead guy, he might have something more to offer on the other players in this mess. Maybe he saw the guy in his restaurant, and maybe he witnessed a meeting between him and a tall, dark haired woman, and maybe he saw a nicer guy. It's possible Jake's story was more a sin of omission, but the rest is true."

"Maybe," Zellie allowed. But her expression said volumes about her doubts on that score. I decided to lower expectations.

"And maybe the Easter Bunny has wings and files to the North Pole to talk to Santa Claus."

Zellie laughed in spite of herself.

"Now you're talking sense," she said. "We need to find this Easter Bunny character and make a citizen's arrest."

My joking aside, I knew what concerned Zellie. We'd known Jake most of our lives. Local residents had an almost religious devotion to him. And the breadth of that loyalty extended far beyond Middletown and Red Bank. I'd heard stories of visitors from foreign countries visiting Jake's establishment as if it constituted an important tourist stop listed in the guidebooks. More than that, Jake owned a sterling reputation as the gruff, but kind proprietor of an eatery clinging to old world quality and values. And our aim appeared clear. Puncture that reputation.

"I know this is serious," I said to Zellie. "We need to approach this confrontation, if you want to call it that, with extreme care."

"I wish we could find a time when he doesn't have customers or employees around."

That hadn't occurred to me. We couldn't just barge into the deli and expose the gaps in Jake's story, explore his feelings about our client's interference with Bessie's estate and ask him to explain her familial ties with the Abogado family.

"Do you know where he lives?" I asked.

"No, but I bet I could find out. What do you have in mind? Visit him at his home?"

"It's better than asking the man to fix us a sandwich, and then blast him in front of his customers and employees."

"We won't blast him. We need answers, that's all. But I don't want to do it at the shop, either."

"We could call and ask for an appointment," I said.

"No...I don't think so. We don't want to clobber the poor guy, but we do want to surprise him."

"Makes sense. But you need to accept that our sweet old deli curmudgeon may have murdered Ferdinand Darrow."

Zellie glanced at her watch. "Okay. It's almost time for lunch. I'll find Jake's home address and phone number, and we'll plan to go visit him at about five o'clock. The shop closes at three-thirty, and I suppose he has clean-up and accounting stuff to do before he leaves for the day."

"Confrontation at five o'clock. Got it."

* * *

We remained silent on our approach to the bridge over the Navesink River, and crossed into Red Bank. Jake's house sat just a short distance from the bridge, and we turned onto his street a few minutes later. We parked a short distance away, and walked to his front door, where we rang the bell. We heard footsteps, and Jake opened the door. At the same moment, we heard several loud blasts, and the windows just to the right of us shattered.

CHAPTER THIRTY-SEVEN

Zellie and I dropped to the ground, and Jake slammed the door. Two shots whistled over our heads and ripped into the heavy wood.

We heard a car drive away, and I looked over to make sure Zellie was okay. I struggled to my knees, and to my feet, and looked over my shoulder to view a street cloaked in eerie silence. Zellie and I embraced, our relief palpable. Jake's front door remained closed, with two bullets lodged in its center. The shots shattered the windows to the right of us, with shards of glass littering the mulch around the bushes planted in front of the house. We surveyed the damage for a moment, looked at each other, and I knocked on the door.

"We should call the police," I whispered to Zellie, while we waited for Jake to answer the door again. If he answered at all.

"We will," Zellie whispered back. "Right after we talk to Jake. Anyway, I bet someone called them already. Maybe Jake. And we need to talk to him before the police get here, and he clams up for us."

I couldn't fault her reasoning, but we're law abiding folks, and when someone commits a crime, you call the police. But I had to admit to an overwhelming curiosity about what Jake would say after someone tried to kill him. And I thought about that. Maybe it was an attempt on our lives. I looked at the bullets lodged in the door, which would have hit one of us if we hadn't dropped to the ground when the glass shattered in the windows. And on the heels of the hit and run, which also almost killed us. This investigation was getting hazardous to our health.

I had no chance to worry any further, as the door opened a crack, and Jake Rothberg peered out at us. He looked toward the street, appeared satisfied that the threat no longer existed, and opened the door.

"Come in and be quick about it." He motioned us inside and closed the door behind us. "What are you doing here?" Jake demanded, once we were in his house.

"We needed to see you in a quiet place away from the shop, without any nosy people listening to our conversation," Zellie said. "We know about Bessie's estate, and your dealings with Ferdinand Darrow."

Jake gave Zellie a long, hard stare. Then his throat seemed to constrict, and his body trembled. He was crying.

We waited in respectful silence for Jake to settle down. When he stopped, he gave us a long appraising look, as if uncertain how to proceed. Satisfied with something in our expressions, Jake motioned us to the living room, where we sat down and waited for him to proceed.

He cleared his throat a few times, adjusted his torso in the wingback chair on which he sat, and paused for a moment to collect his thoughts. Or to plan a line of complete bull, I couldn't be sure. But he looked sincere, and I was willing to give him the benefit of the doubt, at least for the time being. I glanced over at Zellie, but her stoic expression revealed nothing. I guessed that she viewed Jake's sudden willingness for candor with the same skepticism I felt.

"I thought I was done with them," Jake began. "And now I've dragged you into it. I'm sorry about that. They could have killed you." His eyelids twitched, showing his anxiety. He looked at us. "You are all right, aren't you?"

We assured him we were unharmed, and he continued.

"I don't think they intended to kill any of us. Just a warning, and a very pointed one, to be sure."

That jived with my thinking, and I said so. Zellie plunged forward.

"C'mon. Out with it. The whole story, Jake. We have little time. I'm guessing the police will arrive any minute."

Jake held up his hand, palm facing us. "Okay. The whole story. I guess a part of me wanted you to look into this."

"Hence, the initial cryptic comments to us at the deli," I interjected, trying to move Jake along. "But then you worried about involving us, and finding out too much of your personal business, but it was too late."

"That's about right," he acknowledged. "Anyway, did you come across the name Herman Garrett?"

"Sure. The guy who drove the car in the accident that killed Freddy Darrow," I said.

"That was no accident," Jake said, with vehemence. "And Garrett is no upstanding citizen. He's an enforcer for MCP."

"Many Counties Properties? They need muscle?" Zellie asked.

"What? No, not them. They're legitimate, as far as those *gonifs* can call themselves legitimate. But another subsidiary of the parent company, Many Counties Industries, also has the acronym MCP. Many Counties Protection. It masquerades as a security firm, that's what the advertising *spiel* claims. But, it's a protection racket. I'm guessing someone thought it cute to call an extortion business a protection company. The realty company is my landlord at the deli. The protection company provides protection against...well, them."

Jake's expression was one of a mixture of bitterness and contempt. He took a breath. "In the beginning, things were just fine. MCP the landlord treats you pretty well if you pay the rent every month, and I had no problem doing that. But then Elizabeth got sick, and I needed more and more money for doctors and specialized care, and, well, the rent took a back seat. When you get behind in the rent, they hit you with a double whammy. The terms of the lease provide for large interest payments on the past due balance, so you get further and further behind, until you have no chance of repaying them. That's when the protection part of their operation kicks in.

"They have you over a barrel, and they know it. You don't have a choice. You don't want them to evict you, and you know you can't catch up with the rent. They give you a kind of carrot and stick. Agree to their protection plan, and they'll give you more time to pay the back rent. You take their less than magnanimous offer, because you have no choice. It gives you time you wouldn't have otherwise. And you can't pay doctor bills without the income, so letting them evict you is out of the question.

"I ended up way behind on both the rent and the protection payments, and they don't look on kindly on that. Business was good, but the deli didn't generate income that could handle the extra payments along with all of our personal expenses."

"What did they do?" I asked, fascinated with Jake's story, and my skepticism fading. I tried to stay neutral, but he told a compelling story.

"They leaned on me. Hard."

"Did they harm you?" Zellie asked.

"They threatened, but never assaulted me. But no doubt existed as to their intention if I didn't agree. And I told them, Elizabeth was only a one-half owner of that place, so I couldn't agree to anything. And it had little worth without a huge investment, anyway."

Zellie and I looked at each other. Jake had skipped a significant part of the story. The "place," for instance, though we knew the property to which he referred.

"Details, Jake. Now," I said. "Who was the co-owner, and what was the place that was co-owned. And what investment?"

Jake looked up, startled. "Freddy Darrow. Didn't I say that? He and Elizabeth co-owned a property in Bergen, New Jersey, that their grandmother left to them. About four acres, in a prime location. Valuable, too, but only if developed, and none of us had the money to do that. We couldn't sell it to pay our debts, not only because we needed Freddy's consent, but because it would not be worth much as undeveloped land. To a real estate company, however, it could be worth a million bucks."

"What was Elizabeth's relationship with Freddy?" I asked.

"Her half-brother. I guess that made me his half-brother-in-law. Anyway, MCP sent Garrett to kill him. In their minds, that solved two problems. It put the property in Elizabeth's name alone, and it scared the living daylights out of Elizabeth and me. Then Elizabeth died, and the property became part of her estate."

"What about the claim filed against the estate by Ferdinand Darrow?"

"He may have been Freddy's brother, but they were nothing alike. He was just a two-bit con man. Bessie loved Freddy, but couldn't stand Ferdinand, or Ferdy, as the family called him. No way on earth Bessie gave him a share of that property.

But he had an abundance of *chutzpah*, filing a sworn claim in a court proceeding."

"I don't get it." Zellie said. "I understand why you felt the need to deal with MCP's protection racket, but why didn't those thugs come down hard on Ferdinand?"

"Search me." Jake said. "You're the detectives. But I can guess."

Zellie nodded for him to go ahead.

"I don't think MCP was happy with Ferdy, but they wanted a smooth administration of the estate more than they wanted to stop him. They wanted to get paid their back rent, overdue protection payments, and exorbitant interest payment as soon as possible. Ferdy threatened to hold up the estate forever, or at least until he got a piece of the action. So MCP told me to settle. I didn't have that kind of money, so they forced me to sell the property to them to finance the payment and to repay everything I owed them. So, they got a million-dollar property for under $200,000, and I didn't receive a cent."

I looked over at Zellie, and could see our usual telepathy was working. She had the same thought I did. MCP might have let our client get a chunk of Elizabeth's estate because it suited their purposes. But that didn't guarantee they wouldn't deal with him later. With extreme prejudice.

Given that Patsy Bruder worked for MCP, I wondered if Jake knew her. When I asked, Jake looked surprised.

"Patsy? Sure. She's Helga's sister. Um, Helga married Bessie's favorite cousin, Bertrand. A good man, Bertie. He died a few years back. We all used to spend a lot of time together, Bessie and me and Bertie and Helga. Patsy, too. She's a nice kid. Very supportive when Bessie died. We still have lunch regularly. Why are you asking about her?"

"Did you know she worked for Many Counties Properties?" I asked.

"I guess so. It's a huge organization. She's a building manager. That has nothing to do with the protection business. She needed a job, and she's good with tools. No way she had any involvement in threatening Bessie and me. No way."

At that moment, the doorbell rang. The police had arrived. Jake's face almost showed relief, glad our inquisition had concluded. But then it turned to concern. He'd have to explain something to the police. He rose and shuffled to the front door.

Before he reached it, the impatient police pounded on the door. No doubt they just noticed the bullets lodged there. Jake opened it up, and looked at three police officers, as if he didn't have a care in the world.

He gave them a pleasant smile. "What can I do for you, officers?"

The two Red Bank policemen identified themselves as Caldwell and Gates. A third man stood behind them and kept silent.

"Are you kidding, sir?" Officer Caldwell spoke first. "Your neighbors reported gunfire, your window is shattered, and two bullets are lodged in your front door. We want answers, and right now."

"I wondered about that," Jake said, gesturing toward the window. "I assumed that some unruly neighborhood kids got a little out of hand. Boys will be boys, you know." He turned his head toward the door. "Whoa. Look at that. Lucky for me that door is solid wood. Not like the hollow garbage they sell nowadays." Jake began talking about the old days, but Officer Gates cut him off.

"Enough of the nonsense, sir. You know local boys didn't do this. What happened here?" He looked past Jake and saw the two of us standing. "You two," he said. "Get over here."

I didn't appreciate his sharp tone, but given Jake's attempted filibuster, I could understand his frustration. We walked over to the door, where we all assembled.

"Can we all come in and talk about his?" The third man joined the conversation, and I knew why he chose that moment. He'd spotted us, and we knew him. Well, in fact. State Trooper Michael Mullen.

CHAPTER THIRTY-EIGHT

Hi Mike," Zellie offered. I just nodded at him. This wouldn't go well, I knew it. Mike was a friend, but he looked all business today, and pretty ticked off. I couldn't blame him. We knew we'd pushed the envelope on acting without a license and played on his good graces beyond anything one could consider reasonable. We hadn't acted like friends, and Zellie and I knew it. I could tell by her expression that Mike was the last person she wanted to see right now.

"Ms. Morgan. Mr. Fischer."

Uh oh. It's worse than I thought. He's gone all formal on us.

"Trooper Mullen," I responded. "I think Mr. Rothberg meant to invite all of you in, and to show you to his living room. Isn't that right, Jake?"

Jake's response was less than enthusiastic, but he mumbled agreement, and pointed in the right direction. We all filed back to the living room and sat down, and looked at Mike. He'd taken charge.

Mike gave a hard look at Zellie and me and held it for a few seconds without speaking. We said nothing, and an uncomfortable silence lingered, which I guess Mike intended. But we held our ground, and he broke the silence.

"What happened?" he asked. "And please don't give me any of that nonsense about neighborhood boys. I heard over my radio that a shooting had taken place at a residence in Red Bank, and I headed over to help out my fellow officers in the Red Bank Police Department. And what do I find here? A couple of all too familiar civilians playing private detective."

Ooh. That hurt.

Mike continued. "This is serious, and you..." he pointed at Jake... "are neither cooperative nor truthful." He looked back at us. "And what are you?" he thundered. "His enablers? I want the truth. All of it."

I was pretty sure Zellie knew better, but she's very fiery sometimes. And Mike had challenged our honor. I tried to warn her with my eyes, but she ignored the silent admonition.

"We're not playing at anything, Trooper Mullen, sir," she said, emphasizing the "sir," and her voice dripping with sarcasm. "We're just talking to an old friend. Isn't that right, Jake?"

"Um, yes. That's right, Zellie. Just old friends chatting."

Uh oh, I thought. That's what we're going to do? Go with that story? Now we're screwed. Mike is our only friend on the police force, and we're going to yank his chain? I'd better temper this before it gets out of hand.

But I didn't get a chance. Mike's face turned crimson.

"You think I'm an idiot? His voice had grown as hard as I ever heard it, and Mike's a tough guy. We were hearing his cop voice for the first time.

"I know you're continuing to act as private investigators, violating New Jersey law. You're also in peril of obstructing justice. I should run you in right now."

"Mike, wait," I said, holding up my hand in a gesture of peace. "We know. We always fully disclose our lack of a license.

Also, we received a letter from the Attorney General giving us ten days to get a license."

Mike's jaw dropped. "Are you serious? Your defense to my arresting you both is a letter telling you to cease and desist from illegal activity?"

"I told you, it gave us ten days." As soon as I said it, I realized how stupid that sounded.

"Arnie, it's not an extension of time. It's telling you to stop breaking the law. It's making a gracious offer of a short time for you to get licensed before someone like me comes to haul you away." He paused. "But you knew that, didn't you? You're just stalling, so we all calm down. Okay, it worked."

He looked over at Zellie. "Shall we start over?" She nodded. "Okay, then. What happened here?"

I spoke first. "We don't really know, Mike." He started to get angry again, but I held up my index finger, asking for more time to explain.

"What I mean by that is that we don't know who fired the shots, or even whether they were directed at us or Jake, although we assume that one of us was the target. But my opinion is that they were intended to warn, not kill."

Mike looked at Zellie and Jake. "Do you agree?"

Zellie nodded. Jake looked less certain.

"I don't know," he said.

"Start at the beginning," Mike said.

I looked at Zellie. "You're best suited for that," I said. I figured that if we wanted to continue working on the case, we shouldn't give them a complete account of our activities and I knew Zellie agreed. But we needed to tell them something that didn't sound like stonewalling. And I'm better at saying nothing than I am at summarizing without sharing inconvenient facts. That's Zellie's department. And she can do it without lying, or even misleading. She's a talented public relations expert.

So Zellie told a story about us not acting as private investigators at all, given we had no license, but circumstances thrust a case upon us through the simple act of looking for office space. She held up her hand, palm facing Mike.

"To rent, in the event we were at some point able to conduct lawful business. We didn't look for a corpse," she told the officers. "It literally fell on us. So, without a client," she pointed out, "and as private citizens, but with acclaimed experience in investigation, we looked into the matter. So," she added, "we had no paying client, and thus broke no laws."

"All we've done is talk to a few people, and look things up in various internet databases," I interjected.

"Uh huh. Sure you did," Mike said. He looked at Zellie. "Okay, what did you find out?"

Zellie summarized the parties to whom we had spoken, and some of the things we'd discovered. She excluded any conclusions from her factual recitation, and if Mike noted the omission, he didn't acknowledge it.

"You've been busy," he observed.

"We have a personal interest in all of this, given we found the body," I said.

"Understood. But it's time to leave it to the police. This is getting dangerous. First the car accident, now this. I'm ordering you to stop."

"Ordering us?" Zellie started to say something else, but caught the involuntary jerk of my head in her direction, and stayed silent. We were almost out of the woods, and I didn't want to start the battle over again. We wouldn't stop, but no need to fight with Mike over it. Yet.

***

"Don't worry. We're not giving up the case," I said as soon as we got in the car and headed home. "I gave you that look to stop you from starting another fight with Mike."

"He was pretty mad as us, wasn't he?" Zellie said with a smirk, and I knew then she didn't intend to belabor the tension between her and Mike.

"I've never seen him so angry. And you were pretty irritated, too."

"I didn't like his tone, that's all. All high and mighty and treating us like children. He had a heck of a nerve."

Okay, maybe she'd belabor it a little. I changed the subject. "That was some story Jake told," I observed.

"Yes, but I don't think we narrowed anything down. It just added Jake as a suspect."

I thought about that. No question, he had a motive, although I couldn't see where he had the opportunity. And the use of poison. My recollection from somewhere, I didn't know where, was that poison is most often used by women, not men. I resolved to check that out.

"We need to go back to the beginning," Zellie blurted.

I waited for her to explain.

"We've gotten too mixed up in pursuing leads and have not done enough cold analysis of what happened, and how it was done."

"What are you thinking?"

"Let's ignore Freddy Darrow's murder for the sake of discussion."

"Okay. Done."

"We have a murder of a guy in his office. We've learned he's a con man, who's ripped many people off."

"Which leaves many people with motives to cause him harm," I supplied.

"Right. And we know that someone poisoned him."

I nodded. "He didn't poison himself."

"No. And that kind of thing suggests premeditation. Someone planned this."

"Probably a woman," I said, giving voice to my earlier thought process.

Zellie's expression was priceless. "Where did that come from?"

"It occurred to me just a little while ago. I'm pretty sure women use poison way more than men. But I haven't checked it out," I admitted.

"Well we should do that pronto," she said. "But in the meantime, why don't we continue to assess the facts, and apply our theories afterwards."

"Okay," I said. "We have an unknown person hating our client enough to poison him and somehow getting him up into the attic and trapping him there to die."

"That's about the size of it," Zellie said. "So, who had the opportunity to get into his office and poison him?"

"And how did they get him up into the attic?"

"It had to be someone he knew," Zellie said.

"I agree."

"Russ told us he heard a woman arguing with our client, and your understanding is that women are the most likely poisoners, so let's take another look at the various women we've met in this case."

"Jayne Merriweather; Patsy Bruder; Greta Abogado and her assistant, Helga Bruder Abogado; and Melissa," I ticked each one off on my fingers.

"And Flora," Zellie added.

"Oh gee, do we have to include Flora?"

"Yes, we have to include Flora," Zellie replied, arching an eyebrow. "Why not? You want to send flowers to another love-sick person?"

"No. Well, maybe. I have no one in mind. But Flora didn't strike me as a killer."

"Me neither. But you never know."

"True. So, we include Flora. What next?"

"I don't think we ignore the male suspects, but for the sake of trying to refocus our investigation, let's consider the opportunity each suspect had to commit the crime. Let's assume that we know the means and the motives of each."

"We don't know how Melissa and Flora are even connected to our client," I pointed out. "And we're speculating about the motives of everyone else."

"True enough. But we have to focus on something. If we can rule out people with no opportunity, we don't even have to look at motive."

"But how do we figure out opportunity?" I asked. "Anyone could have visited the office, almost at any time. Well, maybe not any time, but at least during business hours."

"That's an important distinction," Zellie responded. "Who had access after regular business hours? Given the nature of the crime, someone had to commit it when the office was closed, right?"

My brain was working at a breakneck pace. "We need to visit the office again," I declared.

"Why?"

"I think I know how the murderer committed the crime."

CHAPTER THIRTY-NINE

Zellie jumped to her feet and grabbed her purse. "Let's go."

"Aren't you going to ask what my theory is?"

"On the way. We do our best talking in the car."

I had to admit the truth of her statement. "Okay, let's go. I need to take another look at the bottom of that attic trap door."

Zellie stopped in her tracks. "The bottom? The view from where you stand and look up at it?"

"That's right, what about it?"

"Would a picture do it for you?"

"Maybe. You have a picture?"

Zellie reached into her handbag and fished out her phone. She tapped a couple of times and held it up. The view I wanted.

"How many pictures regarding the case do you have?"

"Oh, lots. These things come in handy," she said, tapping her phone.

"I'll say. You have detailed notes, and pictures, too."

"I'm kind of used to this. In my career, pictures were essential, as well as detailed notes about the people we wanted to publicize. In the most favorable way possible, of course."

"Obviously." I smiled at her. Zellie was great at this, and I told her so.

"So are you," she replied. "We make a good team. Complement each other's skill sets." She touched the back of my hand and ran a soft finger up my arm. The effect was like an electric shock to my brain. Several passionate kisses later, we disengaged, and we looked together at the picture on her phone. I pointed to the marks we had noticed when we visited.

"Just what I thought," I said. "Look at that. See where there is a small dark line leading to the clear spot we figured resulted from some sort of wedge used to hold the attic door closed?"

"Sure. I remember. What about it?"

I traced my finger over the line. "I bet this is where the killer dragged an extendable pole to wedge it between the floor and the trap door."

"Where did you get the extendable pole theory? That came out of the blue. Although the more I think about it..." she paused. "It makes sense."

"I think so." I pointed over her shoulder at the curtains hanging in the kitchen window. "Look over there."

Zellie looked. "The windows?"

"The curtains," I replied. "Remember you helped me hang them? And we went to Curtain Warehouse to get the hardware? And they had maybe ten thousand different ways to hang curtains?"

Zellie brightened at the memory. "Including what seemed like dozens of different tension rods, including huge ones that could expand up to twelve feet. We wondered what kind of window would require such a big tension rod. Had to be a big commercial building, we figured. And the murderer could have used it to prop against the attic door. Sharp thinking, Arnie."

I waved my hand and executed a majestic bow, as if acknowledging the cheers of an imaginary audience, while Zellie indulged my theatrics.

"How do you figure it went down, Sherlock?" Zellie asked, after waiting patiently for the conclusion of my self-congratulatory ministrations.

I turned serious. "If we assume the killer used a tension rod, it opens up interesting possibilities. A tension rod is expandable, which means it's collapsible. And so compact someone could carry it in a large handbag, or maybe a shopping bag. Yeah, a shopping bag, that's a little bigger. But mobile and easy to conceal. And it would require little strength. So, a woman our client knew met with him and slipped poison into his drink. She contrived an excuse to get him to go up in the attic, say to get an old file or something. It would take little for her to follow him over there, close the attic door, and prop the expandable tension rod in place, and wait for him to die."

"Which wouldn't take long, because the coroner said it was a fast-acting poison," Zellie supplied. "Then she could just collapse the rod, put it back in her bag and leave. I like it. I bet that's how it happened."

"We know the how, but not the who."

"We can't limit it to women, either." Zellie said. "I wonder if we should restart the investigation. Maybe we missed something."

"Will we hear anything new by asking the same people the same questions?"

"No, we won't. We need to either get new people or new questions. Or, I wonder...."

"Wonder what?" I said, breaking my longstanding rule against interrupting Zellie in a train of thought.

"Maybe we should re-examine the facts surrounding Freddy Darrow's murder."

"Should we go visit Flora again?" I asked.

"No, I don't think so. We've obtained as much information from her as possible."

"And she's kind of ditzy," I added.

"That too." Zellie agreed. "No, I was thinking about the police report about the accident. We've never seen it. And the only thing we know about it is from the article in the newspaper, and what Flora told us."

"That may be true, but we have a little problem. They won't give us the report."

"You're right," Zellie said, pursing her lips. "I'd just hoped that it might give us an unexplored avenue of investigation."

"We need someone to put in a good word for us up there," I said. "Someone who knows an official in the police department. And no way Mike will do it, even if he knows someone."

We stared at each other and said the name in unison.

"Josh."

"He seems to know everyone," I said. "And while I'm sure I'm pushing it with someone I just met, I'll call him. Nothing ventured, nothing gained."

Josh answered the phone on one ring. "Checking to see how your matchmaking went? I love a *yenta* that follows up."

"So how did your date go?" I asked.

"Great, Arnie, just great. But she still doesn't believe you exist. And I'm not pressing the issue, believe me."

"I'm glad to hear it. Thrilled for you. Um…"

"You're not calling to check on my love life, are you?"

"Well, yes and no. Yes, I'm interested in how it went, and no, that's not the only reason I called."

"I don't know anything more to tell you about Freddy. I'm tapped out on that front."

"I was hoping you might know someone in the Hudson police department."

"As it happens, I do know someone. A buddy of mine from high school is a lieutenant in the Hudson P.D. What's this all about?"

Cornered. I had no choice but to blurt it out. "We need to get a look at the police report from Freddy's accident." I expected Josh to yell something unpleasant at me, or at the least, hang up, but he did neither.

Instead, he gave a long chuckle. "I guess unmitigated *chutz-pah* is part of your business. Even if I gave you my friend's name, and put in a good word for you, I don't think Rob would do it. He's like Mother Teresa with a badge."

"You know it's for a good cause. And you're a lawyer. Your stock-in-trade is persuasiveness. It's your job, for goodness sake. And look at how you talked Debbie into a date. That's skilled convincing, that's what that is."

"I haven't had much success in persuading you to leave me alone," Josh muttered.

"If not for me, do it for Freddy," I said, sort of as a closing argument.

Josh sighed. "You know, I almost think Debbie isn't worth the price you're extracting from me. Almost," he added. "I'll give Rob a call. But I'm giving no guarantee."

"That's all I'm asking. And thank you. I promise not to re-quest anything else of you."

"If I were you, I wouldn't make promises like that. Some-how, I think you'll be back. Anyway, I'll call you one way or the other." With that, Josh hung up.

"He'll ask," I said to Zellie.

"That's good, right?"

"It's good. But I've gone to that well once too many times. I feel like I'm taking advantage of a new friend's good nature."

"He's a big boy. He won't do anything he doesn't want to do."

"Oh, I know that. But I've only known the guy for a few days, and I've already pressed him like a...."

"Private detective?" Zellie asked, with a twinkle in her eye.

"Perish the thought," I replied. "I'd never act in such a *gauche* manner." I held up my nose in an exaggerated posture of pomposity.

Zellie laughed, and brushed her fingers along my arm. "An unfortunate part of the detecting business."

At that moment, a large projectile smashed into my window, dispersing hundreds of glass shards as it hurtled toward us.

CHAPTER FORTY

A brick landed at my feet. I didn't wait to look at the attached note. I grabbed my gun, which I'd kept in easy reach since the incident at Jake's house, and ran outside. All I could see was an SUV of some sort already at the end of my street. It made a rapid right turn and disappeared. Not even a glimpse at the license plate.

When I returned to the house, I found Zellie examining the note, which contained, in block print, a single word: "STOP."

"Not a very wordy vandal," I observed.

"Not a vandal at all," Zellie said. "Someone is trying very hard to warn us off."

"Yeah, and look at this mess. Be careful, you'll cut yourself on those shards of glass. I better get the broom."

"I'll get it." Zellie said, and headed down the hall. "Should we call the police?" she asked, as she went.

"Why? What can they do? They'll call it vandalism, local boys committing mischief, *et cetera*."

"Well, there's the matter of the note," Zellie said, carrying a broom and dustpan, and sweeping up the mess.

"True. Let's put cardboard on the window until I can get it fixed, and call it a day. There's nothing left to do but wait for Josh to call."

"It's been a long one," Zellie agreed.

We fixed dinner, watched a little television, and went to bed.

***

The next morning, as we sat drinking our coffee, Josh called.

"I have a copy of the police report," he announced, without saying hello.

"Well good morning, Josh," I replied, looking straight at Zellie, who peered up from the morning newspaper.

"Yes, good morning, Arnie, how are you, how's the family, your girlfriend is well, your dog okay, *et cetera, et cetera*. Didn't you hear me?"

"I did. I'm just not used to you fast talking lawyer types."

Josh laughed. "I guess I was a little brusque. But I thought you'd be happy about it. And damn it, a little more appreciative. You don't know what I had to do to get this. My friend now hates me for asking the favor, and he didn't want to do it at all, but he kind of owes me for reasons I don't want to go into, and..."

"Okay, okay. I appreciate it, I do. And I'm sure you had to exercise every bit of your considerable charm, and well-honed persuasive skills to get the job done."

"That's better," Josh said, in a voice that said he hadn't cared at all about being buttered up. "I only did it for Freddy, anyway, but you still owe me. Big."

"Do you need me to fix you up with another girl? Already? What did you do to that nice Debbie?"

Josh chuckled. "Nothing. And I don't need a fix up. That's going just fine. How do you want me to get you this file?"

"How did you get it?"

"My friend dropped off a copy. Do you want me to scan it and e-mail it to you?"

"Perfect." I gave him my e-mail address. "Is your friend aware of what you're doing with it?" I asked, after he finished writing it down.

"Oh yeah, and he's not happy about it. But he gave me the impression he was a little frustrated by how swiftly the department closed the case. And while he hates, underline hates, private detectives, he saw no real harm in your 'wasting your time' as he put it, looking into a closed case. And he seemed glad to not owe me anymore."

"Thanks. I'll find a way to repay you, I promise."

"I'm sure you will, Arnie. In fact, I expect to insist on it. One more thing. My friend needed to eliminate the police seal on the top of the report to protect himself, so the document I'm sending you will just look like blank pages with notes on them. It will be the official report, without looking like one."

"Fine with me. And thanks again."

A message from Josh appeared a few minutes later. It contained an attachment labeled "Betty's Chocolate Chip Cookie Recipe." Josh had concealed the name of the file. Or he'd sent his Mom's cookie recipe. From the way I'd pushed the envelope of Josh's good nature, it could be a computer virus. Anyway, I threw caution to the wind and clicked on the file, and true to his word, Josh had sent a few pages of unmarked notes. It began a few spaces from the top, with a space where Josh's friend had obliterated the police seal.

I printed it out, and Zellie and I read it together, heads a few inches apart, our cheeks almost touching. For a moment, I forgot what I was doing, and brushed my cheek against hers. We both paused for a second and then looked back at the file. It began with a summary of the accident, including a report by the officers who'd arrived at the scene. Straightforward stuff.

It included a diagram of the position of the two cars, which we looked at with interest.

It showed Darrow's car in the middle of the intersection, with Garrett's vehicle almost perpendicular, demonstrating a crash into the driver's side of the car. No surprises there. But it also showed a traffic signal, with no lights lit, presumably because the officers arriving at the scene arrived after the crash, and couldn't specify when the lights had changed.

The officers had interviewed a few people who were viewing the scene, but obtained no eyewitness accounts, other than a few people who stated the same thing – that it had all happened too fast, that they'd looked up only after they heard the impact. All standard responses to an accident scene.

But one person claimed to have seen the whole thing. Our friend Flora, who the police did not interview at the scene, because she did not come forward. She'd shown up at the police department several days later, with a precise explanation of the details of the accident.

A police officer recorded her statement, and the report contained a transcript. It jived with the account she'd given us. An assessment of the quality of Flora's statement and her possible value as a witness revealed the officer's doubts. He didn't question her veracity. He did, however, express skepticism that someone showing up with a prepared statement could have witnessed the accident at the precise moment it had occurred, including knowing whether the light was red or green at the exact moment. The officer speculated that potential motives for her coming forward included a possible quest for publicity for her business, Flora's Florals.

The officer clarified that this only constituted his opinion, but there was no doubt he questioned Flora's intentions, making a point of citing her immediate report to the newspapers.

Without a witness they deemed reliable, the police closed the case.

Zellie and I looked at each other. Who to believe? Jake had told us that Garrett was an enforcer for Many Counties Protection. So we believed Flora. But Jake was the only source of that information. We had not verified it ourselves. What if Garrett was just an innocent person who'd had a terrible accident?

We read further in the report. It contained an interview of Herman Octavius Garrett, who attested that he'd proceeded into the intersection as soon as the light turned green. He admitted "going the split second" the light changed, as he'd been in a hurry to get home, which was at an address reflected on his driver's license as Holmdel, New Jersey, a town adjacent to Middletown. He gave a vehement denial that he moved before the light turned green and, as he possessed a clean driving record, the officer taking the statement believed him. The officer noted the possibility he'd "jumped the gun," and could have been more careful, but discounted that as the proximate cause of the accident, which he listed as resulting from an "unfortunate" sequence of events. He opined that it was a "sad, but all too common" accident, and recommended the closure of the case with no recommendation to prosecute Garrett for manslaughter.

We sat in silence for a few moments.

"It's time to visit Garrett," Zellie announced.

I knew she was right. We hadn't even tried to find, much less interview him. And that thing about him being an enforcer for some terrible people didn't do much for my enthusiasm. But I nodded just the same.

"Yup. Can't put it off anymore."

Zellie's shoulders dropped, and she emitted a brief sigh, as much accepting my agreement as acknowledging the uncomfortable nature of our prospective interview. "Are we taking Matilda, or do you want me to drive? As if I have to ask."

"Um, let's take Matilda."

"Surprise, surprise," Zellie said, but with good humor.

"You know, we haven't called, or anything. We don't even know if he'll be home," I said, as we headed out the door. "And I'm not sure he's the type of guy you sneak up on."

"We don't know that," Zellie said, with a bravado I don't think matched her true feelings about the matter. Her drumming fingers on the passenger side window as soon as we sat in the car revealed significant anxiety.

Before we left for Holmdel, I patted my left shoulder, where I had my gun concealed under a light windbreaker. I didn't know whether Garrett posed a danger, but visiting him unarmed seemed imprudent. Zellie noticed my movement, and nodded.

"A wise precaution," she said.

I pulled up to the address in Holmdel. A mailbox at the end of a long driveway indicated the street number, but nothing else. No name. We peered down the driveway while still sitting in the car, perpendicular to its entrance. A Cape Cod style house sat at the end, with a big green lawn in front. The place was secluded. There didn't seem to be any other houses nearby, and the land was heavily wooded all around and in back.

"Well, here goes nothing," I said, and turned into the driveway.

I inched Matilda down the driveway. As we neared the house, I could see an SUV parked outside the garage. I looked over at Zellie and saw her expression. It was the same type of car that had run us down.

"A lot of SUVs look like that," I whispered to Zellie.

"Why are you whispering?" she asked.

"I don't know. It seemed like the thing to do," I replied, in a normal voice this time.

"Why don't you park right next to it, and we'll look to see if there are any dents when we get out."

I did as she suggested, pulling to a stop a few feet from the garage, and parallel to Garrett's car. Zellie got out of the car and walked around the SUV, checking for dents, or other signs of an accident. She looked up at me and shook her head.

"Nothing. Not even a scratch."

"He could have repaired it," I offered.

"Maybe." Zellie didn't sound convinced. "It's pretty clean. Look for yourself."

I did, and had to agree with her. Either he used another vehicle to run us down, or it was someone else.

"Let's see if he's home."

We walked up a pretty flower lined stone path up to the front door. As we walked, I looked around at the well-manicured grounds. It looked nothing like an enforcer's home. More like that of an accountant, or something. When we reached the front door, Zellie rang the bell. No answer.

"Car's here," I said. "Maybe he's sleeping."

"Or maybe he has another car." Zellie replied.

"Let's look around," I said, fingering my gun through the windbreaker.

"Um, do you think that's a good idea?" Zellie asked, her earlier bravado all but forgotten.

"What's the harm? We can say we saw his car and thought maybe he was out back and didn't hear us." I couldn't believe I'd said that. Usually I was the cautious one. But I was getting tired of being run down, shot at, and threatened. I wanted to do something. Anything to move things along. And if that meant snooping around a possible killer's house, so be it.

Zellie took my arm. "Okay, then. Lead the way. But I'm not leaving your side."

"I wouldn't have it any other way," I said, with more gallantry than the butterflies in my stomach might reflect. We headed to the back of the house, where we encountered that bastion of suburbia, a patio upon which sat a table and chairs and a barbecue grill. There was no answer to my shouted inquiry if anyone was home. Front and back, the place looked vacant. And about as suspicious as whole wheat toast.

"The place looks empty," I said, stating the obvious. Zellie nodded and let go of my arm. Wandering over to the patio, she looked at the sliding glass doors leading to the house.

"Let's take a peek in there," she said. "We might see something worthwhile."

"Might as well. We have nothing yet. What's the harm in a little peeping? It's not like anyone is home."

Having agreed to look, neither one of us moved.

"Let's do it together," I said.

"Maybe one of us should be the lookout," Zellie said. "I volunteer for the job."

I laughed. "Okay, fine, you win. You stand watch, and I'll go look."

I walked over to the sliding glass doors, intent on getting at least some information from our visit to Garrett's house. When I reached the door, I looked inside to a nondescript living room. *And the business end of a Glock.*

CHAPTER FORTY-ONE

I stared at the gun for a split second, and then raised my hand as if to knock on the door. The man didn't buy my charade, because he opened it before I completed my forward motion.

"Keep your hands where I can see them," he barked, and motioned me inside with the barrel of his gun.

"No need for that," I said. "I'm just here to talk." I hoped like heck that Zellie could hear me imply to Garrett (for it had to be Garrett) that I was alone.

"We can talk inside. Now move it before I get unpleasant."

What could I do? I did what he said and entered the house.

***

Zellie jumped out of sight as soon as she heard the door open. Arnie's comment confirmed the wisdom of that action. Arnie was probably in danger, but he still might talk his way out of the situation.

Zellie hadn't seen Garrett's gun. She'd jumped out of sight without getting that information. She'd heard Arnie told to get inside, though, and it hadn't sounded much like an invitation.

Arnie's indication he was alone was a message to her as well as Garrett. But what was the message? Leave and get help? Call the police? Save herself and let him figure it out? She wouldn't leave under any circumstances, she knew that. But what could she do? And should she do anything until the whole thing played out? At which time Garrett could hurt Arnie, or worse... she didn't even want to think about that.

Zellie walked back to the driveway, where Matilda sat next to Garrett's SUV. She wondered a little whether Garrett had spotted her through any of the windows, but she'd avoided them, ducking down each time she thought it might be possible to see the yard from inside the house. He'd known Arnie was there before he looked in the sliding glass door, so she wondered when Garrett spotted him. No new car had arrived, and the two cars blocked the entrance to the garage, so no hidden car had slipped around them.

The garage. Garrett might have a second SUV in there. For a moment, Zellie forgot her mission to figure out how to help Arnie. She peeked into the side window into the garage, and sure enough, it contained another SUV. She bet it was the one that Garrett used to hit them. Zellie was dying to get into the garage to find out, but she came to her senses. She needed to figure out how to get Arnie out of the house and to safety. And she thought of a way. And it had the added advantage of proving Garrett's guilt.

***

As soon as I got inside, Garrett shut the sliding glass door, and closed the blinds, while keeping the gun trained on me. I thought about reaching for my gun while he drew the blinds, but I didn't have the time. I blustered again about my innocent intentions, and that I only sought an interview. He bought none of it.

"Your gun, Mr. Fischer." So, he knew my name. "Slowly open your jacket, and with two fingers, remove it."

I did as he said. I had no other option.

"Toss it over there, he said, still pointing his gun, which looked like a Glock G43. An accurate and deadly weapon. He directed my movement like a skilled professional. He's done this kind of thing before, I thought.

I tossed it on a nearby chair as directed.

"You have quite a reputation as a marksman, Mr. Fischer. I don't want to test its veracity. Now move over and sit in that chair," he said, pointing at a wooden straight back with narrow arms. When I sat down, he tossed me a pair of handcuffs.

"Cuff your left wrist to the right arm," he said, and watched while I complied. He moved over and took my right wrist and cuffed it to the left arm, securing me to the chair with my arms crossed in front, much like a straight-jacket. I didn't like this one bit. I considered kicking him, but with practiced ease, he blocked one leg while securing the other with a zip tie, and completed the job on my other one.

"You've given me a great opportunity, Mr. Fischer. Catching you breaking into my home? And armed, to boot." Garrett gestured at my gun, which lay on the chair next to where he stood.

"A Sig Sauer P220, too. A very dangerous weapon. I was so frightened seeing this burglar breaking into my home, and I could see the outline of a shoulder holster under his coat. I grabbed my gun, officer, which I of course just use for protection out here in this isolated area, and defended myself. Words can't express how terrible I feel about it, officer, but I just did what any God fearing American would have done under the circumstances. How's that sound?"

"I don't suppose that you'd consider 'I scared him away, and no one got hurt?'"

"No, I think not. I've tried to scare you away. Three times, to be exact. I'm done scaring."

My body stiffened, my heart palpitated, and I felt sick, and downright terrified. This guy was a killer, and I had little hope of escaping. I tried stalling, but I knew it was futile. Zellie would call for help, but it would be impossible for anyone to get here in time. I wondered why he'd handcuffed me to the chair instead of just shooting me at the back door, but I didn't need to wonder long.

"I'd have killed you already, if I didn't need something from you."

He meant Zellie, I thought. And no way I would tell him she was outside. I had to deflect. So I blurted out the first thing that came into to my mind.

"If she wanted you to kill me, I'm guessing I'd be dead already. I bet I'm not supposed to die."

If Garrett was thrown by my reference to "she," he didn't let on. "Maybe not, he allowed. But sometimes warnings get out of hand, and people die anyway."

"Like Freddy Darrow."

Garrett shrugged. "Regrettable."

"She just wanted to warn him, didn't she?" I was hoping for a disclosure of a name, but Garrett didn't bite. And anyway, I wouldn't survive to tell anyone.

"She's quite capable of taking care of her own problems. And I think you know way too much for my comfort. Enough of the questions. Where did your pretty partner go?"

Feigning ignorance, I said "I'm alone, and I'm not sure where she's going today."

"Don't make me lose my patience, Mr. Fischer. You know where she went. I'll beat it out of you if I have to."

I wracked my brain for a suitable response. The way he asked the question suggested that he didn't know she'd arrived with me. Otherwise the question was unnecessary. "Okay,

okay, you're holding the gun, and I'm handcuffed to a chair. Anyway, I don't see the harm in telling you she's at home, doing research on the computer."

"I don't believe you. She's here, isn't she?" He looked me straight in the eye, and despite my efforts, I must have reacted, albeit with the slightest blink.

"Well, well. Let's see what we can do about that. He tapped his Glock, and I shuddered, hoping to heck that Zellie had retreated to safety.

At that moment, there was a loud crash, followed by the sound of a car alarm outside.

"Don't go anywhere," Garrett said facetiously. With an ominous laugh, he added "I have target practice to attend to." He headed out the back door.

***

Zellie pulled a tire iron from the trunk of Arnie's car, and hefted it in her hands, gauging its considerable weight. Yes, this will work just fine, she thought. She readied her phone to take pictures, and put it in her front pocket. Then she strode over to the SUV sitting in the driveway. Raising the tire iron over her head, she brought it down on the windshield, putting large cracks in the glass, and setting off a loud car alarm. She then sprinted to the side of the garage, and repeated the action on the side window of the garage. The window shattered, spilling glass both inside the garage and on the ground at her feet. She needed to exercise care and not rush too much. That glass could rip a nasty slash in her arms. But she needed to work fast.

She cleared the remaining pieces of glass from the window by brushing the tire iron along the sides and assessed the resulting opening. A tight fit, she thought, but there was no stopping now. Casting aside the comic image of becoming stuck in the window with her head inside, and her butt and legs hanging out, Zellie wriggled through the small opening into the garage. She breathed a sigh of relief, knowing a tense, and not even remotely humorous moment had passed. But extreme danger remained, and there was no time to lose.

She snapped a few quick pictures of the dented front panel of the SUV inside the garage, and another picture of the license plate, and then entered the house through a door at the back of the garage, just as a shouting and angry Garrett arrived at the driveway, waving his Glock.

***

From my vantage point secured to the chair inside the house, I heard both the shattered glass and the car alarm. I knew it was Zellie. While I'd hoped she would retreat to safety and get help, a part of me knew she'd never leave. She'd have some sort of plan for rescuing me, no doubt one of mildly insane brilliance. I hoped that Garrett didn't catch her outside. That comment about target practice had unnerved me. My insides felt like a giant hand was squeezing my stomach, and beads of perspiration dotted my forehead. I pulled my arms up and down, trying to break the slender chair arms, but I had a terrible angle, and couldn't exert enough force.

Looking in front of me, I spied my gun. In his haste to, gulp, shoot the intruder outside, he'd forgotten about it. I couldn't reach it from where I sat, but if I could just move the chair by forcing my body up and down, I might get close enough to grab it. I moved my body up and down, and the chair lurched forward about an inch. Piece of cake, I thought with pride, and tried the same action again. The chair legs didn't budge. My head and the top of the chair were a different story. I landed face first on the floor, still handcuffed to the chair, and unable to move.

CHAPTER FORTY-TWO

As I contemplated my embarrassing posture, Zellie burst in, her brown-blonde locks flying behind her. She carried a tire iron in her right hand, and stopped short when she saw me.

"Arnie!" She tipped the chair up so I could see her. Without so much as a greeting other than her initial exclamation of my name, Zellie barked an order. "Close your eyes and don't move a muscle."

I was in no position to argue. I closed my eyes and kept still. And a second later felt the whoosh of a heavy object inches from my wrist, followed by an intense vibration, and the sound of cracking wood.

I opened my eyes to the sight of a cracked chair arm. And not my actual arm, thank goodness. I pulled up hard against the cracked wood and freed my wrist, still attached to one end of the handcuffs.

"Close your eyes again and don't move. He'll be back any second."

We repeated the process, and I freed my other arm. I somehow got my shackled hand into my pocket to retrieve my knife, and handed it to Zellie, who knelt to release me from the zip ties. Once freed, I lunged over to the chair and grabbed my gun just as Garrett exploded into the room spewing epithets, and pointing his Glock at us. Zellie and I dropped to the floor, using the narrow chair as woefully inadequate cover. Several bullets smacked into it, and others whizzed over our heads. I looked at Zellie and pointed at the tire iron, which lay next to our location behind the chair.

"On two," I whispered, "toss it in the air, to the right." I nodded in the direction I intended, and she nodded back.

"One, two," I said, and Zellie tossed the tire iron to the right, while I peered around the chair and fired two shots to the right of where Garrett had turned left to avoid the tire iron. As I'd hoped, the shots caused him to continue his momentum to his left and drop to the floor, while Zellie and I skedaddled out the sliding glass door.

We ran to the driveway to get into Matilda to complete our escape, but Garrett had shot out all of her tires, and put two bullets into her windshield for good measure.

I had no time to lament Matilda's fate. In a way, the extra time Garrett had taken to damage my car out of vindictiveness had given Zellie time to free me. I made an instant decision. Pointing to the woods beyond the driveway, I said, "Let's go that way on foot. He can't follow us in there. It's not like we're unarmed, and he'll know that we can just hide behind trees and shoot at him if he follows."

Zellie paused. "Um, Arnie, what about Matilda?"

"It's just a car, Zellie. Let's go!"

Zellie looked at me in astonishment, and I'd kind of surprised myself with the comment. I had never, ever referred to my car as "it" and surely never said "it" was just a car. But sometimes, you have to move on. And no time like when a crazed killer is firing a semi-automatic at you. I grabbed Zellie's hand, and we rushed into the woods.

With a final backward glance over our shoulders, we hurried into the thick brush, and plunged further into the wooded areas of what was turning out to be a confusing array of dense foliage into which we'd sought refuge. I tripped over a rock embedded in the ground and almost fell, but Zellie grabbed my arm at the last second. Dead wood, grass and other detritus of the forest crackled under our feet as we hastened to escape Garrett's clutches.

Out of breath, we stopped for a moment in front of a large oak tree and assessed the situation. In our haste, we'd paid little attention to direction, valuing cover over anything else, and needed to figure out where we were and if Garrett had followed us. There was no sign of him, however, and in truth, we hadn't heard or seen any evidence of a human presence in the woods.

"I don't think he followed us," I observed, looking around as I spoke.

"No, I don't think so. But now that we seem to have escaped, do you have any ideas on how to get out of here?"

"Nope. Don't even know where we are, much less how to get back to civilization."

"Well, we can't go back to where we came from," Zellie said. "I'm not even sure of which way that is."

"Lucky for us, our phones have compasses built into them." I reached for my phone as I spoke, and it wasn't there. Garrett had taken it away.

"Oops. He took my phone. He left my Dad's penknife, though." I held the small object up.

"Well, there's that. Not much use in determining direction though. How about I check my phone instead?" She looked down at it and pointed. "North is that way."

"Um. Great, I think. Do we want to go north?"

"I don't know. We got so turned around running into the woods, I can't be sure even which direction we came from, so I don't know if going north will get us out of these woods."

We looked around. And observed our complete enclosure by more trees than hay in a haystack. And we were the needle.

"Let's go east." I said. "While I'm not sure, I think we came from that direction." I pointed west. "Going the opposite direction seems like a good idea."

"Okay," Zellie agreed.

"These woods can't last forever. We're bound to get out of here if we head in one direction and don't go in circles. How big could these woods be?"

Big, as we discovered. We walked for what seemed like hours, tripping over rocks and low brush, scraping our faces in the brambles, and at one point, soaking our shoes in an unseen stream.

I felt exhausted. I looked at my wrists, still shackled to the handcuffs.

"We need a better plan than just going east. For all we know, these woods extend for miles in this direction."

"Let's call Ted. Maybe he can use some scientific mumbo-jumbo to locate our position and tell us the right direction to get out of here."

"And pick us up," I reminded Zellie. "We have no car."

She nodded, and handed me her phone.

Ted answered on the first ring.

"Fast answer," I observed.

"Oh, it's you. I thought Zellie might have come to her senses and dumped you for me."

"No such luck," I said, chuckling. "And what would Marla think about that?"

"She'd say it is further proof that Ted has good taste in women," Marla replied. Ted had put me on speaker.

"I'd banter a little more with you two, but we need your help, and I don't know how long the cell phone battery will last." I explained our predicament and Ted jumped into action.

"Hmm. I can locate your position, no problem. Yup, there you are. The difficulty is figuring out how to get you out. "Ted mumbled a few things to himself, and after a few moments said, "Uh, oh."

CHAPTER FORTY-THREE

U h oh? Don't say 'uh oh' and then go silent on me. What's the problem?"

"Big stream between you and the road. Hang on. I'm mapping a different route that doesn't require you to cross it. Hmm. Nope. You'll have to get wet. And I don't know how deep the stream is. Maybe you can get across and keep your phone dry, but I don't know."

Ted gave me specific instructions as to the direction to take, and that he and Marla would pick us up. As predicted, we reached a wide stream after just a few minutes more of walking. We both stared at it.

"It's pretty wide," I said.

"And has a strong current," Zellie offered.

"Looks deep."

"Yes."

We looked at each other, and I saw dismay creeping into Zellie's

face. I'm sure I looked the same.

"I think I could swim it with no trouble, if I wasn't wearing these bracelets," I said, holding up my wrists. It's not the weight, it's the awkwardness. Together with that current, it'll be tough."

Zellie pursed her lips, and a large wrinkle appeared on her forehead. "I know. And I think I could do the same, except for trying to keep this phone dry. It's kind of our lifeline, and I'd hate to lose it."

"There's only one answer."

Zellie looked at me. "You take the phone, and I swim across and get help."

I nodded. "I'll call Ted and tell him to bring bolt cutters. We'll figure out a way to get them across. I'll also tell him your expected route, so he can anticipate your position when you emerge from the woods, because you'll have no phone."

Zellie kicked off her sneakers and tied them in a loose knot around her neck. Then she waded into the water and was off. I was nervous about it all, but I knew she was an excellent swimmer. A short while later, I could see her emerge from the water. She gave me a wave and was off. Now I had to wait.

I sat down on a bed of pine needles and thought about the case. Garrett had confirmed our suspicion that a woman was calling the shots. But which woman?

I reviewed all the suspects in my mind until my reverie was interrupted by a whining sound. Looking up, I saw a small object heading in my direction. A drone, carrying a package. It landed right next to me. I leaned over and opened the package, which contained bolt cutters and a note instructing me to put my shoes in the container. Peering across the wide expanse of the stream, I saw the outlines of Zellie and the tall figure of Ted on the opposite bank. I made quick work of the handcuffs. Then I kicked off my shoes, placed them in the drone's container, and swam across the stream. I hugged Zellie, soaking her already damp body, and shook Ted's hand, and he guided back the drone carrying my shoes. I put them on, and we walked to his car.

"Where's Marla?" I asked, when we arrived.

"Back at the office. When you called, she'd just taken a quick break."

"I hope I didn't interrupt anything important," I said, with a raised eyebrow.

"Just wild, passionate sex. Nothing out of the ordinary."

"Uh huh. In your lab."

"Best place. Those test tubes can be pesky though."

We all laughed as Ted put the car into gear and drove us home. Zellie asked him to drop her off at her house for a shower and a change of clothes, while I continued home for the same purpose.

Shedding my wet clothes, I jumped into the shower, and felt much better afterwards. But my wrists still chafed. I shuddered to think of my narrow escape – thanks to Zellie's quick thinking. I knew I had to call the Holmdel police to report the incident, but figured it could wait until after I settled down. Sitting on the couch in my living room, I contemplated stretching out for a nap, when the doorbell rang.

Who is that? I wondered. A salesman, or someone like that. Zellie would just come in with her key, as would Ted. I figured it must be Betsy, Lazlow's dog walker. She had a key, too, but always rang the bell and knocked a few times before she entered. It surprised me a little, as she wasn't due until much later.

I rose and looked through the peephole. Standing at my door was a police officer. I opened the door, and we looked at each other for a moment and laughed. I invited him in, and we sat down in my living room.

"George! You're a policeman?"

"Yes, sir. Holmdel Police Department. Graduated from the academy last year."

"I thought you went to pharmacy school, like your father and grandfather."

"True enough. Turns out I hate it. Not the same as it used to be. It seems like I spent most of my time taking pills from big bottles and putting them into little bottles. Dad and Grandpa got to be chemists and mix stuff."

I knew George both from high school and the shooting range back in the old days. He was a good marksman. And now, I guess his shooting could be for real.

"It's nice to see you, and I'm glad you're here. I was going to call the Holmdel Police in a little while. I just returned home from an ordeal a little while ago. Um, that's why you're here, isn't it?"

George looked uncomfortable. "I'm supposed to give you a warning."

"Give me a warning? About what? The man handcuffed me to a chair and threatened to kill me. If Zellie hadn't saved me, I might be dead right now."

George held up his hand, palm facing me, and I stopped talking. "Listen, Arnie, I believe you. But Mr. Garrett gave a different account. He claimed he stopped you from breaking into his home, and even had to disarm you. In fact, he claimed you discharged your firearm at him. Is that true?"

I nodded. "Two shots, but just to stop him from killing us. I didn't even aim at him, only in a manner calculated to get him to fall down. Which he did, enabling us to escape."

George nodded. "I'm guessing if you'd aimed at him, you'd have hit him center mass. Anyway, he's not pressing charges. Just wants you to get a warning to stay away."

"Makes sense, I suppose. He can't want too much scrutiny, given the business he's in. And it was smart of him to call you right away. Smarter than me," I added.

"If he's as bad a guy as you say, he's had plenty of practice in putting the best face on his actions. Consider yourself lucky that you don't have his kind of smarts."

"Thanks. That's nice of you to say."

"It's the truth. I might be new to the force, but I know his type. And I promise you, we'll keep an eye on him. Any false moves, and he's toast."

"Thank you. And good luck with your new career. I think you'll be great at it."

"Thanks. Good seeing you. Take it easy. He paused at the door. "One more thing. Garrett had your 'junker'... his words, not mine, towed at your expense." George handed me a piece of paper with the name of the towing company. "Call this number, and they'll tell you where to pick your car up. It will be expensive," he cautioned.

I thanked him, and he left.

I sat there for a while thinking about the case. Exhausted as I was, I must have drifted off, but the doorbell woke me up. Who was it this time?

CHAPTER FORTY-FOUR

I peered through the peephole and saw Marla standing there. I opened the door and let her in. She gave me a quick kiss in greeting.

"I have to run. When I spoke on the phone to Ted, he filled me in on the rest of the day's events, and then told me he dropped you here and Zellie off at her house. I figured you'd be meeting up with her soon, so I grabbed the opportunity to see you and deliver this." She thrust a package in my hand.

"Don't open it now. Wait for me to make my escape first before Zellie sees me, and we have to make up more lame excuses." And with that, she departed.

Moments later, my phone rang. Zellie. We made plans to pick up my car the next day. I put the package on the coffee table and went into the kitchen to grab a quick bite. I tried to watch a little television, gave up, and went bed. After a fitful sleep, I awoke with a distinct plan in mind. I dressed, put Matilda's car keys in one pocket, my Dad's penknife in the other, grabbed my wallet and wandered into the living room.

Hearing Zellie's car pull up outside, I spotted the package on the coffee table, and scooped it up and put it in my pocket. Marla and I had taken great pains to keep it from Zellie, and I didn't want to blow the surprise. Zellie came in a few moments later. I kissed her hello, and we headed out on our mission to rescue Matilda.

At the towing company's lot, a heavy-set, greasy looking character with a handlebar mustache advised us of the $500.00 fee for retrieving Matilda. I looked at Zellie, and she shrugged, figuring I was dumb enough to pay twice that price for my classic car.

"Let me see it first," I said to the guy, and he complied, leading us out to a large parking lot littered with hundreds of vehicles in various stages of disrepair. Matilda was no exception. All the tires were flat – we knew that already. But Garrett had finished the job, by smashing the windshield, and torching the interior. It resembled the result of a car bomb. I looked at Zellie in dismay, and she took my hand. No one could repair Matilda, and I knew it. I only wondered how to provide a decent burial for her. It would take hiring my own tow truck and paying the exorbitant price to retrieve my car. The junkman's $500.00 fee was an attempt to con me before I saw the damage. Making a snap decision, I turned to the guy, and said, "Keep it." With all the dignity I could muster, and still holding Zellie's hand, I strode out of the lot and out to where Zellie parked her car.

"Let's get out of here," I said, setting my jaw.

Zellie took one look at me, and without a word, put the car in gear and headed out of the lot. To say I was angry was an understatement. His destruction of my car was sheer vindictiveness. As I calmed down, I tried to put the incident in perspective.

We had invaded his space, not the other way around. We'd poked the lion with a stick, and he'd bitten back. Not surprising. Sure, the handcuffing in his house was over the top, but I had lurked outside carrying a lethal weapon. And he didn't kill us, nor did we have any evidence he'd planned to kill anyone.

He'd warned us three times, and he'd warned, but didn't kill Jake. It was possible that Freddy's death was another warning that went too far. In contrast, our client's death was a cold-blooded murder.

"I wonder if we're looking at this right," I said, and told Zellie my thought process.

"You found your words. Good boy," Zellie responded, with a sideways glance. "But I'm in no mood to look at his conduct as justifiable. The man is deranged, and he almost killed us. And I thought you'd say, 'That SOB murdered Matilda, let's find him and run him over. Twice. Backwards and forwards."

"Um, yeah. Put me down for that, too. I guess it is crazy to look at Garrett as anything other than a psychopath. Forget I raised the issue."

"What's next? I'm driving around with no direction in mind."

"I think we bring matters to a head. Can I borrow your phone? I haven't replaced mine yet."

"Sure. It's in my purse. What are you thinking?"

"A trap. With us as the bait," I said.

"Great. Bait, that's what we've come to."

"Oh, I don't intend to put us in any danger. At least not much. And not for long. I think."

"Very reassuring. Okay, out with it. What do you have in mind?"

I explained my theory, and Zellie hemmed and hawed a little, but agreed that harebrained as it was, it had a slight chance of working.

"Okay, make the call," Zellie said. "I'm sure she'll do it."

Melissa agreed, as predicted. "I'll call them right away," she said, after I told her what I needed.

"Okay, it's all set. Melissa will text when she makes the calls." I handed Zellie back her phone.

"So now we wait."

"Yes. And no telling how long. Time to head over to the cottage to see what develops. I'll drive."

We arrived at the cottage a few minutes later and parked a discrete distance away. We could see the front door from our parking spot. The street was quiet, with few cars, and no people around. I was confident we'd see any arrival long before it occurred.

"This could be a long wait," I observed, after a few minutes.

"Part of the job," Zellie said. "You want to be a detective, long, boring stakeouts are part of the deal."

"I wonder if anyone will show up," I mused.

"Now you wonder? This is your plan, remember?"

"Someone will show up," I said, evidencing more confidence than I felt. I feared we could wait for hours, but I kept my mouth shut.

"Melissa texted me she made the calls, so it can't help riling someone," I added.

We sat in silence for a while, afraid to do anything but eye the front door.

"Maybe we should take turns watching," I said, but received no reply. I looked over and saw Zellie staring at the window on her side of the car.

A gun. Pointed at Zellie. *And Herman Garrett fingering the trigger.*

CHAPTER FORTY-FIVE

He motioned for Zellie to roll down the window, which she did.

"Okay, here's what will happen. Mr. Fischer, you know the drill. With two fingers, remove your gun from your shoulder holster, and hand it to me. Keep the barrel pointing at yourself. No tricks or Ms. Morgan is a dead woman."

I did as he requested, thinking he was smart to make me hand it across Zellie. Leaning like that, I had little chance for any trickery, even if I intended to risk Zellie's life, which I emphatically did not.

Garrett had disarmed me for the second time in two days. I didn't like our chances this time, but there was no choice. We had to keep our wits about us and hope for an opening to escape. Again.

My gun ensconced in his pocket, Garrett barked additional orders. "Remove the keys from the car and throw them out your window along with your cell phone."

"You already have my phone," I said to Garrett. "I don't have a new one yet."

Garrett sneered in response. "I smashed it with a hammer. You won't need a new one." He pointed at Zellie with his free hand. "You, hand me your phone."

Zellie handed it over. There was no way to resist. We were trapped in the car, like zoo chimpanzees in a glass cage. Unlike them, however, we'd imprisoned ourselves. Garrett could shoot us on the spot. And how on earth did he sneak up on us like that? We were so fixated on the front door we didn't watch behind us. And how did he know we'd be there? Melissa's call. It tipped him off, too. My big idea had backfired in the worst possible way.

He ordered us out of the car and marched us right up to the front door. Pulling out a key, he handed it to Zellie and directed her to open it. This accomplished, he marched us inside.

As we entered the cottage, Garrett directed us to the open area in front where we'd envisioned a waiting room. The floor was covered with linoleum, patterned with a light paisley print. The room was bereft of furniture, and our only escape would be through the door through which we'd just passed, or the big windows in the back. Both stood about ten feet away.

"Get down on the floor," he barked at us. "I want you sitting back to back."

We both looked at Garrett's gun and sat down on the hard floor as he directed. He pulled a large roll of heavy-duty duct tape from his jacket. Slapping one end hard on my arm, he wrapped the tape around us, pinning our arms straight against our sides, with us back to back and our legs extended out in front of us in opposite directions.

Garrett looked at his work with satisfaction. "Given a few hours, you might wriggle free. But you don't have that long. And not much chance of one of you coming in to save the other, is there?" We didn't answer his rhetorical question.

"That will teach you to invade my home," he added. "No one threatens me and gets away with it."

"We didn't threaten you," I said. "We were looking for information. It was a misunderstanding. Now let us go. We won't visit your home again. We received the warning you requested the police give us, and fully intend to honor it. And we received your message, loud and clear. I know you're tough, but I don't think you'd commit pre-meditated murder."

Garrett looked at us. "You don't get it, do you? You're not going to visit my home again, because you're going to die today. I tried multiple times to warn you off your investigations. The warnings end today. The police report was just a ruse to keep the focus off of me. I'm pretty good at convincing them."

"Like you convinced them that Freddy Darrow's car crash was an accident," Zellie accused.

"One of my finest acting jobs. Should have received an Oscar, or an Emmy, or something, for that one."

"Was that a mistake? Did you mistake him for Ferdinand Darrow, then realize the error and poison his brother right here in this cottage?"

"Oh, it was no mistake. And I poisoned no one, much less the late, great confidence man and extortionist Ferdinand Darrow. Someone else did that. But you'll have no chance to figure it out. You've become too much of a nuisance. And this place has become an albatross to MCP. The good news, to MCP, not you, is that it's insured against fire. I can kill two birds with a single match. Goodbye. It's been a distinct pleasure."

He turned to exit, but stopped short. Another person had entered the cottage.

Jayne Merriweather strode into the room. If we expected her to help us, we were mistaken. She looked over our bonds and expressed approval.

"You didn't use accelerants?" she asked Garrett.

"I'm a professional. No gas, nothing. All natural."

"Good. We don't need pesky questions from the police or an insurance adjuster. You have his gun?"

Garrett nodded.

"Give it to me."

Garrett handed it to her.

She flipped off the safety, and raised her arm, poised to fire.

Zellie and I stiffened, waiting for the inevitable. I'd hoped to grow old with Zellie, not die with her now, killed by my own gun.

Jayne began to pull the trigger.

CHAPTER FORTY-SIX

At the last second, she turned her hand to the right, and shot Garrett right between the eyes. He fell backwards, his lifeless head bouncing off the hard floor.

Tied back to back, Zellie's posterior was to the scene. I was grateful for that. But she heard the whole thing. And I had closed my eyes, so I didn't see it until I realized I wasn't dead. I felt Zellie's uncontrollable shaking, her quivering back pressed hard against mine. Or maybe it was me. Probably both of us. Neither of us had ever witnessed a murder, whether by sight or sound. I hoped I hadn't wet my pants. I wasn't sure how I felt, other than shock at the brutality. I couldn't even feel relief at Jayne shooting Garrett instead of us. But maybe, just maybe, she'd shown up in a rescue attempt.

No such luck. As Jayne explained, it was Garrett who wanted to give us a final, terrible scare.

"Herman was a liability," she said. "Wanting to let you go was the last straw.

I paid him to make messes disappear, not create situations where nosy people ask a lot of questions. His work became much too public – a cancer on our cultivated image. I had to remove the diseased part. And it gave me an opportunity to kill three birds with one stone." She laughed at her little joke.

"You're crazy," Zellie said. "You're acting like a mob boss, not a real estate executive. Let us go."

"Can't do that. You know too much now, including the demise of Mr. Garrett over there. This place is a death trap. Ferdinand Darrow died in this cottage. We had nothing to do with that, but I will deal with you. It's time to burn the place down."

She removed a small cloth from her handbag. She used it to wipe down my gun, and leaned down to press the handle into my hand, and removed it.

"Perfect," she said. "Let me tell you a story. You were visiting the cottage you intended to rent as your new office, when a dangerous criminal accosted you, and threatened your lives. Well known as a skilled marksman, you killed him before he could do the two of you harm. The police would deem it self-defense, and no charges would result. A fine result, but for the unfortunate circumstance of a terrible fire. Little evidence would exist. The only thing remaining would be your gun. If the police could lift any fingerprints, they would only be your own. What do you think of my story?"

Ignoring our pleas and vehement protests, Jayne turned and left.

We struggled against our bonds, to no avail. I had to think of something.

"She's going to torch the place with us in it, isn't he?" Zellie asked, a slight tremor in her voice.

"I think so. We need to figure out a way to get loose before that happens."

"I can't move my arms, but I can wiggle my fingers." With that, she pinched my butt. Irreverent to the end, I thought. And I hoped it wasn't the end. But it didn't look good.

We were about to die, and we still didn't know who killed Ferdinand Darrow.

CHAPTER FORTY-SEVEN

Let's try to move side to side, or up and down. We'll see if we can loosen the tape. Even a little bit might be enough for what I have in mind."

We tried moving side to side first and had a little luck. Moving up turned out to be almost impossible because we were sitting flat on the floor with our legs extended.

I tried reaching into my pocket, where my father's penknife sat tantalizingly close, but just out of reach. Zellie's angle was a little better.

"My penknife is in my front pocket," I said. "Try to reach the top of the pocket and pull. Maybe you'll be able to pull the lining up."

Zellie wriggled her fingers, but couldn't quite reach. After trying several times, she stopped and sniffed the surrounding air.

"We need to hurry. That smell is smoke. Jayne is burning this place down with us inside."

With an anguished groan, she reached her fingers back to my pocket, grabbed onto the fabric at the top of my pocket and pulled as hard as she could. Nothing happened.

"I don't think I can reach," she said, desperation creeping into her voice.

"We'll get out of here," I said, in a tone intended to sound more confident than I really thought. "I'll try to lurch as hard as I can toward the side, at the same time as you reach for the pocket. One, two, three, go!" With a groan, I heaved my body as hard as I could. Shock waves of pain ripped through my arms, and I pulled us both down on our sides with a jarring thud. But from my vantage point on my side, I saw my pocket knife lying on the floor a few inches away from a small box that had popped open in our fall.

"You did it," I exclaimed. "Now we need somehow to move ourselves forward and get that knife open." I was trying hard not to acknowledge, at least for the time being, the shiny object next to the knife.

"Um, Arnie..." Zellie started. "Are you going to just ignore the beautiful diamond ring sitting right there next to the knife?"

"I thought we should try to escape the clutches of a deranged arsonist first, but I would hate to die before I did this, so here goes, in a shortened version of the nice dinner, gorgeous flowers and rehearsed speech I had planned.

"Zellie Morgan, I love you more than life itself. You're my best friend, and the most wonderful sweetheart in the world. I want to spend the rest of my life with you as both friend and lover, and also as your husband. Let's get married."

"I thought you'd never ask, and I'm certain I didn't imagine you'd pop the question under these circumstances," Zellie said. "But yes, a thousand times, yes, let's get married and spend the rest of our lives together." She looked around. "Which won't be long if we don't get the heck out of here."

I looked up and smelled the air. More smoke. I saw none yet, but we had no time to waste. We needed to get that penknife open somehow and cut ourselves free. Working together, we wriggled up to a position where Zellie could lean on the knife while I pulled at the blade with my fingers. It took a few agonizing tries, but we reached the point where I knew we'd be successful if we kept at it. After a grueling effort, the blade popped open.

I picked it up and started sawing through the duct tape near the crook of Zellie's arm. I couldn't see what I was doing, and she yelped when I nicked her a few times, but I made steady progress. I wasn't sure if it was fast enough. The smell of smoke was stronger now, and I could feel the heat coming from outside of the house. I needed to hurry. I sawed as fast as I could, but still the tape held firm. We were in real danger now, and we both knew it. You can die from the smoke as easily as from the flames, and we were still stuck on the floor.

But with a sudden pop, I made it through the tape. I could feel Zellie wince as the knife blade jabbed into her, but she freed her arm. Working with deliberate speed, she ripped the tape off of us, and we headed for the door, which was by now engulfed in flames.

"It's the best way out," I said. "We'll have to make a run right through it."

Zellie nodded, and I took her hand and we burst through the door, with the smoke stinging our eyes and the flames licking at our skin. We tumbled out the door, coughing our guts out and a little singed, but otherwise unhurt.

We got to our feet and moved away from the cottage, where we watched the flames for a few minutes, thanking our lucky stars we'd escaped. Dusk had gathered while we were inside, and the light of the fire contrasted with the growing darkness.

"Arnie," Zellie whispered. "The ring! We left it in there."

I reached into my pocket and pulled out a gleaming diamond ring, and slipped it on her finger, which I caressed and held for a moment. I got down on one knee right there in front of the burning cottage, and said "Zellie, you're the most wonderful woman I have ever known. It would be my honor and privilege to have you as my wife."

Zellie smiled down at me.

"It would be my honor, too. Let's get hitched."

I arose and took her hand, and we started walking to the car, but I tripped on something. A dead body.

CHAPTER FORTY-EIGHT

We stared in disbelief. The corpse was none other than Jayne Merriweather.

Before we could say anything, a woman's voice spoke. Patsy Bruder, holding a gleaming handgun.

"Touching proposal. But I'm sorry, the wedding will never happen. She looked over at the burning cottage.

"Don't get me wrong. I'm happy that that stupid cottage is burning down. Courtesy of the late Jayne Merriweather. She looked down. I'd hoped that piece of garbage would finish the job for me. I can't have you snooping around anymore." She looked at the burning house again.

"Although the extendable bar is burning now, so the evidence is gone. But you know too much, and could cause me too much trouble. It ends here. I'm sorry you got involved." She raised the gun as if to fire, when a hand reached out from behind, and pulled her arm down.

"No more killing, Patsy. These two are like my kids. Please hand me the gun. It's over." He said it in a soothing voice, and she responded, handing him the gun and burying her head in his chest. We could hear the sobbing, as Jake Rothberg patted her head and whispered consoling words.

CHAPTER FORTY-NINE

Did you know Patsy killed him?" Mrs. Minniefield asked, as we enjoyed the comfort of her living room. As usual, Zellie and I sat together on the couch, Mrs. M occupied her dainty armchair, and Ted and Marla sat in the two over-stuffed chairs.

"Well... we didn't know, but we thought so," I started, and looked at Zellie.

"She was the only one with motive, means and opportunity," Zellie finished.

I took it up from there. "We ascertained means and opportunity pretty early," I said. "Once we figured out how the murderer committed the crime, those two elements pointed at either her or Russ."

"Explain," Mrs. Minniefield directed, in her abrupt manner.

"It took a while, but we figured out that the killer poisoned Darrow first, and then locked him in the attic by propping an extendable pole up against the attic trapdoor, and left him to die."

Mrs. M. nodded for me to continue.

"It thus had to be someone with both access and knowledge of the office layout. The murder could not have occurred while he was meeting clients, unless a client knew enough about the office layout and could orchestrate Darrow going up to the attic during business hours, when anyone, including Russ and Patsy, could have shown up at any minute. It didn't seem possible. We thought the killer could only do it while Darrow was busy doing something else, like archiving files in the attic."

"So, it wouldn't have been the person Russ heard arguing with Darrow – the mysterious dark-haired woman," Zellie added.

"Who was that, anyway?" Ted asked.

"It's only speculation, but I think it was Jayne Merriweather," I said. "Russ told us he only dealt with Patsy, and never met anyone else at MCP, and I think he told the truth. So, he wouldn't have known Jayne. And she and Darrow had things to discuss, given their competing claims on Elizabeth Abogado Rothberg's estate, but we're getting ahead of ourselves here.

"It thus had to be someone Darrow was accustomed to having there while he did routine work. Someone, for example, who cleaned the office, such as Russ, or who often worked there, such as the building manager, Patsy Bruder. Both had means and opportunity, but we couldn't figure out their motives.

"They both seemed like ordinary workers, unconnected to the crime, so we moved on to other characters, such as Jayne Merriweather and Herman Garrett. Both were criminals," Zellie said. "Garrett just happened to be more comfortable and overt in getting his hands dirty. But Jayne turned out to be much worse, running an extortion racket right here in Middletown, and as we now know, killing without remorse."

I nodded. "Because we concluded that Garrett killed Freddy Darrow, it was logical to view him as the number one suspect in Ferdinand Darrow's murder. He made that conclusion easier by the various attempts he made, or at least seemed to make, on our lives. First the hit and run. Then the shooting incident at Jake's house, then the handcuffs and threats at his home. Not to mention the final incident which came later," I added, with an involuntary shudder. "We kind of became distracted from what was right in front of us."

"We lost focus," Zellie said. "In particular, after we figured out that Patsy Bruder was a member of the extended Abogado family, and Jake confirmed his personal connection to her. Once we established that relationship, we had our motive, albeit one without definition. We had a motive for Russ, too, in that Darrow cheated his sister, but $5,000 didn't seem like enough of a reason to kill the guy."

"Hard to keep focus when you're being crashed into, shot at, handcuffed, lost in the woods and almost burned alive," Marla observed.

"Maybe so," I said, "but we might have figured it all out a lot earlier if we'd stuck to the facts."

"I think you can give yourselves a pass on that under the circumstances," Mrs. Minniefield said. "But I think your behavior might have been a bit reckless, don't you agree?" She said it with as much kindness as she could muster, but there was little subtlety with Mrs. Minniefield.

Zellie spoke up. "If we did it over, I think we'd figure out a different way of trying to trap Patsy. That turned out to be dangerous, no question about it. But the visit to Garrett's house? We just wanted to interview him as the party to the hit and run that killed Freddy Darrow. We couldn't have expected his crazed reaction to our visit."

Mrs. Minniefield just looked at us for a long moment, saying nothing. Zellie remained impassive, I had to admire her fortitude under the scrutiny. I squirmed a little, I admit it.

"We might have had an idea he was dangerous. I brought my gun after all," I said, breaking the silence. "Dangerous, yes. But reckless? I don't think so. No sense arguing the issue though, Zellie," I added, and she nodded.

Point made, Mrs. Minniefield continued. "So you figured that she had a motive to kill Ferdinand Darrow. What was it?"

"Jake." Zellie and I said it together.

They all looked at us with eager anticipation, and I explained.

"In her confession, she admitted that she'd always loved him, and they both acknowledged being lose friends. It's not like she and Jake had any affairs, or anything like that. By all accounts, Jake and Elizabeth Rothberg remained a happy couple for many years.

"When Elizabeth died, however, Patsy saw how tortured Jake was at the 'bloodsuckers,' as she called them, who operated their extortion ring right in front of her. She tolerated what she saw until it involved Jake, and while she couldn't do much to help him, she bided her time until she could execute her carefully conceived plan. And it worked to perfection, just as she'd imagined. While Darrow did his monthly archiving, which required frequent trips to the attic with boxes of files, she acted. Pretending to work on a problem with the window, she waited until he was upstairs with his first box, then slipped the poison into his mug of coffee, and went back to work. Darrow dutifully took a swig or two, then picked up another box to bring upstairs. As soon as he left the room, she grabbed the pole holding the curtains and swooped over to close the attic door. She propped the extendable pole into place, and waited until his shouting subsided. Then she removed the pole and replaced it with the curtains, where it remained. We in fact saw it each time we looked at the place, but made no connection."

"Ingenious," Ted said, with obvious admiration. "Simple, but clever. Two questions. When you set the trap, who did you ask Melissa to call, and what did you tell her to say?"

"I asked her to call Jayne Merriweather's assistant at MCP to let the building manager know her clients wanted to remove the curtain rods to examine and measure them for the purpose of deciding what drapes to hang when they rented the office, and that she'd given her clients the okay to do so, and had provided the combination to the realtor lock to give access to the cottage. She also was to ask them to let the cleaning service know the same thing, as extra cleaning might be needed the next day for the same reason.

"I should say now we wanted to create the implication that our true intention was to examine them for fingerprints, or scraped paint from the trap door on the end of the rods, or evidence that Patsy was the only one who handled them. It was a bluff, as Patsy was the building manager. It was feasible that she was the only one who handled the rods, anyway. In fact, she might have installed them in the first place, if not an interior decorator, the curtain store, or Darrow himself. And the attic door paint was the same as the window trim paint, so it might not have made any difference. But it was worth a shot, and it worked out."

"Also," Zellie added, "we thought it possible someone else would reveal him or herself – Jayne; Flora, although I don't know how she'd receive the message; or Russ; or Melissa herself, but we didn't think so. And we didn't expect Garrett to show up. We were lulled a bit by his call to the Holmdel police. As if that was the end of it. I assume Jayne told him about it – but we don't know. And Jayne – we thought it was a possibility, but we didn't expect her to show up, or to be so ruthless. Even more cold-blooded than Garrett."

"That's the story," I said. "The rest is us becoming distracted."

I explained that Garrett was just trying to stop us from finding enough evidence to convict him of Freddy Darrow's murder and he became more and more desperate. He had nothing to do with the death of Ferdinand Darrow. But he was a violent man. It's what he did for a living. And we were dumb to provoke him. It almost cost us our lives. Ironically, Jayne killed him for not being enough of a killer. And Patsy killed Jayne to avenge Jake's mistreatment. Flora told the truth from the outset. She was right about Garrett, and as I told the group with a broad smile, it made me happy she was innocent, so I could keep her as a florist. And Jake...poor Jake. He'd done nothing other than love his wife. And for that, he'd become involved in a family embroiled in extortion and murder.

"How did Jake know to come to the cottage when he did?" Marla asked. "Fortuitous, wasn't it?"

"Life-saving, in fact," I said. "Jake explained it. He said Patsy and he had a regular lunch date at his deli, but she'd telephoned him she'd be late that day, as she had to run over to the cottage to take care of something. He had begun worrying that she'd become unhinged, and he remembered our connection with the cottage, so he decided on the spur of the moment to head over there, and we're lucky he did."

"There's one thing I still don't understand," Marla said. "What was the whole *Brothers Karamazov* thing all about?"

Zellie smiled. "It had nothing to do with the case, and it didn't sidetrack us. It was just an odd coincidence and interesting observation by Freddy Darrow. You read the book, right?"

"Sure, you know I did," Marla replied. "What about it?"

"What was the gist of it? You told us at breakfast."

"Evil dad has four sons, one of whom is a half-brother, by a different mother. That's the son who killed him. That's as simple as I can get."

"Freddy Darrow inscribed 'Does life imitate art, or does art imitate life' in Josh's copy of the book. It wasn't literal, he was just describing his messed-up family, including himself, his no-good brother, and a half brother-in-law, Jake. He also forecast a murder. In fact, two murders. I wouldn't read much more into it than his desire to share a good book with a friend, together with a spur-of-the moment scrawl on the flyleaf based upon his distraught state of mind."

"There wasn't a fourth brother?" Marla asked.

Zellie's eyes twinkled. "Not a real brother. A facsimile of one. And we'll let you figure it out. I'll give one clue and write it down for you." She scrawled the name Herman Octavius Garrett on a piece of paper, and handed it to Marla.

"Garrett. How is he Freddy's brother?

""He's not."

She looked for a few moments, muttered something about his initials spelling HOG, and shook her head.

"Need help?" Zellie asked with a grin. "One more clue – you speak fluent Spanish."

"What?" She looked down at the paper again and laughed. "Herman O. Garrett. Hermano means 'brother' in Spanish."

"Yes," I said. "We know Freddy had Spanish background, and he must have known or heard Garrett's full name when he was being threatened. He noted the odd correlation with a book he liked. Why he gave the book with the inscription to Josh, we'll never know. My guess is that he intended to recommend the book to him and added the inscription as an afterthought. Maybe he intended to tell Josh what it meant at some point, but that's pure speculation."

"There's one other thing," Ted said. "I couldn't help noticing that shiny rock on Zellie's finger. Nice piece of jewelry. Does it have any significance?"

I glanced over at Zellie's ring, feigned mock surprise, and said "Zellie, what is that?"

Zellie looked at her finger. "Oh, a diamond. I must be getting married. I wonder who the lucky man is?"

Marla, who of course knew all about it, and Mrs. Minniefield, who Zellie probably called right after she called her parents, already knew, but Ted expressed his fervent congratulations, and we all embraced.

We parted from Mrs. Minniefield, and Ted and Marla went their own way. Zellie and I headed down the street to my house. As we walked, I spotted someone hurry into a mid-sized foreign car parked in front of my home. It was a woman, standing about five foot eight, with long, dark hair. She shut the door and sped off. I knew that shape, and that posture, and I didn't need to see her face to know the identity of the visitor, and neither did Zellie, who'd frozen right next to me. My criminal ex-girlfriend, Jennifer.

***

Dear Reader:

Thanks for reading my book! I hope you enjoyed Arnie &
Zellie's latest adventure in Monmouth County, New Jersey.
If so, stay tuned for their continuing exciting unlicensed
detective work, as the series continues. Arnie, Zellie, Ted,
Marla, Mrs. Minniefield, and Rupe will all return, along with
many new friends and enemies. And yes, Jennifer is back!

Online reviews are much appreciated, so it would be great if
you took a few moments to write a review on Amazon.com,
BarnesandNoble.com, or any other review site. Thanks!

Just click on a link (or type it into your browser), and scroll
down to where it provides for a review.

Brazen Gambit:

http://www.amazon.com/dp/0998859206

http://www.barnesandnoble.com/s/9780998859200

A Tale of Two Freddies:

http://www.amazon.com/dp/098859231

http://www.barnesandnoble.com/s/098859231

Eric Small

About the Author:

Retired government attorney Eric Small began writing a cozy mystery series featuring the investigations and adventures of Arnie and Zellie in their fledgling detective agency, set in the environs of Middletown, New Jersey. Brazen Gambit was the first in the series, and A Tale of Two Freddies continues from where that left off. Eric grew up in Middletown, and now lives in Florida with his wife, to whom he's been married for over thirty years.

Ordering and Contact Information:

At Amazon.com, Barnesandnoble.com, and other online booksellers.

Brazen Gambit:

http://www.amazon.com/dp/0998859206

http://www.barnesandnoble.com/s/9780998859200

A Tale of Two Freddies:

http://www.amazon.com/dp/098859231

http://www.barnesandnoble.com/s/098859231

Contact Information:

Eric Small Books
P.O. Box 840003
St. Augustine, FL 32080
Eric@ericsmallbooks.com
www.ericsmallbooks.com